100

The Beach Road

The Beach Road

Sarah Diamond

ORION

Copyright ©2000 Sarah Diamond

The moral right of Sarah Diamond to be identified as the author
of this work has been asserted by her in accordance with
the Copyright, Designs and Patents Act 1988

First published in Great Britain in 2000 by
Orion
An imprint of The Orion Publishing Group Ltd
Orion House, 5 Upper St Martin's Lane,
London WC2H 9EA

A CIP catalogue record for this book
is available from the British Library

Typeset in Great Britain at The Spartan Press Ltd,
Lymington, Hants

Printed and bound by
Clays Ltd, St Ives plc

For Catherine, the wind beneath my wings

'A stranger's just a friend you haven't met yet.'

American saying

Prologue

A murder was committed in the alleyway outside Maxine's nightclub, on Christmas Eve, 1998. Flats faced on to the alley, and the screams brought people running: the cynical look-the-other-way ethos of the big cities didn't exist in sleepy small-town Underlyme. The killer was arrested almost immediately.

The story was sold to the British public like a big-budget Hollywood movie. The tender ages of its central figures recalled De Palma's prom-queen telekinetic; the provincial setting evoked *Twin Peaks*. Style of murder owed rather more to *The Texas Chainsaw Massacre* than to *Seven*, but the case made up in spectacle for what it lacked in sophistication. In Brixton and Golders Green, in Richmond and Moss Side, popcorn was cracked, boyfriends cuddled close and eyes opened wide in horrified fascination. It was a good show.

Like something that shines brightest just before it goes out, the height of the murder's notoriety marked the end of it. Time passed, and extracts from a book about the case were moved from the centre pages, then tailed off abruptly. Soon after, Liz Hurley was snapped in a new kind of lipstick, and another IRA bomb went off in Manchester. Life moved on. In national terms, the Underlyme murder was yesterday's news, and yesterday's news doesn't sell papers.

But in Underlyme, Dorset, the memories stay alive.

The seaside town of Underlyme (pop. approx. 20,000) isn't as small as it seems. To judge by the little town centre or the one-horse railway station, you'd think it wasn't much more than a village, but from where you're standing you can't see the full view: the two comprehensives, the three council estates, the sprawling prosperous area in the suburbs. Literally and figuratively, there's more to Underlyme than meets the eye.

If you take the beach road out from the town centre today, you'll be hampered at first by the weight of the traffic. The tourists like Underlyme in July. But if you're patient and keep going, you'll find it clears as miraculously as heavy congestion often does, evaporates into thin air at a crossroads further up. This is the point where the blurred line between tourists and residents ends. No more cheap cheerful shops with rubber dinosaurs hanging outside and rude mugs in the windows: you pass nothing but four-square respectable houses, getting a little more luxurious every minute you're behind the wheel. Cars parked in driveways give way to cars parked in garages, then garages become detached, cartwheels and coachlights grow on elongating gates. Occasionally, far away in the sunlight, there's the glint of an outdoor pool. A few minutes more, and you'll be in the part of Underlyme where the wealthy live.

If you stop at 20 Goldcroft Drive, your idle-sightseer status instantly switches to that of ghoul. Drive on, sicko. The once-famous murder didn't even take place here. What exactly are you expecting to see?

Oh, all right, then. If you must.

Since you've come this far, the bushes round the back won't deter you, and you'll probably be able to sneak round and peer through them without being noticed. You'll see a wide flat carpet of daisyless green bisected by a meandering stone path, stone bird tables, a kidney-shaped outdoor swimming-pool with candy-striped loungers ranged round it. But there's nobody in the pool and nobody on the loungers, and the garden's as silent as a graveyard. Far away, there's the distant hum of a lawnmower.

About a hundred metres down from your vantage-point, through the garden, past the patio, you can see the rear windows of the house, uncurtained in self-conscious reference to the seclusion of the area. You see a clearly focused photograph of a dream kitchen cut off at odd places. Occasionally it's disturbed by the movement of a woman. She's blonde, slim, attractive, wears a red-and-white-striped apron so the olive oil won't splash on her blouse. At first, you think there's something oddly familiar about her. But perhaps it's just the resemblance to a girl who appeared two years ago on the front page of three tabloids at once.

On the side-table under the corkboard, there's a silver-framed photograph. From this distance it's hard to make out properly, but you think you can see a flash of bright blonde hair, and your imagination fills in the lovely laughing face beneath it. Perhaps you're right. Perhaps it is the same snapshot that once smiled out from the *Mail* and the *Sun* and the *Mirror*, all on the same morning.

I think it's best if you moved on now, left the blonde lady to her cooking, the garden to its silence.

If you return to your car and take the beach road into the town centre, all you need to do is turn left at the first roundabout you come to, then right at the lights and right again, and you'll be entering the Darlington Estate. Funny how twenty minutes behind the wheel can change the world. The Darlington Estate's as half-hearted a nod to genuine poverty as were the suburbs you've just left to genuine wealth. The occasional graffiti's perfunctory and harmless, and you don't need to check the bushes to be sure there are no used needles lurking. Number 3 Spring Lane is easy to find in the neat grid of connecting streets, easier than it has any right to be.

There's an old man walking out of the front door, along the three-foot-long path that runs through the unfenced postage-stamp of lawn and leads straight on to the pavement. You look at him with some disappointment. Even though he was a peripheral, rarely mentioned figure in the case, you'd expected something more than that. He's shabbily respectable, balding, perhaps sixty-five. He could be anyone. His head's bowed, and he looks down as if there's something on the pavement that interests him. He'd never admit it to his wife, but he gets scared himself these days . . .

Drive on. There's nothing for you here. Leave the old man in peace. If you take the main road from the suburbs, you should be back at home by five at the latest. It's a lovely summer's day, and you can leave the roof down while you're driving. You've seen all there is to see in Underlyme.

It's funny, now there's nothing left to see but the ashes, that people try to work out how it happened.

When the fuse was burning slowly away into nothing, nobody noticed anything at all.

August

1

Jane had not expected such beauty. The perfection beyond the car window held her hypnotised.

'It's a nice little town, Underlyme,' said her grandmother, from the passenger seat of the elderly Ford. 'You'll be ever so happy here, Jane, dear.'

Jane barely heard her. Her eyes were wide and dazed. The melting summer afternoon, the chuckling radio and the nauseating smell of fabric upholstery had stopped mattering. This beauty dwarfed it all – the rolling green lawns and the wrought-iron gates, the tantalising glimpses of tall ivy-veined houses and other people's happiness. A young man in cut-off shorts washed a car in a driveway, and the picture was as perfect as a still from an advert. 'Well, we're in the suburbs,' said her grandfather, from the driving-seat. 'What do you think, love?'

'It's beautiful,' she murmured. She looked and looked, soaking in every detail of a beauty that had come out of nowhere. 'It's so beautiful.'

'Well, the estate's not quite up to this standard,' said her grandfather, with a vast and hollow joviality, 'but it's as good a place to live as any. Isn't it, Mary?'

'It is that,' said her grandmother. 'We've got your room done up lovely for you, Jane, dear. You'll be all settled in in no time.'

Jane barely heard her. It was like the hunger after a fast: she gorged herself on honey-coloured brickwork and glittering window-glass and ivy, on shadows in the windows that hinted at the real lives behind them. People were in there somewhere, as tangibly solid as she was herself, and she found the thought somehow thrilling. 'I've never seen anything like this,' she said. 'Not in Streatham. Not ever.'

'Yes, it's a lovely little town,' said her grandmother cosily, turning to smile at Jane over the passenger-seat. 'We'll be at the estate soon.'

Jane watched the suburbs fading like a dream around her – she twisted in her seat, and her eyes shrieked goodbye to something beautiful. It felt like her second bereavement in as many weeks. Her mother had died eight days ago.

2

Although Emma had been to Bev Green's house countless times since the two of them had met in the playground three years ago, she always felt vaguely awkward walking up the drive. It was just the way the house towered above her, reminded her how small-scale her own life was by comparison. The Green home was a three-storey mock-Tudor affair, nestling in Underlyme's wealthiest street, complete with an outdoor pool and every mod con. Bev's father made a pretty good living for a second-hand-car-dealer.

Emma walked up the sloping driveway, seeing what she always saw: the tall tree in the weedless front garden, the intricate, mullioned windows glittering in the light. As usual, a kind of self-conscious inadequacy gripped her at the sight, and she saw herself in her mind's eye – a dark-haired, sensible-looking teenager with freckles and nice eyes, perfectly suited to the little semi five minutes' walk away from school, utterly out of place in the here and now. She wondered what it must be like to be Bev Green, with the perfect house, the perfect family, the perfect *life*.

When she reached the house, she raised the big iron knocker and banged it down. She heard muffled voices through an open window – 'I'll get it, Mum,' Bev was calling, 'it'll be Em' – and then Bev was there.

'All right, Em?' asked Bev. 'Come on in.'

In the bright summer light, it was like looking straight at the sun. It wasn't hard to see why the boys at school regarded Beverley Green as a kind of movie star, or why she'd received the record total of eight Valentines last February. Golden and glorious were the only words that really fitted – a thick cascade of gleaming blonde hair, smooth tanned skin without a hint of pink, startlingly blue eyes. The perfect figure, of course. Sometimes, Emma almost hated her well-liked best friend. 'You started packing yet?' she asked, as Bev closed the door behind her.

'Only just. Shit, we're flying out first thing tomorrow. You don't mind giving me a hand with it, do you, Em? We can sunbathe after we've finished.'

'Sure. Whatever,' said Emma, and they started up the stairs.

Up in Bev's room, they packed shorts and T-shirts and bikinis and crop-tops, and talked mainly about boys. They discussed the boys at school Bev didn't fancy, and the couple Emma did, and the ones in the public eye they both agreed on, and the music from Bev's stereo pounded out cheerfully, like their voices. Melting summer flooded the room. 'I bet you get off with an amazing lad out in Florida,' said Emma, folding a nightshirt. 'American lads sound well tasty.'

'As if. I'm not exactly going to get off with someone with Mum and Dad and Toby hanging round me the whole time.'

'You might.' Emma squashed the nightshirt down atop a mountain of clothes. 'You're going to have a wicked time out there, anyway. Wish I could go away one summer.'

'You went to France last year. You said you loved it.'

'I suppose.' Emma remembered the ugly little bed-and-breakfast overlooking the sea, her father's woefully inadequate French, her mother looking dowdy and embarrassed in a pink-flowered swimsuit. Somehow, she couldn't reconcile it to the perfect tan suitcases overflowing on Bev's stripped-pine floor. 'It wasn't the same, though.'

'Don't see why not. A holiday's a holiday,' said Bev, easily. 'God, I'm thirsty. Let's go down and grab a milkshake.'

From the kitchen, vast windows faced out on to the pool.

Bev's cool, tasteful mother sat talking with two cool, tasteful friends, and their conversation broke off as Bev and Emma came in. 'Hello, darling,' said Mrs Green. 'Oh, hello, Emma. How are you?'

Emma always felt slightly awkward in Mrs Green's presence – she remembered her own mother's middle-aged spread and fondness for silly jokes. 'Hi, Mrs Green,' she said, as Bev mixed strawberry milkshakes at the counter. 'I'm fine. How are you?'

'Very well, thank you.' Bev's mother smiled her polite indifferent dismissal, and returned to her friends. 'Anyway, Betty,' she said, 'Trisha and Martin are redoing their house from top to bottom, and . . .'

Emma felt the cold weight of the glass in her hand, and followed Bev back through the shadowed hallway with an inexplicable sense of reprieve. 'I never know what to say to your mum,' she said, when the two of them were back in Bev's room. 'Or your dad. Haven't they ever embarrassed you or anything?'

'How do you mean?'

Emma thought of drawing Bev's attention to her own father's entire wardrobe, but loyalty stopped her. It was true, she thought, Bev really didn't know what she meant. Even Bev's little brother was perfect, in his dumb, skateboarding way. 'I don't know,' she said eventually. 'I'm just being silly.'

'They're not that scary,' said Bev. 'They're just people.'

Emma looked at Bev. *Like hell they are*, she thought.

And, looking at Emma, Bev thought, *Please God don't let her go too soon. Please let her stay for a little while longer.*

3

As the car slowed down and parked, Jane experienced an overwhelming disappointment. She'd hoped for more than this – this dowdy, well-scrubbed little terrace, with its net-curtained windows and tiny front lawns. She'd dreamed of so much more.

'Well, Jane, dear,' said her grandmother Mary, 'welcome home.'

The three of them stepped out into intense heat and an almost absolute silence. A bird shrieked far away, and the sound seemed to echo.

'We'd best get you unpacked and all,' said her grandfather Alf, as he hoisted her suitcases out of the boot. 'We've got all new furniture in the spare room for you, love. You'll be right at home in no time.'

Inside, the little terrace smelt clean and false and impersonal; the sun cast neat squares across the carpet, and china dogs stared down from the sideboard with empty eyes. Jane remembered dark rugs peeling away from ancient lino back in Streatham, and a sense of loss touched her deep inside. 'It's lovely,' she said, realising she was expected to say something, 'really lovely.'

'We're glad you like it, dear,' said Mary. 'After all, it's your home now.'

In the bedroom, fussy *faux*-princess frills adorned the single window, and the pink duvet cover was turned back to reveal pink-flowered sheets. 'Well, here we are,' said Alf, puffing as he set down Jane's suitcase's on the bed. 'I'll leave you girls to unpack, then. I'll be out in the garden, if you want me.'

Jane stood awkwardly, and watched her grandfather's departing back. 'Does he do a lot of gardening?' she asked eventually.

'Oh, he loves his garden, your grandad.' Mary walked over to the window, and pulled the net curtain aside. 'Look.' Jane looked. She saw a neat little fenced-in back garden beneath an empty blue sky, garish flowers in orderly, serried ranks. 'He's got an allotment, too,' said Mary, 'just up the road. He grows vegetables.'

Jane's eyes fixed on the garden outside. She remembered the third-floor flat in Streatham, and the strange greasy cooking smells that lingered on the stairs. Homesickness gripped her like a cramp. 'I never had a garden before,' she said, and then, 'It's really nice.'

'Oh, Jane, dear,' said Mary, 'if only we could have had you sooner.' She put an arm round Jane and hugged her awkwardly.

Jane breathed a cloud of scent as bright and false as air-freshener. 'We'd best unpack your things, anyway,' she said. 'Get you settled in.'

Something stiffened inside Jane. A new and sudden apprehension overcame her. 'No, Nan, really,' she said. 'You don't have to bother. I don't mind unpacking on my own.'

'Well, if you're sure, dear.' Mary moved over to the door. 'I'll leave you to get settled in on your own for a bit, then.'

Jane stood in the too-hot little bedroom and listened to her grandmother descending the stairs. When she was sure Mary wasn't going to pop back up for something, she opened her suitcase. The small package she'd wedged in right at the bottom was easy to find. Her eyes scanned the unfamiliar room for a possible hiding-place. Finally, she stuffed it under the mattress. As she stepped back from the bed, her breathing came quick and shallow. It felt exciting to have a secret, something that would shock other people, something that they wouldn't understand at all. Something in the world that really felt like her own.

But even her small nervous high couldn't last long here. She folded her few clothes neatly, and was left far too soon with nothing to do. A memory of beautiful houses haunted and mocked her. Outside, the sun blazed down.

4

She's going to say it any second now, thought Bev. She and Emma had finished the packing about an hour ago, and were now lying on the poolside loungers, soaking up the last of the afternoon's rays. *Any second. Bet you.*

'Oh, God, I'd better go,' said Emma, looking at her watch. 'My mum'll kick my arse if I'm late home.'

As always, the attempt to keep the sunlight, even as she saw the clouds moving overhead. 'You can stay, if you want. My mum could call yours. You could stay for dinner.'

'I'd love to,' said Emma regretfully, 'but I can't. Listen, have a wicked time in Florida, yeah? And remember to send me a postcard.'

'Sure. I'll call you as soon as I get back.'

Emma rose from the lounger, and Bev rose with her. They came into the house via the kitchen. Bev saw her mother's friends were gathering their things together, too. 'My God, it's a mass exodus,' said one, and the three women laughed.

At the front door, Emma said, 'See you later, then, Bev. Have a great time,' and then she was walking away. Bev stood and watched her retreating back for long, slow seconds. She thought how Emma didn't really look like she belonged here, in this tasteful stage-set of a home. She thought she envied Emma for it.

She wished she could talk properly to Emma. But she couldn't. She just hadn't been brought up to talk about the things that mattered. It had been with her from her earliest days – the constant training in sweeping things under the carpet and pretending that they weren't there. Now she came to think about it, the only real bollockings she'd received from her mother had come when she'd forgotten to do that, when she'd let too much slip out without thinking.

One time, when she'd gone round to Emma's house for dinner, she'd wondered if maybe it was the same with Emma's family, after all. She'd carved her gammon steak and sipped her Diet Coke with her mental antennae on elastic, exquisitely attuned to the possibility of undercurrents. But it had been like running a radio dial through dead silence. There wasn't any tension here at all, she'd realised – Emma's mother placidly gathering up the plates, Emma's dad telling some long story about a recent coach-trip to Cherbourg, Emma herself contriving to look both bored and horribly embarrassed. It had occurred to Bev that they'd be just the same when she'd gone, and real jealousy had twisted in her guts at the way Emma didn't have to pretend all the time, the way Emma was allowed to be herself.

Bev ascended the stairs. She stopped and lingered on the first-floor landing, hearing the voices from the kitchen approaching the front door. 'Well, goodbye, then, Melissa,' said one, 'have a marvellous holiday.' Bev heard the front door open and shut. She heard her mother walking back towards the kitchen. Something in the tiny, solitary sound chilled her soul: a black cloud passing over the late afternoon's sepia sunshine, a sudden sense of eclipse.

5

Sometimes, Bev felt as if her own family was two different families. There were the Greens who came out in company, the Greens whom her mother's friends and her brother Toby's friends and even Emma all thought they knew – attractive, rich, loving, enviable. They were the public Greens, who emerged and performed for visitors. When the visitors left, that version of the Greens ceased to exist.

The second version of the Greens was something that never got talked about. It was deliberately ignored, like a fart or a tasteless joke, something unpleasant that took place, and you pretended you'd forgotten it right away after. But – although they never mentioned it – Bev knew that they all sensed it. It was why her thirteen-year-old brother Toby spent more time in his friends' bedrooms than he did in his own, why her mother lived for dinner parties, and decorating, and anything that could make her forget what it was really like at home when her father came back from work. It was why she never wanted Emma to go home.

It was everywhere and nowhere, the trouble at home. Nothing that could be named, but something vast and towering all the same. There was never any physical violence in the household, or even any direct verbal abuse. But, when they were all together in the evenings, it was somehow worse than either . . .

Bev remembered how it had been over dinner last night, the familiar tableau of the four of them in the kitchen. Her father constantly asking her mother for this or that or the other, in the most offhand voice imaginable – 'Can I have some more peas,

Mel?' he'd said. 'Turn the radio down, will you?' when he'd been far closer to it than she had, when it had been glaringly obvious he could do it himself. And she remembered the familiar apprehension of seeing her mother's face right after he'd spoken. How it froze for a split second, in a sort of unconscious grimace, a setting of the jaw, a pursing of the lips as if she was biting down on some unthinkable retort. As always Bev had been terrified that her mother would finally explode, but she never did. Just did whatever he said with a smile that didn't fool anyone, and a 'There you are, darling,' before she sat back down to eat, and the uneasy silence gathered around them all over again . . .

It didn't sound like such a big deal, Bev thought – if she'd tried to describe it to Emma, it would have looked like she was complaining about nothing – but when you saw the same tense interplay over and over again in different situations, it began to look like a pretty big deal after all. To Bev, being alone with her parents felt quite a bit like sitting in a closed room that was slowly filling up with poison gas.

There were more specific problems, almost never mentioned in Bev's presence, though over the years she'd stumbled on them by accident. Her maternal grandfather was in an old people's home, which was what she was allowed to know. But she'd also found out it was her father who paid for it, and that her father complained about each monthly cheque. It seemed a simple enough sort of thing – her father always complained about how much things cost, although he always bought plenty and he never bought cheap. But there was something complicated there that she didn't understand. It was in her mother's expression when her father occasionally brushed up against the subject, and at those times it was in her father's expression, too – something dark and sinister that Bev tasted full in the mouth, and couldn't define.

She'd come across other issues as well, by accident, at one time or another – things that never got discussed out loud. Why she and Toby hadn't ever met their relations on their father's side, why their parents never even mentioned them. Although she'd sometimes wondered, she'd been eleven before she'd found out for sure. Standing by the kitchen door, eavesdropping, she'd heard her father's voice. 'I had to choose between you and my family,' he'd said to her mother. 'You made me choose and I chose you.' It should have sounded romantic, Bev thought, but it hadn't at all.

She considered other things, too: her father's long hours at work, how it was when he sometimes came home late at night, her mother surprised once in the bathroom, crying over the wash-basin. The endless silences at the dinner-table and the overwhelming tension. That was what it was like, when it was just them. The Perfect Greens, As Seen On TV, were something like best china or silver cutlery, hospitable luxuries that only emerged when there were guests.

Bev went into her room and shut the door behind her. The late-afternoon rays slanted through the mullioned windows and cast squares of sepia light across the floor. She saw that Emma had left her empty milkshake glass on the dressing-table, and found the sight ridiculously poignant. Soon, her father would be home from work. For now, there was only the silence.

6

It was the sight of herself in the dressing-table mirror that told Jane she had to get out. In the light of a perfect summer evening, she saw her reflection against the backdrop of a stranger's room: podgy, plain, lank-haired, scared-eyed. It depressed and alienated her, as it always did. She wasn't anything in particular, she realised, her tragedy didn't matter to anyone in the world – and then she was hurrying out of the room, down the stairs, away from the truth of herself. More than anything, she wanted to see the beautiful houses again.

Mary was dicing carrots in the kitchen – a small knife moved expertly. 'Hello again, dear,' she said as Jane came in. 'Finished unpacking yet?'

'Yeah,' said Jane. 'I hung everything up nice and neat. You

won't have to do it again.' Through the half-open back door, she saw her grandfather out in the garden, his worn face intent upon his roses. 'Listen, Nan,' she said, 'you don't mind if I go out for a walk for an hour or so, do you?'

'Well, of course not, dear,' said Mary. 'Be back by six, mind. I'm cooking for you specially tonight.'

Jane left by the back door. Her grandfather didn't seem to notice her as he pruned and trimmed. Something in the set of his diligent respectable shoulders reminded Jane by default of her mother – the sour smell of wine, the loud harsh laughter, the dead white flesh in the bath. She found it impossible to believe that her mother had come from this place. Its peace and tranquillity were terrible to Jane, haunting, somehow unreal.

Out of the back gate, she had no idea where to go. For a long time, the scenery around her seemed caught on a tape-loop: she passed what seemed like a thousand identical red-brick semis, a thousand well-tended little gardens. A fat woman sat on a doorstep watching a fat man mow a lawn, and Jane wasn't sure whether to smile a neighbourly greeting or not. She didn't. She walked on, to nowhere, away from the insubstantial little bedroom and the paralysing sense of loneliness.

Eventually she began to see landmarks she recognised from the drive here – a small newsagent, a second-hand-clothes shop, a shabby little furniture store with a letter missing from the sign – and the deadly silence gave way to a kind of vivacity. People passed her and paid her no attention, but Jane hardly noticed them. Regretfully, she realised she'd never make it to the suburbs where the beautiful houses were before six o'clock. But she could always go there some other time. And there must be something else to see, here in Underlyme.

She came to the small harbour she'd seen out of the car window earlier. Little boats bobbed on glinting blue water. Across the bridge she saw the beginnings of the town centre that the car hadn't travelled through. She went over, and was there.

Even though the shops were mostly closed or closing, Underlyme's town centre was still busy and bustling – families, teenagers and children all spilled together as the evening came down. Jane saw an anonymous jeweller's with steel grilles pulled down in the windows, a pub with seats outside, a pretty little still-open kitchen shop displaying aprons and fridge magnets, and then her eyes were drawn by something she'd never seen up close before: a crowded promenade, a narrow railing, a distant glimpse of the land melting into the sea.

So this was the seaside people talked about, Jane thought, as she crossed the busy main road. In the strong sunlight, it was like a hallucination: bright kiosks that promised candy-floss and ice-creams, small shrieking children trailing from parental hands, old ladies on deckchairs, and a roundabout on the beach. She walked as if hypnotised, on and on, until gradually she became aware of the crowds thinning around her, and she didn't have to watch out that she didn't bump into people, and then she was alone.

She looked back to the crowds. They'd become ants, now. Here was something else. Here, the road led off in a different direction, not between road and beach, but buildings and beach, and the boarded windows of a long-closed bingo hall stared down at her on her right. On her left, the golden sand had graded into grey-white pebbles, which led down to clear blue water streaked with red-gold. There were no kiosks or bright deck-chairs here. Just the naked beach, and the cold shriek of distant seagulls, and something poignant and evocative that reached out to embrace the world.

Motionless as a statue, Jane stood and looked out to sea. Something out there seemed to join her in her loneliness – the silence and the power. She thought of her mother lying dead in the bath, and she stared into the world beyond the beach road, and the world beyond the beach road stared back.

7

Jane had been ten when she'd first met her, in the launderette where both their mothers worked. It had been the height of summer, and the sweet, suffocating smell of hot fabric and washing-powder had filled the world.

'My name's Anita,' she'd said. 'What's yours?'

'I'm Jane,' Jane had said, and that was how they'd become friends.

It was a good friendship for Jane, whose father had walked out ten years ago, whose mother never paid her much attention. Ever since she could remember, she'd had a bad time at school and home alike. Her peers didn't like her – it wasn't that she was too bright, she knew, but she wasn't thick in the right way either. She lacked a kind of saving brutality, and she was scared of too much. There were girls called Michelle and Chandra and Stephanie who picked on her at school. People always had. She was used to it.

But when she was with Anita, she didn't feel any of that. With Anita, she felt that maybe she could belong, after all.

Anita was nine years old, and went to a different school. At weekends and during evenings and afternoons they shared, Jane came to adore her confidence. Anita carried a kind of bright amiability with her, and she smiled like she knew she'd be smiled back at. She was a slight, dark-haired girl with a quick, staccato way of speaking. She was the youngest of four daughters, her star-sign was Leo and she loved Sheryl Crow and Bryan Adams. Jane soon found out all the facts about Anita, and she felt very lucky that Anita wanted to be her friend.

How they'd walked together, that first slow blissful summer. Jane would always remember it. How they'd walked on summer Sunday afternoons, when their mums were both hard at work in the launderette. On Streatham Hill, they'd bought cold blue drinks in plastic cartons, and they'd poked the thin red straws through the top, and they'd walked aimlessly through sunshine, laughing about bands and TV shows and nothing in particular.

The nice Indian lady in the shop always smiled at them and asked them how they were. Further up the road was a chemist-cum-newsagent that always stayed open on Sundays and, from the shop, they'd always gone there. One time, Anita had nicked a lipstick, and Jane had been both shocked and admiring, and they'd giggled about it all the way back to the launderette. And they'd dared each other to grab down *Viz* and *Zit* from the top shelf, and they'd always managed to get through a cartoon or two before the girl at the counter shooed them out –

To Jane, it was the joy of a togetherness that had nothing to do with the world outside, far from the sniggering classrooms and the noise Carol's friends made back at the flat. Those first summer afternoons with Anita had felt like a refuge – a little place of her own.

Before it had all started going wrong, that was.

Later, it hadn't been the same at all.

8

Melissa was making a start on dinner when she heard Toby come in. She pulled herself back from the brink of tears, and called out brightly, 'Hello, darling!'

'Hi, Mum.' Her son walked into the kitchen, a tallish, handsomeish blond boy with a skateboard under one arm and an expression of amiable stupidity. As always, the sight of him made her feel protective. You're not useless, she thought suddenly, whatever your father says. 'What's cooking?' he asked.

'I'm doing tuna steaks. They should be ready by the time your father comes home.' Always, she thought, the conversation came back to him. She stirred busily, not looking at her son. 'He shouldn't be too late tonight.'

'Yeah?' Toby rested his skateboard against the wall, leaned against it himself. 'Oh, yeah. How'd it go last night?'

'Last night?' In her mind's eye, she saw the little restaurant in Underlyme's town centre, the red wine, the burly male stripper in a policeman's uniform. She heard the shrieking, and recalled her own incommunicable isolation. 'Oh, it was good fun. A typical hen night, really.'

'Yeah?' Toby shifted against the wall. His expensive trainers moved clumsily, but not without a certain street-cred. 'Bev back yet?'

'She's been in all day. Had her friend round.' Suddenly, Melissa remembered what Jack had said before leaving for work – she tensed inside. 'Your father said to make sure you've packed everything. You have made a start, haven't you?'

'Sure,' said Toby, but his guilty, furtive eyes gave him away at once. 'Yeah, I'll, like, go on up and finish it off.' He picked up his skateboard, and dispersed into a clumping of footsteps. Even in trainers, Melissa thought, he managed to be heavy-footed.

She returned her attention to the tuna steaks. Thank God I reminded him, she thought, and envisaged how it would be the following morning if Toby wasn't packed and ready to go at seven sharp. How Jack would blame *her*. He'd yell at Toby, of course, but she'd take the worst of it. The endless sniping warfare. 'I work hard all day for you and the kids,' he'd say. 'And your father. That old fart costs me a fortune. And I don't ask for much, Mel. Just that you can tell that boy to *pack his fucking cases.*'

Carrie's husband beat her up. Melissa had known it for a long time. As the eldest of five daughters, responsibility died hard for Melissa – at any given time, she knew what the other four were up to. But last night, on Julie's hen night, when the conversation had grown maudlin and rambling over their fourth bottle, Carrie had said it out loud. *'That fucking bastard,'* she'd said. 'Two weeks ago, he storms in pissed from the pub and he gives me a black eye. I swear to you, I'm going to leave him next year.' And the conversation had fallen silent, and Melissa's gaze had panned slowly across her assembled sisters at the table: pallid, ugly Lisa who'd never married, fat dowdy Katie who lived with a car mechanic and five kids on the Darlington Estate, shy little Julie, who was finally settling down with an unemployed drifter at the tender age of twenty-nine. And it had been terrible to realise what she had done, that, of all of them, she was the only one who really understood what Carrie must go back to every night, the only one who really knew how it felt to be afraid. The one they all envied, the one who'd escaped. Melissa Green.

Not that she could ever tell Carrie and the others about it, any more than she could tell the women she called her friends in her new life. They all regarded Jack Green in much the same way that teenage girls regarded Leonardo di Caprio – a definitive walking ideal. 'You're so lucky,' they always said, without bitterness but with a kind of wistful yearning admiration. He wasn't just successful, he was *gorgeous*, and whenever they'd met him he'd charmed them, as he charmed all casual acquaintances. Seeing him through their eyes, Melissa always felt an awful loneliness. She sensed she had no right to be as unhappy as she was, that she was probably very ungrateful, that maybe her husband was wonderful to her after all. He'd never been physically abusive to her, never once raised a hand to her. It was just –

It was just that he'd done everything for her and never let her forget it for a second, that he paid her father's nursing-home bills, that he'd ostensibly broken with his ultra-orthodox Jewish family for her sake. It was just that her whole life revolved around paying him back in kind, and he had a hundred thousand tiny ways of criticising everything she did. It was just that she couldn't cook a new recipe or style her hair a new way without first wondering what he'd say and whether he'd like it. It was just that, last night, she hadn't been able to get tipsy with her sisters for fear of a hangover in the morning, when she'd have to get up and be cheerful and fix his breakfast. It was just that his shadow fell across every second of every minute of every day of her perfect life, and she hated his fucking guts.

Melissa mixed the vinaigrette for the side salad in the dream kitchen. She saw her well-tended hands, her little gold watch, the swimming-pool glinting in the gathering darkness outside. She thought of how much she was envied. She waited for Jack to come home.

9

Jack was constantly aware of the silver-framed photograph that stood beside the computer on his big, prosperous desk. It was, he thought, with some pride, as perfect as a still from an advert or a movie: a pretty blonde woman, a handsome blond boy, a stunning blonde girl. The merest hint of smooth green lawn showed behind them as they all displayed dazzling white teeth to the camera. 'What a perfect family,' any observer would have said, and Jack couldn't have agreed more. It was, after all, his own, and he'd worked hard all his life to be able to afford the best of everything.

Jack switched off his computer and rose from his seat. As always, he saw himself in his mind's eye with a mixture of arrogance and insecurity: a tall, lean man with heavy horn-rimmed glasses, hawk-like features, greying dark hair. He wasn't the lanky nerd from Manchester any more, Jacob Green, who'd spent his miserable teenage years slaving away in his dad's shitty little grocery store: he was the boss of Jack's Motors, the most successful second-hand-car showroom in three towns. He wasn't the boy the girls all laughed at any more, because he had a pretty blonde wife in a silver frame by his desk, and a pretty red-haired secretary he'd been screwing for the past two months, and who he was leaving to meet right now.

As he walked out of the office and down the stairs, he saw with some satisfaction Evan hastily stub out the fag he'd been smoking – Jack had recently instigated a blanket ban throughout the building, and liked it when people did what he said. 'You off, then, Mr Green?' asked Evan.

'Yeah,' said Jack. 'I'll have to trust you to keep the place running smoothly for the next fortnight, I suppose. You've got my mobile number, and you've got the number of my hotel. If anything happens, for Christ's sake ring me.'

'Sure thing, Mr Green,' said Evan. 'It's nothing I haven't done before.'

'Good man,' said Jack dismissively. 'Anyway, do your best. I'll see you the Monday after next.'

Out in the showroom, Tim was grease-monkeying under a Ford Mondeo, and Brad and Simon were cleaning a Renault Clio. Jack raised a hand to them in passing greeting. 'Have a great holiday, Mr Green,' called Brad. Jack smiled, and walked out into the sunshine of the car-park, where his gleaming black Merc awaited.

He was a happy man behind the wheel of the top-of-the-range two-seater – the man who wore a Rolex and took two foreign holidays a year, the man who was always perfectly groomed, and whose family thought the sun rose and set on him. The man who'd finally escaped the clinging hands of the past, and whose mistress always said he looked like Michael Douglas.

She was waiting at the bus-stop up the road, as she'd told him she would be, and he saw her as he'd always seen her, a pretty, sharp-featured redhead in her early twenties, with a hard veneer of chainstore glamour, the kind of girl he'd wanted more than anything, long ago. He slowed the Merc, she leaped in and closed the passenger door, the Merc set off again. The whole process had taken maybe four seconds. 'Relax,' she said. 'Nobody's going to see us.'

'There's such a thing as discretion, sweetheart.' His hand settled on her knee and travelled higher; his wedding-band glittered in the thin rosy light of early evening. 'We'll go to that lay-by out by the Harvester,' he said. 'I can't stay long.'

Silence fell in the car. She buckled her seat-belt and looked at him out of the corner of her eye, like she'd been doing in the office all day. 'Did you see?' she asked. 'When Tim came into the office earlier, he kept looking at my legs.'

'Tell him to fuck off,' said Jack, with a half-hearted attempt at machismo – he'd like to have said it to a tough, good-looking girl like this in his youth. 'You're mine, now.'

The lay-by was on the side of a quiet, narrow country lane. Evening bugs flickered like dust-motes in the headlights as Jack pulled up and parked. The headlights went out – the soft evening extended endlessly beyond the car windows. In the car, a quick, brutal, undignified scuffle like two cats fighting in a sack began, continued and reached its inevitable conclusion. His numerous infidelities had never quite lived up to expectation. 'Well,' he said at last, readjusting his clothes.

'What time you flying out tomorrow?' she asked.

'Half twelve,' he said. 'We'll have to leave at seven to get to Heathrow on time.'

'Try and phone me when you get out there, will you?' she asked.

'Sure,' said Jack, who had absolutely no intention of doing any such thing. He refastened his seat-belt. 'Is it okay if I drop you off at Safeway, sweetheart? I'd better be getting on home.'

'Okay,' she said, 'that's fine,' and they set off into the gathering night.

Outside the supermarket on the outskirts of town, he pulled over and kissed her on the cheek. 'Bye-bye, sweetheart. I'll be in touch.'

''Bye, Jack,' said Mandy. 'I'm going to miss you.'

She got out of the car and closed the door behind her. Jack had a vague sense of her standing and watching him drive away, but he paid no attention. He didn't particularly care for her kind of girl any more. It was just a matter of proving he could have one. And besides, at home, Melissa would have the dinner ready.

10

This is what I'd like to tell you, Emma, thought Bev. This is what you never get to see . . .

'Top me up, will you, Mel?' her father was asking, and it was going to happen as it always happened because it always did.

Her mother was on the other side of the kitchen, taking the side salad out of the fridge. Jack was sitting at the table, with Toby and herself. The bottle of wine was right next to him. He could have reached out and touched it, Bev thought. Without stretching.

She didn't need to see her mother's face to watch the

involuntary flicker of fury cross it, before Melissa turned from the fridge in silence, walked over to the table in silence, poured in silence. Then, she went back to the fridge, took out the salad and carried it over to the table. In silence. See, Emma? Bev thought. This is what I mean . . .

They'd been eating for a good six minutes before her father spoke again, this time to Toby. 'You finished that science assignment yet?'

'What science assignment?'

'Don't give me that. The one you were set end of last term,' said Jack. 'You know what I'm talking about.'

'Oh, *that*.' Bev watched her brother's eyes become guarded and tense, watched him study his plate as if for inspiration. Pity gripped her. 'Yeah. It's, uh, almost finished, Dad.'

Well, if it's not, you're taking your books out to Orlando, and you're working on it three hours a day till it is,' said Jack. 'I'm warning you, Toby. If your mother and I have to come in and see your teachers *again* next term . . .'

It was like an interrogation, Bev thought. She looked out of the french windows at the floodlit patio, and the hint of black shining water beyond it. 'That wasn't my fault, last term,' her brother was saying, sounding embarrassed and petulant. 'They weren't even my cigarettes. I was just looking after them for a friend.'

'More fool you,' she heard her father say unfeelingly. 'You're too easily led, that's your trouble. Look at your sister. Same school, same peer pressure, and she's never been in a second's trouble since she started there.' Her hands gripped each other convulsively beneath the table, knowing exactly what was going to come next.

'That's true,' said her mother. 'And I've never known your sister get less than a B in anything.'

'You'll have to work hard if you want to match *that* school record in two years' time.' As always, Bev thought, it was as if her parents were competing on some private battlefield: who could admire their daughter most. 'And there's no question about your sister going on to college – is there, Bev?'

Shut up, she thought, with sudden fury, shut up and stop making him hate me. She shrugged. 'I suppose,' she said.

'You *suppose*,' said her father. 'We *know*. That's why you're going to be getting an iMac for Christmas. Over six hundred quid's worth, mind.'

'It'll come in useful for your A-level essays,' said her mother. 'You see, Toby, it's worth doing well at school. If you went on to college after your GCSEs, you'd get an iMac, too.'

Bev glanced across the table at her brother. In his expression, she saw a dozen other faces looking back at her; the indifferent, watchful jealousy united them all. She felt alone, and trapped. 'Okay, okay,' said Toby. 'I'll bring my books out to Orlando with me.'

'Good,' said Jack. 'I'm sure we can spare you for a few hours every evening. Give me some more salad, will you, Mel?' The salad bowl, of course, was inches from his elbow, and Bev watched her mother's lips tighten and draw together as she rose from her seat. Silence fell once more.

See, Emma? Bev thought, savagely. This is what you're missing, and she sat and stared at her plate, keeping her thoughts to herself, not rocking the boat. It was what she was best at, when the visitors had gone.

11

They had visitors that night. An elderly, mild-mannered couple called Bob and Joyce Andrews, who lived a few roads away. Jane had a feeling they'd been invited round to inspect her.

'Now you don't have to tell me what you want,' said Mary, smiling by the little cocktail cabinet. 'That's a small sherry for you, Joyce, and Scotch and a splash for Bob. Am I right?'

'You missed me, love,' said Alf. 'I'll have a Scotch on the rocks, while you're at it.'

To Jane, there was something forced and hollow in their joviality. The neat little lounge felt like a stage-set, and its ostentatious cosiness chilled her. She thought about the beautiful houses on the outskirts of town, and promised herself she'd go back there soon. 'How you been bearing up then, love?' asked Joyce.

Jane was staring at her hands, and didn't realise for several seconds that Joyce had spoken to her. For a moment, she didn't know what to say. 'Me?' she said stupidly. 'Oh, I'm okay, I suppose. Yeah. I'm okay.'

'She's being very brave about it, bless her,' said Mary. 'But it's been a terrible time for her. Hasn't it, Jane, dear?'

Jane felt like a bug under a microscope; all eyes were upon her, and her throat was tight and dry. 'Yeah,' she said. 'I suppose.'

'I mean, it was an awful shock for all of us, really,' said Mary. 'Me and Alf hadn't heard from Carol in over ten years – or seen poor little Jane since she was knee-high to a grasshopper – and, well, you can say what you like about Carol but she was our only child. And then we just get this call from some social worker out of the blue. Saying Carol's killed herself. Can you imagine?'

'Oh, how *awful*,' said Joyce. 'I *am* sorry, Jane, dear.'

'Well, there you are,' said Alf. 'If there's a silver lining, it's that we were able to take her in. God knows what would have happened to her if we hadn't.'

'Or if the Social people hadn't been able to get hold of you,' said Bob. 'If you hadn't kept the same address all these years.'

'It doesn't bear thinking about,' said Mary 'You hear such stories about these children's homes. Not that Carol could have given a damn. I'm not one to speak ill of the dead, but she was no kind of mother at all to poor little Jane.'

'At least she's with people who care about her, now,' said Joyce kindly. 'She'll know Underlyme like the back of her hand in no time.'

'We're going to look at a school for her next week,' said Alf. 'You must have heard of Underlyme Grammar.'

'Of course,' said Joyce. 'I hear it's a wonderful school.'

'It's the best place for Jane, all right,' said Mary. 'Well, we're keeping our fingers crossed they'll take her. From what we've heard, her school marks weren't up to much in her last place. But she seems like ever such a good girl.'

30

'And maybe her marks'll improve, now she's got you and Alf to encourage her,' said Bob.

When Bob and Joyce had finally gone, Jane went up to her room. Nameless fears overwhelmed her, and she experienced a sense of anonymity. She could be anyone, she thought, and she listened out for footsteps on the stairs as she went over to the bed. She lifted the mattress and extracted the little package from beneath it. Its hard edges were reassuringly lumpy beneath an old handkerchief.

She knelt on the pink carpet, and unwrapped what she'd picked up back in Streatham. Familiar objects stared back at her, beautiful with secrecy. An old-fashioned metal compass of the kind you used in maths; a cheap blue plastic cigarette lighter. The sight warmed her. They thought they could create her all over again, the neat respectable strangers downstairs, but the fingerprints had already been baked into the clay. She'd arrived here with baggage they didn't know about. For now, the knowledge was enough. She didn't want to do the ritual too often. She was afraid it might lose some of its power.

Jane replaced her secret under the mattress, and went to sit down at the dressing-table. She stared at her reflection for a long time. As the wall beside the mirror slowly faded from gold to charcoal-grey, the houses she'd seen in the suburbs lingered in her mind like an obsession. Soon, she would return there. She'd see all there was to see.

12

As the hotel came closer Bev gazed out of the car window. She listened to her parents talking.

'Oh, now,' said her mother, from the passenger seat of the hired Cadillac, 'isn't that lovely?'

'Should be,' said her father, from behind the wheel. 'The amount I'm paying for the damn place, I'd have expected Buckingham Palace.'

Why does he always have to ruin everything? wondered Bev furiously. She saw her mother's face tighten in the rear-view mirror, saw Toby obscurely blaming her for the science text-books in his suitcase. And it could so easily have been wonderful. She looked out at the soft exotic evening, the building that looked like the home of some billionaire film star, the bright lights blazing from the windows. They told you about that in the glossy brochures she'd read, but they didn't tell you about the tense silences that fell in the car and the kitchen, didn't tell you that you'd carry the Underlyme suburbs with you wherever you went. 'Not bad, is it?' she whispered to Toby, but he just stared moodily out of the window, shrugged and said nothing.

At the entrance to the underground car-park, a smiling clean-cut young man approached, and Bev watched her father wind down the window. 'Park your car for you, sir?' the stranger asked, and in a split second, Bev felt the Perfect Greens snap back into character. Her mother became sweet and demure, her father charming and laid-back, she and Toby two happy, well-balanced teenagers exhilarated after a long flight. 'Great. Thanks,' said Jack. 'The cases are in the boot. We're staying in apartment sixty-seven.' And Bev hated the way they all got out smiling and exchanging affectionate glances, and she hated the way they walked towards the main entrance in silence.

If only it was different somehow, she thought, watching her parents run through the intricate reception rigmarole, I could really enjoy this place. It was exciting to look around and see the beginnings of sophisticated night-life in this beautiful apartment complex – the thin rosy lights and the gleaming parquet flooring, the sense of something both alien and close enough to touch. Far away, someone was playing a piano, with the tinkling, arrogant ease of the slick professional. 'Well,' said her father, and she saw him smiling paternally for the girl on Reception, 'that's that, then. Let's get on up and get unpacked, shall we?'

Bev saw without surprise that the apartment was stunning: one double bedroom, one twin bedroom, one kitchen, one living room. Two bathrooms, of course. Peach and white were the dominant colours, and the décor favoured five-foot lamps and vast impressionistic prints to match. 'Jesus Christ,' said her father, as the door closed behind them, 'that bloody boy's just dumped our cases on the carpet.'

The suppressed anger in her mother's voice chilled Bev as it always did – the note of barely concealed hatred. 'Well, darling, where else was he supposed to put them?'

'How the hell should I know? Anywhere,' snapped her father. 'Not just leave them in the middle of the hallway. If I hadn't had the sense to put the light on, I'd have tripped over the damn things.'

As if hypnotised, Bev moved across to the living-room window. She looked down at an impossible fantasy pool, alive with little lights like fireflies in the hot deepening dusk, at crowds of laughing, lounging, happy people. It seemed as distant as an image on a TV screen, even now she was here. 'What do you mean I didn't tip him?' her father demanded. 'Have you got any idea how much this holiday's *costing* me?'

Her mother sounded hesitant and fearful: 'Of course, darling,' she said, 'I was only *saying*.'

And Bev turned away from the tantalising picture with an overwhelming sense of loss. That wasn't reality after all, she realised. The only reality was inside.

13

It's our very first morning here, thought Melissa, in this beautiful apartment, in Florida. I should be *happy*.

She was standing in the anonymous white kitchen, making a start on breakfast. Jack and the kids were still in bed. She'd long ago got used to getting up without waking anyone, had set an internal alarm clock to wake her twenty minutes before her husband. Everything had to run perfectly for Jack. If it didn't, he got so *angry*.

But she was used to running things perfectly. She'd been

looking after a household from the age of fourteen. Standing and cooking breakfast in the light of a bright foreign morning, she found herself thinking of the breakfasts she'd cooked in her youth. After her mother had died of cancer. Her younger sisters had been like her kids then, she remembered. And her father . . . her father had been like her husband.

Her father, elderly even then, demanding and querulous in worn pyjamas. 'Hurry up, Melissa. Why do you have to be so slow?' Her father picking discontentedly over the dinner she'd cooked. 'What have you done with these potatoes? Your mother would be turning in her grave, God rest her soul.' Anger when she wanted to go out to a party like the other girls did, scorn when she failed her O levels, no congratulations even when she took a secretarial course and got a job right after. 'You'll never make much of yourself as a secretary, Melissa. Katie's going on to do A levels. And Lisa's doing well at school.' Giving her nothing but an overwhelming desire to prove herself, to show him she could get the things that mattered after all – the perfect man, the perfect kids, the perfect *life.*

Standing at the cooker, Melissa experienced the luxury around her with a bewilderment close to tears, because she'd somehow attained it all and life still looked just the same.

'For God's sake, Melissa,' her father said in her mind, 'get a bloody move on with those eggs,' and then Jack was coming to sit down at the kitchen counter, and their very first day in Florida was beginning.

14

He's going to ask Toby about that science assignment, Bev thought bleakly, in the back of the hired Cadillac beside her brother. *Any second.*

'Did you make a start on that science assignment before you went to bed last night?' her father asked abruptly.

Against the backdrop of palm trees and blue skies, Toby's

hunted expression looked out of place. 'Dad, it was a long flight. I'll make a start on it tomorrow.'

'You'd *better* make a start on it tomorrow. There's a desk in the lounge, so you won't have to keep your sister awake.' Jack frowned at his son in the rear-view mirror. 'What the hell is it with you? When I was your age, I was running errands in my spare time and saving towards driving lessons. You've got nothing to do but get half-decent school marks, and you can't even manage *that*.'

Bev's long nails bit into the palm of her hand. She looked out at a scene she could have torn straight out of one of the holiday brochures. 'A bustling hive of activity and entertainment,' she remembered, 'you'll find it's all happening on this five-mile strip.' 'Well, here we are,' said Melissa eventually, 'here's the Belz Factory.'

Once inside, Bev started to feel slightly nauseous. It wasn't really a physical sickness, just something leaden and bone-deep that sucked all the fun out of everything. The smell of new merchandise, bright lights and wide aisles, Toby sulking beside her, her parents holding hands for an unspecified audience. She saw other families browsing, as smiling and unselfconscious as Emma's back at home, and a cold iron fist clenched down in her guts. 'Mum,' she said, 'I don't feel well.'

'What do you mean you don't feel well?' asked Jack, turning. She could have been in a witness-box. 'What is it? Food-poisoning or something?'

'I don't know. I just feel a bit rough. Listen, do you mind if I go on back to the hotel? I think I'd feel better for a lie-down.'

'Oh, *great*. Now I've got to drive all the way back there,' said Jack, and Melissa said, 'Darling, *please*, she can't help it if she's not feeling well.' The strained politeness in her voice put Bev in mind of creaking ice over deep water, and the bright consumer lights stared down at them. Bev knew, sure as fate, that she didn't want to go back in the car.

'No, *really*, Dad. You don't have to drive me. I can get one of those funny-looking bus things back to the hotel. We passed loads of them on the way here. You remember.'

'The I-Ride system? Oh, yeah,' said Jack. 'Good idea, sweetheart.'

'*Jack*,' said Melissa, and Bev heard the creak again. It sounded ominous in this colourful public space. 'Will you be all right going back on your own, Bev? Are you sure you're feeling well enough?'

'Mum, I'm not about to die or anything. I've just got a bit of a headache, that's all. I have got buses on my own before, you know.'

'Well, I suppose.' Melissa's pale preoccupied eyes appraised her daughter, and what she saw seemed to satisfy her. She fished in her handbag. 'Here's the room key. Be sure to keep it safe, now.'

'You can say *that* again,' said Jack. 'If she loses it and our things get stolen . . .'

Bev pulled herself out of the conversation as she'd have pulled herself out of sucking mud. She said purposeful, rapid goodbyes, and disappeared through the crowds, through the doors, with the room key now zipped in her rucksack.

Once out of sight of her parents and Toby, her sense of leaden nausea began to disperse. She stepped out on to the teeming strip of International Drive, and started walking in the direction of their hotel. Although she knew they'd all be back at the apartment for lunch, a dizzy sense of freedom overwhelmed her, and she tasted the sunshine with a new sweetness. Maybe, back at the Marriott, she could go and sunbathe by the pool for a while –

'Hey, honey!'

She turned. It was a young man not far off her own age, eighteen or nineteen, perhaps. He was cute, in a scruffy, laid-back way, with bright blue eyes and a dazzling white smile – Central Casting's ideal hippie. 'Yeah?' she asked.

'You dropped this,' he said.

Bev recognised her white lace hair ruffle at once. Her hand flew to the naked elastic band now holding her ponytail in place. She took it from him, smiling. 'Thanks.'

'Don't mention it. Mind if I walk with you for a while?'

Although Bev wasn't consciously aware of it, any number of factors could have made her *mind* a great deal – a preppy shirtfront logo, an English accent, a reference to her looks. But as it was, he seemed ultimately exotic and attractive, and she didn't mind at all. 'Sure,' she said. 'I'm getting the I-Ride a bit further up, though.'

'Where are you off to?' he asked, falling into step beside her. 'Meeting someone?'

'Escaping from someone. Three someones, really. My family.'

'Hey. That's pretty intense.' His bright blue eyes were frankly interested. 'How come?'

Bev looked up. Palm trees towered against a luminous sky. 'You don't want to know.'

He smiled. 'Try me.'

'Okay. My parents hate each other. They make my brother hate *me*. And I hate being around them.' She spoke carelessly and defiantly – she realised that, in three sentences, she'd told him more than she'd ever dreamed of telling her long-term best friend at home. 'Is that enough?'

His expression didn't change. 'I guess,' he said. 'Why don't you tell me more? There's a bar just up ahead. We could have a drink together.'

15

I must be out of my mind, thought Bev, in the cool shadows out of the sunlight, sitting on a stool by the bar, beside a total stranger she'd met maybe six minutes ago. It was ten o'clock in the morning, and she was drinking a Seabreeze cocktail, and if her parents smelt booze on her breath, or if they decided to return to the apartment before lunchtime –

But the fear just seemed to add to her squirming, treacherous excitement. She felt as if she'd broken free in some way, as if she'd shaken off the long silences and the unbearable tension, and was now relaxing in a different world.

'You're staying at the Grande Vista?' he asked. 'That's uptown.'

If he'd shown the faintest sign of being impressed by the name she'd have gone off him in a second, but he just sounded cool, sardonic, slightly mocking. 'I suppose,' she said. 'It's just a bunch of rooms, and my mum cooks in the kitchen. It's not really like being in a hotel at all.'

'You're too young to be that blasé, surely. How old are you, anyway?'

'Sixteen,' Bev lied.

'Jeez. I thought you were older than *that*.' For a second, she thought he was about to get up and walk away, but then he smiled. 'And you're bored with it all already, huh?'

'Not everything. Hardly anything at all.' Bev's hand caressed the stem of her glass idly. 'Just my family and my school and the town I live in. Nothing more than that, really.'

'What's so wrong with it all? Lots of people's parents don't get along.'

'Mine are different.' It was something she'd felt a hundred times before, that she'd never tried to put into words. 'They don't just not get along. They have to make everyone else think that they *do* get along. When we're with other people, we're the happiest family in the world. It's just, like – *pretending*. All the time. And that's why I hate school. Because I have to do it there, too.'

His face was watchful in the half-light. 'How do you mean?'

How easy it was to talk in this alien world, where you drank cocktails at ten in the morning and nobody knew your name. 'It's like I sort of *represent* them at school,' she said. 'I can't just do stuff because I want to. And I can't tell anyone what it's really like. They think I'm lucky.' Something darkened in her eyes. 'My parents just expect me to get everything right. It's not even like they're happy when I do. But they'd go mad if I didn't. I get As and Bs, and that's just for them, and I've got to go to sixth-form college, and that's just for them. And I got eight Valentines this year, and, you know, it's like *that* was just for them, too.'

'I've always figured Valentines were kind of dumb,' he said.

It seemed to set him on a different plane of existence from the stupid, shallow boys at school, who wanted to be Bev Green's first proper boyfriend in the same way as they'd once wanted a better yo-yo than their mates'. It drew her closer to him. 'I think so, too,' she said.

They were sitting and sipping in companionable silence, when Bev caught a glimpse of her watch. 'Oh, my God. Listen, I've got to go. My parents could be back at the apartment any minute. I'm supposed to be ill in *bed*.'

'We should do this again,' he said. 'How about meeting up in here tomorrow?'

'What'll I tell my parents?'

'You're supposed to be ill in bed, aren't you?' His smile was lazy and challenging. 'Just stick to the story.'

'What time do you want to meet up?' she asked, and felt the treacherous excitement intensify.

'I don't know. How about two o'clock?'

'I'll be here. Listen, I've really got to go.'

On the bus-ride back to the hotel. Bev's heartbeat picked up speed. Over and over, she envisaged the cold interrogation as to where the hell she'd been with their room key. But when the key turned in the lock, the door opened to silent sun-drenched emptiness, and crisp folded corners saying that the maid had come and gone. Relief swept over her. She went into the bathroom, and brushed the taste of thrilling corruption out of her mouth, and thought about the young man she'd just met. It dawned on her that she didn't even know his name.

16

'And this is the science lab. We're having a second one installed next year, as you might have heard. I like to think we've got quite an exceptional range of facilities, and . . .'

The headmaster of Underlyme Grammar was a youngish man,

nothing quite as crass as trendy, as charming, smiling and inaccessible as a politician. Mary and Alf flanked him on either side as he walked, oohing and aahing politely over everything. Jane trailed along behind them, and tried to do the same.

There was something strange about walking through the wide, clean, echoing corridors that smelt of paint and polish, glancing through glass door-panels at empty classrooms with the chairs stacked neatly on the tables for the cleaner's sake. To Jane, it was terribly evocative. She remembered the comprehensive back in Clapham with a shudder; she looked at doors and lockers and whiteboards, and felt the present blur around the past. In her mind, she saw Michelle and Chandra and Stephanie. 'Well, it all looks lovely,' said Mary. 'I suppose you've got quite a few names on the waiting-list?'

'More than a few, for the first year,' said the Head. 'But it's quite unusual for young people to be changing schools at third-year level. When Jane joins us next term, she'll be the only new pupil in her class.'

'It's wonderful you've got room for her, Mr Martin,' said Mary. 'To be honest, we were starting to get a bit worried. Term's so close.'

'Eight days, now,' said the Head. His searchlight smile swept over Mary and Alf in turn, then switched off. 'You can always trust a headmaster to keep count.'

They saw the assembly hall and the domestic-science kitchens, the tuck shop and the library and the canteen, and they ended up in the head's trendily disordered office, where paperwork of various kinds was shuffled and distributed and folded into Mary's handbag. 'If you could get this back to the school secretary before term starts, I'd be very grateful,' said the head. 'Well, it's been lovely to meet you both.' There were handshakes all round. Finally, he extended a hand to Jane. 'And you, of course, Jane.' And she took it briefly, and smiled, and said nothing.

'Well, wasn't that lovely?' said Mary, when they were back in the elderly Ford, driving back towards the Darlington Estate. 'He seems like ever such a nice man. Doesn't he, Alf?'

'A good headmaster,' said Alf. 'A good school, too. I don't mind saying, I was worried we'd have to send Jane to St Andrew's.'

'Don't you mention that place to me. Carol was a good girl before we made the mistake of sending her *there*.' Mary cleared her throat, and turned in the passenger seat. 'There, Jane, dear. Aren't you pleased? You'll be starting there the Monday after next.'

'It looks lovely,' said Jane.

Back in the house, Alf went straight out into the garden, and Mary made a start on cooking a late lunch. The time was almost half past two. Jane lingered in the kitchen, and tried to speak noncommittally. 'Nan,' she said, 'you know those suburbs we went through the other day?'

'Of course, dear,' said Mary, chopping busily. 'What about them?'

'What are they called?' asked Jane. 'What's the area called?'

'Out by the beach road?' asked Mary. 'Preston, dear. The area's called Preston.'

'Preston,' Jane spoke almost inaudibly, tasting the word. 'Listen, Nan,' she said eventually, 'you don't mind if I go out for a walk, do you? I feel like a breath of fresh air.'

17

It was amazing how easy it was to find the golden advert world. She walked into town, and spent maybe eight minutes searching out the bus stop that promised Preston, and waited patiently. The bus arrived sooner than she'd expected. She sat on the top deck and stared restlessly into the bright bustling summer afternoon, and prepared herself for that first step into heaven.

It was all that she'd remembered, and more than that – it was an oasis in the wilderness, its loveliness awed her. Without knowing where she was or where she was going, she walked and walked, and drank it all in with her eyes. Beneath a clear blue sky, lightly stonewashed with clouds, green lawns unfolded like velvet, and tall wrought-iron gates stood closed, not concealing but accentuating the beauty behind them. Such absolute and inaccessible beauty. She saw houses of varying styles and sizes: a white Romanish villa with pillars round the doors and a flat roof: big plain four-square family homes: some split-level architectural caprices, all granite and red timber and tiles. A three-storey mock-Tudor residence with the hint of a swimming-pool glittering round the back. Occasionally, she saw flashes of life – a woman moving in a window far away, a boy mowing a front garden, a car turning into a driveway – but otherwise the stillness was absolute, dreamlike, mesmerising. A cool refreshing breeze caressed her face. She walked and walked through the world that filled her dreams, the heart of light.

A bronzed bikini-clad woman sunbathing in a back garden, a family group laughing round a barbecue Jane wished she could smell. Movie stills imprinted themselves on her mind, and every one was as perfect as a fantasy. She'd never forget a single tiny detail as long as she lived, she thought, and walked on dazed and drunk with beauty. At last, she'd found something that would always be in the same place, something that would always be wonderful.

When the summer light started to fade into sepia, she knew she'd have to go home. Somehow, she didn't want to see the garish orange bus-seats right now, and a kind of mental compass led her back into town via the beach road. Walking along it, she felt exhausted with fading passion, and thought she'd like to rest for a while. So she sat down on a chipped green bench that faced out to sea, and the gulls screamed above the empty water as she lapsed into a reverie.

18

Anita had lived in a crowded little terrace on Tulse Hill with the big fat capable mother who worked in the launderette with Carol, a taciturn father who rarely appeared, three teenage sisters, an endless succession of relatives who came and went from week to week, and a large hairy mongrel Jane was vaguely afraid of. The house was always in a mess. Everywhere you looked, you saw the cheerful disarray of crowded lives – travel brochures picked up on a whim, boxes of the video blockbusters they'd rented last night, curling tongs and French-manicure kits belonging to the teenage sisters, who talked of nothing but beauty and clothes and gossip. To Jane, there was something wonderful about the chaos. It was far from the beer-cans and overflowing ashtrays Carol's friends left behind at night, something open and friendly, that welcomed you with a smile no matter who you were, something that didn't need to know your name to let you in.

Anita's room was like all of it, and more than any of it. It was even smaller than Jane's own at the third-floor flat, but there was none of the bleakness Jane had come to associate with small rooms. Just a kind of amiable, extrovert busyness that exploded from every possible place: corners of bright material poking out of drawers, stickers on the dressing-table mirror, the table itself a forest of hair-ruffles and combs and pens and the occasional stolen lipstick. Schoolbooks were bundled carelessly underneath it, and a motley mob of old teddies colonised the bed, so the bright patchwork of the counterpane was only occasionally visible. It was such a wonderful room to be in, with the sun streaming through the tiny window, the ancient stereo pounding out cheap cheerful pop. You could sit around, and chat with Anita, and forget this wasn't home after all.

One time, the two of them had taped a radio show in that room. Not one off a station, a radio show of their own. It had been amateurish, to say the least, the record button pressed down and their tinny voices calling out to each other in a parody of DJ cool, introducing songs ('And here's MC Anita, movin' into the afternoon with Sheryl Crow') telling stupid jokes, talking about their respective schools. When she was with Anita, Michelle and Chandra and Stephanie didn't exist, Jane was popular at school, she was happy at school, she and her mates smuggled fags in and couldn't wait for the lunch-time bell. It had been the best fun in the world. When the afternoon had started fading into evening, Anita's mum had poked her head round the door. 'Do you want to stay for tea, Jane?' she'd asked. 'I can call your mum and tell her you'll be late home, if you like.' And the relief of accepting had been immense. She'd always remember that single slow, lazy, beautiful afternoon round at Anita's, and in that second, Jane had known it deep inside: nothing in her life would ever be better than Sheryl Crow on the stereo, Anita giggling beside her, the sisters gossiping in the lounge and the wonderful smell of slowly cooking meatloaf.

19

Melissa came to look in on Bev before she and Jack and Toby left for the Epcot Center. Thin streaks of sunlight slanted through the bedroom window's half-drawn blinds. Where they touched Melissa's face, they made her look pale and tired. 'You sure you're going to be all right on your own, Bev?' she asked.

'Of course, Mum. You don't have to worry.'

'But I *do* worry. You've spent almost every day laid up in bed since we got here. I do wish you'd ask your father to call a doctor.'

'No, Mum, really,' said Bev hastily. 'I haven't got some dreaded lurgy or anything. Honestly. I just feel a bit manky, that's all. I'll be better in no time.'

'But still,' Melissa began, and then the voice drifted out of the living-room – 'Mel, get a bloody move on. The queues are going to be hell,' and Melissa's face froze, and she turned away from the bed. 'Coming, darling,' she called.

In the doorway, she looked back at Bev for a second. 'Well, if you need anything, just tell Reception. We shouldn't be back any later than five.' And then she was gone.

Bev's heartbeat pounded slowly in her ears as she listened to the three of them leaving. When she was sure they'd gone, she got out of bed. She went to the window and opened the blinds, and felt the bars of light flash into a perfect summer afternoon.

In the bathroom, she brushed her hair out loose and applied a little makeup – blusher, lipgloss, a touch of brown mascara. It was wonderful how these afternoons felt, both furtive and guiltless, like an innocent prisoner plotting an audacious break-out. Of course, she'd told him all about it, and he'd laughed. Over the last six days, she'd told him just about everything.

Bev hadn't ever suspected you could have this kind of unity with anyone else, let alone a boy. That you could really talk about the things that mattered, and know you wouldn't be stared at with shocked, judgemental eyes when you finished speaking. The sense of liberation she felt was extraordinary – there was a life beyond the slick pretences, after all. A life her parents and Toby would never know existed.

His name, as she now knew, was Bradley. He was a nineteen-year-old aspiring artist, and he occasionally worked at Walt Disney World, in one of the merchandise shops. She knew it wasn't a CV her parents would approve of, and the knowledge made him all the more attractive in her eyes. For the first time in her life, she was doing something just for her – the afternoons in shadowed bars, Seabreeze cocktails and the taste of his lips when they said goodbye – a small, private part of her mind that her parents couldn't touch or take away. She felt that, in some way, this summer romance belonged to her more completely than the promised iMac ever could.

He was just so *real*, like this new happiness was. The way he never flattered her, never sucked up as she occasionally suspected Emma of doing. It made her feel good. With him, she didn't feel like Bev of the Perfect Greens at all. Just somebody three-dimensional and human whom someone else could honestly like and be interested in, just somebody *normal*. She'd never felt anything like this about a boy before. She thought maybe she loved him.

Bev changed into a vest top and shorts; she bent to tie the laces of her trainers. Her parents had left her the door key, so she could come and go if she needed to. She picked it up off the side-table. She'd be back here to let them in in plenty of time, she thought. It was only one o'clock now. She was meeting Bradley in the bar at half past. He'd said the day before that they could go back to his flat.

20

The smell was the first thing that hit Bev as she walked through the door behind him. It was an insidious, unpleasant smell, like aerosol deodorant and old trainers and wet towels all at once. And something else underlying it, something sickly sweet and pungent. She'd never smelt it before, but instinctively recognised it as illicit. 'Well,' he said, 'welcome to the palace.'

For the first time in his company, Bev didn't know what to say. She'd expected a stylishly sparse loft apartment with bare floorboards and uncurtained windows, a kind of careless, arrogant squalor. But there was nothing careless or arrogant about this – the ugly patterned carpet and the squashy plastic three-piece suite, occasional socks and video-boxes discarded on the floor. He laughed at her ongoing silence. 'Not impressed, huh?'

Bev felt embarrassed. She told herself her unease was ridiculous and snobbish – she'd already known he hadn't any money. 'Oh, no,' she said. 'It's not that. It's just . . .' and she tailed off, realising it was the first time she'd ever lied to him.

'Take a seat. I'll fix a joint. You ever smoked a joint before?'

It was terrible, how she felt shocked. It embarrassed her all over again. How suburban and safe she was after all, she thought, with contempt, how perfectly fitted to the tense silences and the nice little lies. 'No,' she said. 'But I'd like to try.'

'So now you can.' He opened a drawer, got out the paraphernalia and sat down beside her on the ugly plastic sofa. He flicked a lighter and crumbled hash expertly; the sickly sweet smell flared strongly, filling Bev's mind. You baby, she taunted herself, you pussy, but it didn't make her feel any better. Despite herself, she was ill-at-ease. The sunlight showed up everything with awful, uncompromising clarity, and she saw the sordidness of the scene, the slight shake of her hand as she reached to take the joint. 'You're shaking,' he said, sounding amused and slightly patronising, 'you're *scared*.'

'I'm not scared.' She raised the joint to her lips and dragged deeply. She'd never even smoked a cigarette before, and fought not to cough as the strange thick smoke invaded her lungs. It left her feeling weak and dizzy and slightly nauseous. 'There,' she said, with a bravado not her own, 'your turn.'

He held on to the joint longer than was strictly sociable, but Bev couldn't have cared less. She didn't feel at all high like people said you were meant to; she felt the effects of the hash as an intensification of her unease. He looked so different here, in this ugly little room. Sleazy and unkempt. 'Have the last of it,' he said, passing her an inch or so of wet-tipped horror. 'It's the best bit.'

She didn't want to smoke it, but couldn't think of anything else to do. Dizziness came in a wave, and the room rotated. She stood up, her head swimming. 'What do I do with it now?'

'Give it to me. I'll flush it down the john. You'd better sit down.' She sat, to a jarring symphony of plastic creaking, feeling nausea clench and unclench in the pit of her stomach. She heard a toilet flush. He came back into the room, and sat down beside her, putting a hand on her thigh. 'You feeling high?'

'I feel weird,' she said. 'Really weird.'

'Good, huh? Come here,' and his mouth closed down on hers, hard. She wasn't sure what to do. The whole afternoon seemed to be running at the wrong speed, like a Walkman whose batteries were failing. She felt weak and sick. And his mouth tasted all wrong. His lips were too hot and wet, and his tongue recalled the taste of the joint in sickening detail. She couldn't think of how to tell him to stop without sounding babyish and pathetic, so she just went with it. Maybe they kissed for a minute, maybe an hour before she became aware of his hand burrowing up her shorts. In a second, it snapped her out of her drugged apathy. She pulled away. 'Hey,' she said. 'Don't do that.'

'Ah, come on, honey,' he said, 'just relax, let it happen,' and his mouth came down again, and his hot clammy hand was going further up the leg of her shorts, hurrying into her knickers, into *her*.

From a standing start, her heartbeat was racing, and she tore herself away. 'Look, *stop it*,' she shrieked, and then he was pulling her back.

'Come on, honey,' he said again, 'just *relax.*'

And then – how had it all happened so quickly? – she was fighting harder than she'd ever fought before in her life. It was impossible that she could fight that hard and still be unable to move. But she couldn't move, and his hands were everywhere, wrenching down her shorts, her knickers. She heard fabric tear, and the sound of his breathing. It was like a wild animal's, a bull perhaps. Puffing and snorting. Her unease had snapped into terror in the space of a couple of seconds. His mouth left hers, and she screamed for a split second before his open palm came down over her mouth, puffing and snorting and grunting until he was on her, in her.

When he finally came and went limp, she was able to wrestle him off her. She leaped up, weeping, and yanked up her torn knickers, her still intact shorts. He said something and started after her, but she was too quick for him. Although she didn't know the flat she remembered where the front door was, and she ran out, still weeping, running as if for her life.

She ran for a long time, until the hysterics gave way to dead nothing, drawing strange looks in a strange land, neither knowing nor caring. A kind of homing instinct led her back to the Marriott Grande Vista on autopilot. The apartment was silent. She went straight to the bathroom and began to run herself a bath.

It was a terrible feeling she had, a nightmare feeling – like maggots crawling inside her, something rancid that she couldn't wash off. A feeling that she'd been spoiled somehow, in a way invisible to the casual eye but maybe discernible if you looked hard enough. Above all, she felt that she was not the same person who'd left this apartment earlier. She looked back to Bev of the Perfect Greens, the girl who'd laced up her trainers in the hallway that morning, and found that she couldn't identify with her at all.

She sat in a too-hot bath and scrubbed her flesh till it reddened – the thick, foresty smell of alpine Badedas drifted on wisps of steam, and sunlight slanted through the blinds, across the bubbles. Aside from the sounds of splashing water and her own breathing, the world was in absolute silence. It echoed in her ears – the terror, the bewilderment, the new and over-whelming sense of nothing.

What would they think if they knew? Suddenly this thought obsessed her. Her parents and Emma and Toby and the boys at school who thought she was perfect. If they somehow realised how she'd been damaged, it would never be the same. But perhaps it *could* be the same, if she kept on pretending everything was just as it had been that morning when the world had looked different and she'd been a stranger. Perhaps she could even get to feel like that stranger all over again.

She would never tell anyone. Nobody would ever know a thing about that afternoon and what had happened. A smile of terrible fragility touched her mouth as she pulled out the plug and rose from the bath. As she looked in the mirror, her smile crumpled into tears, because her eyes had a judgemental look not her own, and she felt as if she was being scrutinised by an enemy.

Mandy walked through the town centre alone, thinking about Jack Green. She always thought about Jack Green now. She thought he was the best thing in her life.

'Try and phone me when you get out there, will you?' she'd asked, and he'd said 'sure,' but she hadn't heard from him yet, and was beginning to worry he might call her now, when she was out.

In the little café in town, Tracey and Caroline were already sitting at a table by the window, smoking and talking and drinking coffee. She came in and said hi and joined them. They'd all been at school together, not so long ago. She despised everything about their lives, but she still met up with them several times a week, so she supposed they still counted as old friends.

'I was just saying to Caroline, me and Wayne are having our engagement party next month,' said Tracey. 'Course, you're invited, Mand.'

A spotty teenage waitress lumbered over; Mandy ordered cappuccino. 'Where you having it?' she asked indifferently, when the waitress had gone.

'Function room at the Rose and Crown,' said Tracey. 'My dad knows the manager. We're getting special rates.'

Mandy gazed out of the café window. Outside, the last of the summer's tourists milled and quarrelled in novelty hats and T-shirts, and the sun blazed down. She saw peanuts and stale crisps in a miserable little suburban function room and spoke without thinking. 'Don't you want anything else?'

'What do you mean?' asked Tracey.

It was terrible to realise that Tracey and Caroline really didn't know, that they were happy to feel life slipping past them, here in the middle of nowhere. You married a boy you'd known at school and announced your engagement in the *Underlyme Echo* and got a cheap, nasty little house together, and then, before you knew it, your daughter would be doing the same thing. It had always been like this, but it chilled Mandy just the same. 'A real party,' she said. 'A real man. Doing *real* things.'

'There won't be anything wrong with my party,' said Tracey, nettled. 'Or my man.'

Mandy envisaged Tracey's boyfriend Wayne – fourteen stone of thick, twenty-year-old plumber. In her mind's eye, she placed him beside Jack. 'I never said there was,' she said, 'but we all used to talk about doing more.'

'That was just talk, though,' said Caroline. 'Everyone wants to get married. Don't you?'

'To the right man,' said Mandy, and the picture of Jack rose again behind her eyes – smiling in his perfect suit, in his perfect office. 'Someone who could take me away from all this.'

'God, Mandy, you're such a drama queen,' said Tracey. 'All *what*?'

'I don't know.' Mandy thought of shabby little celebrations and the Merc's powerful headlights zooming away into the night. *He* wouldn't be like Tracey's boyfriend, if she could get him to leave his wife, he'd do things in style. 'I'm just fed up with Underlyme, maybe. *Our* bit of Underlyme.'

'What's the alternative?' asked Caroline, laughing.

'I don't know,' said Mandy, but she knew perfectly well – her affair with Jack, the possibility of it becoming something more. It felt like a lifeline to her, as it had from the start: Prince Charming in a black Mercedes, a door leading out from this predictable provincial hell. Over the last few months, he'd come to mean everything to her. 'It doesn't matter,' she said. She sat and gazed out of the window, hearing Tracey and Caroline begin talking about the engagement party again. He hadn't called her from Florida, but perhaps he hadn't been able to. He could still rescue her. She looked out at the red-faced tourists, and realised he'd be back the day after tomorrow.

23

Jack was looking forward to going back to Underlyme. He always felt vaguely insecure away from the home he'd made his own. Out here he wasn't *the boss* any more, just another fairly prosperous tourist in a town awash with fairly prosperous tourists, and he longed for the safety of Jack's Motors and absolute deference, and an adoring, undemanding mistress who appeared whenever he wanted her, and vanished the second he clicked his fingers.

He was homesick.

He was sitting with Melissa and the kids in a crowded Texan-themed restaurant the holiday brochure had recommended with four stars and a tick. Melissa watched him anxiously. 'What's the matter, darling? You've hardly said a word all evening.'

'It's nothing.' They were all quiet and edgy tonight, he thought, even Bev. Across the table, he watched her pick indifferently at her *chilli con carne*, obviously thinking herself unwatched. 'What about the science assignment, Toby?' he asked. 'You got it finished yet?'

'Last night, Dad,' said Toby, with a kind of listless relief.

'Good.' Jack thought he saw Melissa looking at him strangely across the table, and felt the usual self-righteous rage move inside him: he only pushed Toby for his own good, he told himself. If only his parents had pushed him a bit harder academically, when he'd been Toby's age. Jacob Green, stuck working evenings and weekends in Dad's grocery shop. It was a miracle he'd made anything of himself at all, he thought, with a background like that. But the pride and exhilaration wouldn't come this evening, somehow, and the silence at the table made him feel slightly uneasy. 'Your mother and I'll be expecting renewed efforts all round, next term,' he said. 'Won't we, Melissa?'

She smiled and nodded. He told himself that it was all right, that she agreed with him on everything. Still, he didn't feel quite himself. He sat and ate mechanically, as Melissa and the kids did, listening to loud, bright strangers' voices ringing out all around

him. Thank God, he thought, that they were going back to
Underlyme tomorrow.

24

'Just think, Jane, dear,' said Mary, 'this time next week, you'll
have started at school.'

They'd just eaten dinner, and were now sitting in the cosy
little lounge, gathered round the television screen – a garish true-
stories programme cackled mindlessly at them through the glass.
A wave of terror washed over Jane at the mention of school. She
kept thinking of Michelle and Chandra and Stephanie, and felt as
if she was being prepared to meet them all over again. 'I know,'
she said.

'You should have a great time there, love,' said Alf, his eyes
not leaving the screen. 'Soon make some nice new friends. You'll
have settled right in in no time.'

How it had been when the lunch-time bell rang and how she'd
dreaded it – how she'd longed for the weekend, when she could
hang out with Anita and feel as though she belonged. Tonight
she could sense it all waiting in the wings for her, preparing to
leap. 'I know,' she said again.

The television roared with laughter, and nobody spoke. Jane
shifted in her seat, trying to find a quick route to her only means
of escape. 'I think I'll get an early night,' she said eventually. 'I
feel a bit tired. I'll see you in the morning.'

She said goodnight to her grandparents, and started up the
stairs. All the way up to her room, a sense of purpose shadowed
her thoughts. She'd denied herself the ritual for too long, and it
was for exactly this sort of situation that it had first been created
– the overwhelming tension, the claustrophobia, the fear of
tomorrow. She went into her bedroom, put on the bedside light
and closed the door. A part of her listened out for footsteps on
the stairs as she extracted the little package from under the
mattress.

She sat down at the dressing-table, and laid the compass and the lighter out in front of her. In the mirror, her face was pale and set and shadowed. Rolling up her sleeve, she peeled back the greying bandage round her forearm. She always wore the bandage beneath her shirts and sweaters, in case someone somehow saw what they weren't meant to and asked her questions she couldn't evade or lie to. Nobody seemed to notice that she always wore long sleeves in the height of summer. At least, nobody ever remarked on it. Perhaps, she thought, they just didn't care.

Above a point about half-way up her forearm, Jane saw her flesh with a sneaking revulsion. Perhaps there was half an inch of unbroken skin between the crusted lines, but she thought it was more like a quarter of an inch. Although none of the marks was all that severe on its own, seen together she thought they were somehow terrible, on her inner arm up as far as her elbow-joint, as if she'd been savaged by tiny, vicious animals. Most were dark and scabbed, a couple fresh and raw-looking. One was still yellowish and unhealthy. She'd been afraid it might get worse, but it seemed to be getting better. She was relieved about that. She'd worried that she might have to go to the doctor, and she couldn't ever have explained the ritual to *him*.

Sitting at the dressing-table, Jane flicked the lighter, and held the compass point steady in the flame. After a few seconds, she extracted it and laid the lighter down on the table. Then she raised the heated metal compass point and carved her flesh till the blood came, and she tasted the brief seconds of wonderful nothing that made it all worthwhile.

25

She'd discovered the ritual some three months ago, in the tense silence of her bedroom back at her mother's flat, at the height of her mother's madness. The compass in her school pencil-tin and a tension that demanded release – she knew they'd been made for each other. The addition of the lighter had come only last month, when the yellowish, unhealthy-looking wound had led her to fear blood-poisoning. She'd read somewhere that, if you held a point in a naked flame, it became sterile. So she'd bought the blue plastic lighter from a newsagent's for forty pence. Though she hadn't expected it, the pain of the hot metal had quickly become an integral part of the experience.

She didn't know exactly why she did it, but it struck her as giving the same kind of satisfaction she'd got out of biting her nails ever since she could remember. She'd graduated in different kinds of pain – the gnawed pinkish flesh round the fingertips, the thumbnail bitten down to the quick – but the compass point was more satisfying than any of it. The pain took up the tension and every other part of her life, and gathered it together like papers in a fist, and for a few wonderful blissful perfect seconds she could feel all of it flying in the wind, leaving nothing inside but an infinite and godlike emptiness. There was no real reason beyond that. She did it because it was what it was, because it felt like it did.

When she'd finished with the ritual, she felt dizzy and drained. She folded tissue paper into a small square, and taped it over the bleeding cut with the Sellotape that wasn't important enough to hide. She'd begun by using plasters, but, once, the blood had seeped through to mark her shirt. She was cutting herself more and more deeply now, and tissue paper was safer and more absorbent when you folded it as thickly as she did.

Then she wrapped the compass and the lighter back in the handkerchief, and replaced them under the mattress.

She tied the bandage back round her arm, changed into her long-sleeved pyjamas and went into the bathroom. She washed and brushed herself ready for bed. When her head hit the pillow, she feared nightmares of Michelle and Chandra and Stephanie but, for whatever reason, the nightmares didn't come. Her mind was running on a different track.

She dreamed about the suburbs.

September

1

The night before her first day back at school, Bev had a terrible dream.

She was in the ugly little flat in Orlando, frozen in the first slow moments of terror as he puffed and grunted his way on top of her. 'Ah, come on, honey,' he whispered in her ear, 'just relax, let it happen,' and she looked up as if in slow motion, and registered what she saw with horror. A coach-party stood in the doorway, watching them; her mother and father, Toby and Emma and a handful of her peers from school. They wore matching T-shirts and identical expressions of cold disgust. 'And this is Bradley's flat,' the tour guide announced brightly from the doorway, 'and this is Beverley Green.' And she realised that her legs were open and he was forcing himself into her, and the coach-party stood there silently, and stared at her with eyes that didn't blink.

She fought and struggled to free herself, to tell them not to tell anyone else what they'd seen here, that everything could be all right if they didn't tell their friends when they got home. But her movements were as slow as if she was swimming through treacle, and the sound of her screaming was almost inaudible. A thin keening sound like a buzzing in her head pierced through her sleep with a sharp sudden pain, and as she jerked awake she realised it had been a physical pain that had awoken her after all, that gnawing in the pit of her stomach that always preceded her period.

Bev padded out of bed and down the hallway to the bathroom. The cord flooded the world with white light, and the silence was absolute. Her watch said it had just gone four. She got the

Tampax out of the bathroom cabinet, and crouched above the toilet bowl. The sight of her own blood should have relieved her, but it didn't. Her heart hammered in her ears in the clean, sterile silence, and she experienced a nameless terror darker than the simple fear of pregnancy could ever be. The loneliness of four a.m. echoed in her head.

Back in bed, she pulled the duvet around her and tried too hard to sleep. But sleep wouldn't come back. There was something inside her that people couldn't see, and it obsessed her for long hours before the first dawn light slanted through the curtains and the birds began to twitter far away, and the alarm by her bed told her it was time to get up for school.

2

The morning was far too beautiful. It taunted her through the kitchen windows with the power of innocence – blue and tender, a distant memory that stayed close enough to see.

'Are you all right, Bev?' asked Melissa, after Jack had left for work and they were alone together. 'You look a bit tired.'

It jolted her: maybe she hadn't covered over the cracks carefully enough. She spoke defensively. 'I'm fine,' she said. 'I slept like a log last night.'

'You look tired,' Melissa repeated, anxiously. In the clean summer light, Bev thought her mother looked tired too, her eyes a little bloodshot, her hands darting to clear the breakfast plates. 'I hope you're over that bug you picked up in Orlando, Bev. You haven't seemed quite yourself since then.'

The terror of a disguise that could be seen through too easily appalled Bev, like a vital piece of evidence left carelessly in the open. She cowered behind her school uniform and carefully styled hair, and fought for the right note of casual irritation. 'I'm fine, Mum,' she said. 'I've just been missing school.'

'Well, that's easily cured, at least,' said Melissa, with brittle gaiety. She stacked the last few plates in the dishwasher and rose, smoothing down her skirt. 'Where's Toby got to? You're both going to be late if he doesn't hurry up.' Then his footsteps were crashing down the stairs, and they were all walking out to the garage.

In the back of the Mitsubishi Shogun, Bev gazed out of the window. Her fingers twined restlessly in her lap as she watched them leaving the suburbs. 'I'm going to see Dad today,' said Melissa, from the driving-seat. 'I'll be coming back your way. I can pick you up after school, if you like.'

'No, thanks, Mum,' said Toby. 'I'm going round to Pete's. You remember, I told you.'

'Well, what about you, Bev?' asked Melissa, with a kind of desperation. 'There's no sense in me driving all the way back on my own, is there? It's nicer than getting the bus.'

'Sure,' said Bev absently. 'I'll see you by the gates at four,' and her eyes flickered out of the window again. As she saw the pastel-blue sky and the gentle morning light, something gripped and twisted in her guts – something dark nibbling at the outskirts of the world, something dirty and secret that didn't belong there, and only she could see.

3

'We'll pick you up at four,' said Mary, from the passenger-seat, as the elderly Ford slowed down and parked. 'Right here, by the gates.'

The taste of fear filled Jane's mouth. Schoolgirls and boys swarmed beyond the car windows, and she could hear them laughing. 'Okay, Nan,' she said mechanically. 'I'll be here.'

'I mean, it's only right, for your first day and all,' said Alf. 'You'll be getting the bus with the others tomorrow, but we'll pick you up today.'

'Okay, Grandad,' said Jane. 'I'd better go, anyway. I'll be late.'

'Well, have a nice day, dear,' said Mary. Jane got out of the car, and the voices rang out around her with a new clarity. She waved off her grandparents quickly, smiling a rictus of terror.

After a solitary walk, collecting her thoughts and readying herself slowly, Jane would have felt far more comfortable than she did in the here and now, thrown straight in at the deep end and left to sink like a stone. She felt inadequately prepared, lost and alone among the confident of all ages: confident eleven-year-old boys running like a herd of buffalo, confident young women flicking styled hair from pencilled eyes and exchanging metallic confidences in voices that locked out the outsider. 'You've changed your hair,' one girl shrieked to another as Jane passed, 'God, you're so *brown*,' and Jane moved through the crowds towards the main double doors, wearing her loneliness like a leper's bell.

Inside the sprawling main building, it was quieter and shadowed. She saw big noticeboards with photographs mounted behind glass panes, and a hundred faces smiled out at her remotely. A harassed-looking middle-aged woman passed her, carrying a sheaf of papers. Jane stopped her. 'Excuse me,' she asked, 'where's 10H?' The middle-aged woman didn't smile. 'Straight down that corridor,' she snapped. 'Turn left at the coats.' She turned and walked away.

Left at the coats, the wide sunny corridor gave way to a kind of twilit clearing, a forest of coat-hooks and lockers, double doors leading on to something Jane couldn't see. Four or five girls of around her own age lingered by the lockers, flaunting an arrogant and ostentatious popularity with their improbable trainers and trendy little rucksacks. 'Yeah, but she's a fucking slag,' one was saying. 'She's got off with *everyone*.' Then they noticed Jane, and conversation stopped, and they watched her walk past them in silence. Jane hurried with her eyes fixed straight ahead. Disturbing echoes of Michelle and Chandra and Stephanie whispered in her mind.

Through the double doors and down another corridor, she saw the open door marked 10H, and walked through it into a big sunny empty classroom that smelt of fresh paint. She sat down at a table near the window and gazed out. She was just beginning to relax when a deafening bell rang. Within minutes, the room had filled up. Eyes glanced at her as at an inanimate curiosity, and two girls sat down at her table. They carried on talking as if she wasn't there. She sat and studied her bitten nails, and tried to look as if she didn't care about a thing.

'Michael! Toby!' a voice shrieked from the doorway. 'How was Florida?' Jane looked over and saw the corridor girls swaggering in like a football team and going over to the noisy central table. She didn't want them to see her, but somehow couldn't help watching them. How intimidating they looked, she thought, and wished she could believe they wouldn't be playing a part in her new life here.

The teacher, when he entered, turned out to be a cold-eyed man in early middle age, with an air of contemptuous and patronising exhaustion. As he ran through his jovial joyless patter, someone coughed and someone else giggled loudly, and Jane felt as if her guts were slowly twisting themselves into knots as the teacher's cold eyes met hers. 'Oh, yes,' he said. 'We've got a new addition to the class this term. Stand up, Jane.'

Blind terror caught hold of her, and she stood. She looked down at the table as if to distract herself from a great height. 'I'd like you all to meet Jane Sullivan,' the teacher was saying. 'Melanie, could you show her around for the next few days?' And then Jane looked up, and saw what she'd been dreading: Melanie was one of the corridor girls, staring at her with cold eyes as hard as granite.

4

The classroom was slowly filling up for registration, and Bev was sitting alone in a pool of sunlight by the window when Emma came in and sat beside her. It was the first time Bev had seen her since Florida. She thought that Emma looked different somehow in the same school uniform – smaller, rounder, younger.

'Where were you?' asked Emma. 'I waited by the gates for yonks.'

'I didn't know we were supposed to meet up.'

'What are you on about?' said Emma impatiently. 'We always meet up before school.'

'So I didn't feel like *meeting up*,' said Bev. 'I was running late.'

Emma looked at her closely. Her scrutiny was like a search-light. 'What's up, Bev?'

'Nothing,' said Bev quickly.

'Must be something. You hardly spoke to me when I rang last night. It's like you were on another planet.'

'I had to go. What did you want to say?'

'I still haven't told you, have I? You've been so hard to get hold of lately.' Emma squirmed and giggled. 'You know I was working in the Spar this summer? Well, after you left for Florida, I only got off with Darren Ellis in the stockroom.'

In the chattering classroom, Bev sat and looked at Emma in silence. Her jealousy combined with an inexpressible loneliness. It wasn't fair that she should feel so much older, that she'd been forced to learn so much more. It wasn't about giggles and Valentines and pride, after all: it was what kept you awake in the small hours with a mind full of nothing. An image of an ugly little lounge flashed behind her eyes. She spoke coldly. 'So what?'

'It might not be a great big deal to *you*,' said Emma, stung, 'but I've fancied him for, like, two years. I thought you might want me to tell you.'

'And that's all you wanted to tell me?' Through the window, Bev saw a flock of birds taking off behind the football field; solid blackness throbbed at the edge of her vision. 'Oh, *please*.'

'Well, excuse me for breathing. Next time I'll keep my news to myself.' An uneasy silence fell between them. 'What the fuck happened out in Florida?' Emma asked eventually. 'You're acting really weird.'

'I told you. Nothing happened. You're just getting on my nerves.' Bev told herself it was true in a way. 'Stop being such a baby, can't you?' She could see Emma taking a long, deep, disbelieving breath and preparing to retort, but it didn't matter because then the teacher came in and the morning registration started.

5

After registration came Assembly, and then it was back to 10H for the distribution of their timetables. Sitting on the edge of the noisy central table, Jane felt as if her stomach was slowly filling with cold water. They hadn't paid her any real attention yet, but she knew they would soon.

Already, she'd begun to arrange them in order of fear: Melanie, the cold-eyed leader; Josie, a dark girl with a face like a well-honed hatchet; Tiffany, who was pretty and curly-haired, with an inane giggle and the little white teeth of a ferret; loud blonde Davina, who wasn't anything in particular. The boys at the table meant nothing to her, as they'd meant nothing to her at her last school. She'd never seen boys as impinging on her life at all.

'Well, I'm sure you all can't wait to get back to work,' the teacher said from the front of the class, with contemptuous joviality. As if on cue, a bell rang. 'Class dismissed. Off you go.'

They were getting their bags from the cloakroom when Jane heard the laugh behind her, and turned. Melanie and the other girls were smirking, and she guessed Melanie had been imitating the way she walked. 'I love your bag.' Melanie fell into step beside her as the others closed in on both sides. 'It's ever so trendy.'

Fear gripped Jane deep inside with a sense of déjà vu. She raced to get to the joke first. 'It's horrible, isn't it?' she said. 'I didn't choose it. My nan got it for me.'

She couldn't think what she'd said wrong, but the others exploded with giggles around her. 'My nan chooses all my stuff, too,' Melanie said airily. Then, as the giggles escalated, '*What? It's not funny, Davina. She does. Really.*'

'Your nan's got well good taste,' said Josie, and they all pressed in closer. A cloud of cloying scent invaded Jane's senses. 'She get your shoes, too?'

'No,' said Jane unwillingly. 'I did.'

'They're way cool,' said Tiffany. 'We always get our shoes from Clark's, too.'

'Does your nan get her shoes from Clark's?' asked Melanie politely, and then they were all in the classroom for English.

It was big and sunny and teacherless, almost filled to capacity already. Jane saw more strangers staring at her. She was about to sit beside Josie, when Josie set down her little rucksack on the seat. 'You can't sit here,' she said, 'my bag's sitting here,' and the others burst out laughing. So Jane had to sit beside a colourless fair-haired girl she didn't know, who stared hostilely at her before carrying on her conversation with the girls in front of her.

When the teacher came in and the lesson started, Jane could hear Melanie and her friends sniggering behind her. She distracted herself by thinking about the dream houses of the suburbs. In her mind, she was back there, seeing the glittering windows and the intricate brickwork, and the images were so persuasive that she could almost smell the fresh-cut grass from the garden the boy was mowing.

6

'I hear our Julie's getting married,' her father said. 'Is it true?'

Melissa sat across from the frail old man in the institutional common room, bolt upright, guarded as a job-interview candidate. The TV was on in the corner, and an elderly lady was watching it. A uniformed nurse was reading by the door. 'Not till next year,' said Melissa. 'She's having a long engagement.'

'She didn't tell me,' he said. 'I got a letter from Katie. Short letter. She'd write more to a friend.'

'I'm sure she didn't mean any harm,' said Melissa. 'Maybe she was busy.'

'They're always busy. They never come and see me.' He

fidgeted and muttered, a shaky, pathetic figure in a dressing-gown and pyjama bottoms. 'Nobody else ever comes. Everyone else has visitors.'

Melissa gazed out of the window at the bright afternoon and the well-tended gardens. She felt a mixture of despair and fury. '*I* visit,' she said. 'Don't you want to see *me*?'

He might as well have not heard her. 'She won't invite me to her wedding, you know,' he said. 'They don't want me there. They never come and see me here, you know. None of your sisters. Just short cold letters once a month. Wouldn't invite me anywhere.'

It was for this, Melissa realised, that she suffered so much at home. This was her one luxury that Jack resented, her private extravagance. 'You came to *my* wedding,' she said. 'I visit you every fortnight. Every other Thursday. I drive down and see you.'

'I want to go to our Julie's wedding,' he said. 'Make her invite me, Melissa.' She realised with horror that her father was crying.

The nurse laid her book down and hurried over. 'Now, then, Jim,' she said. 'There's no need for that, your daughter's come to see you.' The nurse mouthed a silent *sorry* at Melissa, and Melissa smiled numbly, feeling inadequate, realising nothing had changed since she'd been a teenager. He still didn't think she was important enough to smile for, even now that he was just a lonely old man her husband paid for. 'Make her invite me, Melissa,' he sobbed. 'I want to go to the wedding.'

Her eyes darted away. Ricki Lake was on the telly. 'I mean, that's just nasty,' a fat blonde girl was saying, 'that's just *nasty*.'

Melissa picked up her neat little clutch bag. 'I'll try,' she said quietly. 'Listen, Dad, I'm going to have to go now. I said I'd pick Bev up from school.'

She was walking fast through the corridor when the nurse hurried up behind her. 'I'm sorry about that, Mrs Green. He's not himself today, bless him.'

'You don't have to apologise. I'm used to it.' Melissa attempted a smile and kept walking. The nurse matched her steps. 'He's been a bit funny since Mum died. A bit difficult.'

'How long ago was that?'

'About twenty years. I was fourteen,' said Melissa. 'He hasn't been the same man since. My sisters don't mean to upset him by not visiting, you know. I don't blame them. They've got their own lives to lead.'

'You find time,' said the nurse. 'You're a good daughter.'

'I'm not. I went to live in Manchester when I was seventeen. Met my husband there. I should have stayed.' Immediately she was ashamed of her bitter eloquence. Her smile returned. 'It's nice of you to be concerned, but everything's all right.'

Out in the bright September sunshine, old people moved slowly, and the silence was unbroken. 'He looks forward to your visits, you know,' said the nurse. 'He'd be terribly upset if you stopped coming.'

'I'm sure you're right. Well, I'll be back in two weeks. I never miss a visit.' The nurse smiled awkwardly and turned away. As Melissa walked towards the parked Shogun, she saw a tiny plane crawling across the sky, and tasted a dark, infinite sadness. She'd pick Bev up from school and they'd talk about nothing all the way home, where she'd cook dinner for a man who didn't give a damn about her – who never let her forget he paid the bills for another man who didn't give a damn about her, and never had.

7

When the bell rang for the end of lessons, Jane could feel Melanie and the others packing her away in their minds without care, and had a half-reassuring thought: they'd made her life hell today, and they would tomorrow, but they'd always forget about her when home-time came. You could see it written on their faces – that they had better things to do when school was over.

'You coming round to my house tonight, Davina?' asked Melanie. 'Josie and Tiff are. We're watching a video.' Jane gathered her things together and scuttled out, pleased to have become invisible.

Out of the classroom and down the corridor, Jane's fellow pupils swarmed around her, and the noise of home-time was a hysterical aviary shriek as she left the main school building. As she walked, she thought about the compass-point and the beach road and the suburbs, and she couldn't work out which image held the greatest power in her mind.

When she reached the main school gates, the time was almost five to four. She leaned back against the sun-warmed metal, and watched strangers chattering and giggling past her. There was no sign of her grandparents. In a way, she didn't want them to arrive at all. She couldn't tell them how it had really been for her that day. She didn't want them to see how empty her life was.

It was then that she saw the car, right across the road from her. It was a big, shiny four-wheel-drive of a charcoal-grey colour – an expensive car, the kind of car she'd seen in the suburbs. With a mounting fascination that cut straight through what she'd been thinking before, Jane watched it park. She saw an elegant blonde woman behind the wheel, and two girls a little older than she was approaching it, one dark-haired and ordinary-looking, the other blonde and achingly beautiful, and she watched the blonde girl getting into the passenger seat for a second that lasted an hour.

Her first thought was that the blonde girl looked like an illusion. The whole picture that she carried with her had been transplanted into Jane's world from nowhere, like a movie poster you pinned on your bedroom wall and looked at far too often. She stared and stared at the beautiful blonde girl, who radiated such pure, uncomplicated happiness, at the wave of her hand to her erstwhile companion, at her careless bounce into the gleaming family car. In those slow moments of wonderment, Jane had time to realise that this girl belonged to one of those lovely houses in the suburbs as surely as anyone had ever belonged to anything, and then the car was gone, leaving the sleepy afternoon indifferently in its wake.

After that, Jane's grandparents arrived far too soon.

8

'Tell us some more about your first day, then, dear,' said Mary. 'You've hardly said a word.'

They were sitting in the neat little kitchen having dinner. The air was far too hot, and shadows flooded the corners of the room. By the cooker, the radio played old love songs that crackled. A froth of suds glittered in the sink, a fly circled the lamp and Mary swatted at it. 'It was all right,' said Jane, chewing a tasteless mouthful of roast pork. 'It was fine.'

'Make any nice friends, then?' asked Alf.

'Yeah,' said Jane. 'I've met ever such a nice girl. Her name's Anita.'

'That's the way, dear. Get in with some nice girls,' said Mary. 'Don't go falling in with the wrong crowd whatever you do.'

'You can learn from your mother's example,' said Alf. 'Carol was a good girl before she fell in with the wrong crowd.'

'They lead a young girl astray, some people,' Mary said darkly. 'That was Carol's trouble. She never had the strength of mind to just say no.' There was a short silence before she spoke again, in a different tone. 'What's she like, then, this Angela?'

'Anita. She's really nice. She lives in Preston.' The surprise in their eyes drove her to say more. 'I saw her mum picking her up after school today. You wouldn't believe their car.'

'Well,' said Mary, 'what's her father do?'

'I don't know. She didn't say,' said Jane. 'I expect she'll say soon. She says I can go round to her house some time.' She realised she wasn't thinking of Anita at all. 'She's ever so brainy. She wants to go on to college when she's done her GCSEs.'

'Well,' said Mary, sounding impressed, 'she sounds like she'll be a good influence.'

'We're glad you've made a nice friend, love,' said Alf. 'We were worried you'd be lonely, in a new school and all.'

When dinner was over, Jane went up to her room. In the too-thin, too-bright lamplight, she lifted the mattress, got out the paraphernalia from under it and sat down at the dressing-table.

She rolled up her shirt-sleeve and peeled back the greying bandage. The dizzying relief of the ritual was over far too soon, and she replaced the little package under the mattress with a huge yet subtle disappointment. Then she got her books out of her bag, sat down at the dressing-table that now did double duty as a desk, and tried to make a start on the homework she'd been set in maths.

It was no use. Whatever point she tried to fix her thoughts on, they kept sliding back to the blonde girl in the four-wheel-drive. It seemed impossible to Jane that such perfection could exist outside a daydream, but she'd seen the girl as surely as she'd seen the suburbs – there was no mistaking beauty like that, it hallmarked itself. Her eyes slid over the angles and grids in her textbook without really seeing them at all. She kept remembering the golden advert girl, and how her hair had shone in the light, and how she had looked like a goddess.

9

When Jane had been a child, she'd seen her mother as a kind of goddess. In some way both superstitious and ultimately practical, it explained the distance between them that had always been there, a distance that might otherwise have seemed too painful and bewildering. It wasn't just that she was the wrong sort of daughter for her mother: Carol couldn't have been approachable and matey with a different kind of girl. She'd have been slightly distant with any daughter in the world, because she was the goddess of beer-cans and loud, raucous laughter, and Jane's fear of her had nothing to do with Jane at all.

Carol had had Jane when she was fifteen. Although she looked much younger than the other mums Jane knew, there was nothing soft or girlish about her appearance. She was a thin woman of medium height, with dyed black hair straggled back in a ponytail. She wore a studded leather jacket, and carried with her a hard, scrawny arrogance that Jane had lived with all her life and still found alien. Carol wasn't scared of anything that wasn't an immediate physical threat, and had no patience with her shy, too-imaginative daughter. Jane was accustomed only to hearing her mother's laughter from a distance – across a room, through a wall, when Carol was with a friend or a boyfriend or anyone but Jane.

In the past, before Carol had met the man called Dave and everything had started slipping, Jane had been almost reassured by her brutal confidence and the way she was always the same. Jane had no real friends at the comprehensive, where she lived for her weekends with Anita. She tagged round after a group of contemptuous, indifferent wannabes: she dreaded Michelle and Chandra and Stephanie, who epitomised everything the sad little group most wanted to be. But in the narrow corridors, in winter, when the radiators gave off a faint smell of boiled glue and got too hot to touch, when the Christmas decorations stirred something infinite inside her, she'd sense the third-floor flat deep in her head, like an open fire, a blanket against the cold. There'd be something waiting for her when the bus-ride ended, and although it was shabby and intimidating and never paid her much attention, it was there for her all the same – something deep inside like the other girls had, a little place of her own.

Before Dave, Carol had always had friends round at the flat. When she wasn't working at the launderette she invited people round, and they drank beer and cider from cans, and talked in loud voices about people who weren't there. Jane came in and fixed herself dinner and went to her little bedroom and listened to them laughing together. Sometimes she liked to pretend they were all her family: the father who'd walked out and whom she couldn't remember, the aunts and uncles and cousins she'd never had. It was good when the pretending swept her away and she could make believe she had something like Anita's life. There was a lady called Lorraine she might have loved. Jane knew the girls at school would call Lorraine a slag, but behind the tangled bleached-blonde hair and jammy lipstick, she was little and nervous and kind – she gave Jane a Christmas card and asked about her day as if it mattered to her. Jane liked to imagine Lorraine was her auntie, that she had a kind of family, after all.

Of course, it had never really worked like that. Whenever Lorraine or one of the others tried to detain her on her way to the bedroom, Carol's voice cracked out impatiently, 'The girl's all right, Lorraine, let her go.' And Jane scuttled away, feeling disappointment and reassurance fade into the shadows of her life. Sitting on the bed, she saw Christmas lights blur through a mist of rain, and felt a kind of contentment, a kind of reality, a kind of home.

It hadn't been that bad in the flat. Not then.

But once Dave had arrived, it had all started going wrong.

10

'You didn't call me over the weekend,' said Mandy.

It had just gone seven, and Jack was parked in the little lay-by in the middle of nowhere, readjusting himself in the aftermath of sex. He looked at her with faint surprise. 'I never said I'd call you over the weekend.'

'Yes, you did. Don't you remember?'

Beyond the gleaming car, he saw that it was almost dark. Tiny red lights sparkled from the dashboard, and something rustled and hooted far away. 'I don't remember,' he said. 'When?'

'On Friday. You must remember. When we came here after work.'

'Oh, that.' Jack remembered a standard goodbye that hadn't meant anything in particular. 'I didn't mean I *would*. I just meant I *might*.'

'And what's that supposed to mean?'

'It means I can't just call you whenever I like,' he said, with deliberate patience. 'I'm *married*.'

'Well, you could have sneaked out and called me from a phone-box or something.' He saw anger stir in her eyes. 'We're supposed to be seeing each other, aren't we?'

Looking at her, Jack experienced a premonition. He wondered if maybe he'd bitten off more than he could chew with this girl. Far from alerting him to possible pitfalls, his previous affairs had lulled him into over-confidence. They'd all been so easy, so undemanding. Now, in the half-light, he saw something beyond Mandy's usual chirpy passivity: a subtle but genuine desperation. 'We're not at school any more, sweetheart,' he said. '*Seeing each other*. What the hell does *that* mean?'

'You know. That it's more than just sex. That there's a kind of commitment.'

She might as well have uttered some Nazi oath. He felt wary and watchful and cold. 'I never said anything about a *commitment*,' he said. 'I can't make a *commitment*. That's what *married* means.'

'Well, what are we doing together, then?' she asked.

'I'd have thought it was obvious.' Out in the bushes, he heard something rustle again. 'Come on, sweetheart. We both went into this with our eyes wide open. I never lied to you about making a *commitment*.'

She stared at him hard, and he saw her face close like a fist. 'So it's just this. But what if I don't want *just this*?'

'Then find someone else.' He tried to speak gently, objectively. 'A nice boy of your own age. Someone you can settle down with.'

'But I don't want to settle down with someone *my* age,' she said. 'Not some stupid boy I knew at school. You know that. You *must* know that.'

'I know I'm going to be late home. We'd better get going.' He started the car, and they drove for a long time in silence.

Outside Safeway, he stopped and turned to her, trying to put things back on their usual easy-going footing. 'You don't mind if I drop you off here, do you, sweetheart?'

'I don't care what the fuck you do. You don't understand. You don't even *care*.' She jumped out of the car, and the passenger door slammed hard behind her.

An overwhelming tension haunted Jack for the rest of the drive. Her betrayed and hating eyes lingered in the car and followed him all the way home. Suddenly he suspected his vivacious, willing secretary of a deep and potentially dangerous seriousness. As he parked in the garage, he knew their affair couldn't go on for much longer. He told himself he'd have to do something about it, and soon.

11

More and more recently, Melissa hated this kitchen in the evenings. Although it was in almost total darkness, the lamp above the table cast a perfect circle of pale light that was far too bright and made her think of a spotlight fixed on the four of them. For endless minutes, the only sound was the slight buzzing from the lights along the kitchen counter, the wind outside, the clink of cutlery on china. It gave her the creeps. They all seemed to be on edge this evening, she thought.

'You got that science assignment back yet?' Jack asked Toby abruptly, and she flinched inside.

'Yeah,' said Toby.

'What did you get?'

Melissa could see the thoughts passing over her son's face like words on a screen-saver – wanting to lie, considering lying, not quite daring to lie. She felt helpless, protective, trapped. 'I got a D,' Toby said eventually.

'Well, Jesus *Christ*. I thought you said you'd worked *hard* on that?'

'I did work hard on it.' Toby sounded sullen and fearful both at once. 'A D's not bad.'

'Not bad? What's your definition of *fucking awful?*'

In his peremptory voice, Melissa caught a terrifying echo of her father, long ago – a god to be feared and hated and escaped from – and she was very aware of what Toby must be feeling. 'Jack,' she said sharply.

He ignored her. 'It's that useless crowd you hang out with at school. They get Fs, so if you get a D, you think it's some kind of achievement. You want to stop hanging out with those losers.'

'They're not losers! Everyone in our year wants to hang out with us!'

'Yeah. You can be the coolest eighteen-year-olds in the dole queue. Your sister never wasted her time trying to keep in with the in-crowd, did you, Bev?'

Bev looked at her plate. In the harsh overhead light, Melissa noticed, she looked tired and embarrassed. *Christ*, thought Melissa starkly, *what are we doing to our kids?* And then Bev spoke. 'I don't like crowds,' she said listlessly. 'I've always just hung out with Emma.'

'Well, if I only had one friend in my year, everyone'd just think I was sad,' muttered Toby. 'People wouldn't think it was cool if it was *me*.'

'Your sister doesn't care about being cool,' Jack snapped. 'That's why she's going to be at sixth-form college this time next year. That's why she's going to pass all her GCSEs at the higher grades. And you're not even embarrassed about getting a D in something you worked bloody hard for, that you –'

Sudden fury flared in Melissa's mind and she couldn't stop herself from speaking as she did. 'Oh, for Christ's sake, Jack. The boy's thirteen years old. Leave him alone.'

There was a silence before she spoke again. She felt three pairs of eyes fixed on her, curious, apprehensive. 'It's not fair to him,' she said. 'He's just not academic. Your parents never pushed you like that, when you were his age.'

'What do you know about my parents?' Jack asked tonelessly. 'How often did you meet them? Twice?'

'How often did you *let* me meet them?' she replied. 'Twice?'

'As often as they wanted to meet you. I didn't keep you apart. They just didn't want to know.'

His hypocrisy maddened her – his politician's way of enhancing or concealing facts to make himself look better. 'Convenient for you they didn't,' she said.

The air cooled twenty degrees. Something darkened in the shadows beyond the table. 'What's that supposed to mean?'

She remembered the one and only family dinner she'd attended *chez* Green in Manchester, the barely concealed distaste on Jack's face as his mother dished up the soup in the shabby, overcrowded kitchen. 'Well, you weren't exactly heartbroken when they wouldn't come to our wedding, were you? You didn't exactly try to talk them round.'

'What are you trying to say?'

There was a flat, final note to his voice that she found more ominous than anger. She saw that Toby and Bev had laid down their cutlery and were sitting, wary and unblinking, prepared for the unthinkable. The sight unnerved her. She didn't want a furious argument with Jack, she thought – she couldn't *cope* with a furious argument – and her rage vanished into nothing. She scurried back to submission with a coward's relief. 'It doesn't matter,' she said quietly. 'I shouldn't have said it. Let's just change the subject.'

Jack shrugged curtly and carried on eating. Melissa picked up her cutlery and did the same. It should have felt like a reassuring truce, she thought, but it felt like anything but.

For a while, the four of them just sat and ate under the circle of white light, the silence absolute, the air tingling. Melissa picked at her chargrilled chicken salad indifferently. She supposed the dinner was good, but she had no appetite. None at all.

12

Bev wasn't getting enough sleep. The nightmares woke her up and dared her to close her eyes again, and she was never quite up to the challenge. In school, she found she couldn't concentrate, and only a soulless autopilot kept the right answers coming when the teacher called on her. A hundred nameless terrors throbbed along with her heartbeat. She didn't want to be here, and she feared going home.

Geography was one of the few classes she didn't share with Emma, and she sat alone – there was no stigma in her isolation, the other girls envied her. She sat and pretended to listen and felt the lunch-time bell coming closer. She decided she'd walk another way after it rang. She didn't want to run into Emma in the hallway, and have Emma ask her for the hundredth time what was wrong.

The bell shrilled and the lesson ended. Bev rose, gathered her things together and turned left instead of right out of the classroom door. Right was the canteen, the tuck shop, the main double doors and the playground. Left was nothing in particular. The distant shrieking voices grew quieter as she walked down the shadowed corridors, and the near-silence both soothed and unnerved her. Streaks of sunlight slanted across the floor. She was alone.

The toilets by the sports changing rooms were dingy and rarely used. Bev walked in, and the door wheezed shut behind her. Here, the silence was absolute. An insidious smell lingered on the air, and the dirty windows filtered the golden light through grey. She walked into a cubicle and bolted the door. As she did so, she took a small involuntary step back, because a crude phallus had been carved across the door's tangle of graffiti with what looked like the point of a compass, and she felt as if her nightmares had somehow followed her here.

13

Melanie and the others kept throwing balled-up sheets of A4 at her. Kept on throwing them when the teacher turned her back to write on the whiteboard, and the teacher didn't seem to notice anything, and the colourless fair-haired girl beside Jane kept frowning at her, like it was *her* fault. Tiffany's high-pitched giggle exploded across the aisle. Jane had been hearing it on and off all morning.

'And for your homework this week, I'd like you all to have a go at something creative,' the teacher said earnestly to the whiteboard. 'I'd like you all to write a short essay about your family. Of course, I hope you'll remember good spelling and punctuation at all times. I'll be collecting them in the Monday after next.' Then she fell silent, and carried on writing something about grammar.

Jane heard the words with leaden uninterest. So she'd have to write an essay about Carol and Dave and how it had all gone wrong. It didn't matter. Already she was thinking five minutes ahead, to the end of the lesson and the lunch-time bell; already she was surreptitiously gathering her things together, so she could be out of the door before Melanie and the others could pass her and laugh at her.

When the bell rang, she was the first to leave the classroom. She saw the colourless fair-haired girl leaning across to the girls in front. 'That was sooo funny,' one of them said, 'it almost cracked me up when . . .' Jane walked out, into the teeming corridor, and moved against the crowds like a salmon upstream, seeking out solitude, silence and peace. She had heard too much laughter that morning.

She always used the girls' toilets by the changing rooms. It was a part of the world Melanie and the others didn't seem to know about, and its bleak ugliness provided a kind of sanctuary. When she walked in, it was silent, as always. She went into a cubicle and bolted the door behind her, and the tangle of ancient graffiti filled the world.

She was just pulling her knickers up when she heard a toilet flush, and realised she hadn't been alone here after all. Something in the thought unsettled her. She heard footsteps and running water and the whine of the hand-dryer. Sudden anger overcame her, coloured by Tiffany's laughter. She didn't want to hide in here till whoever it was had gone, she realised – she was tired of hiding and worrying – and she unbolted the door with pathetic defiance. She'd expected to see a stranger's back facing her, a stranger's face reflected in the mirrors, but it wasn't a stranger, not really. It was the blonde girl, the golden advert girl, the suburbs incarnate.

14

If Jane was surprised to see her, the golden advert girl looked every bit as surprised to see Jane herself. Jane guessed she'd also thought the other cubicles were empty. At first, the girl looked an ace away from bursting into tears, then, noticing Jane, she flicked her hair back, got a lipstick out of her bag and started putting it on.

Jane washed her hands far more conscientiously than she usually did, going round every bitten-down nail. Somehow it struck her as very important that she should say something to the golden advert girl, that she might never have this chance again, and suddenly there was only one thing she could say.

'It's horrible in here, isn't it?'

The golden advert girl looked round with some surprise. For the first time, Jane saw how blue her eyes were. 'How do you mean?' she asked.

'I don't know,' said Jane haltingly. 'It's all grey and dirty. It's so quiet.'

'I suppose. I don't know, really.'

The girl returned her attention to the mirror, got a brush out of her bag and started on her hair. It was unquestionably a gesture of dismissal, but Jane couldn't bring herself to leave things where they were. She waved her hands under the dryer and watched the blonde girl's reflection from the corner of her eye. Without surprise, she realised that the brush was perfect, and the bag was perfect, and she *was* a golden advert girl, after all.

'How do you get your hair to go like that?'

It was a stupid thing to say, and Jane knew it as soon as the words were out – gauche, fumbling words fit only to be sneered at. She'd never understand why the golden advert girl shot her a genuinely friendly smile, why the words seemed to please more than anything. 'What, you mean the wave?'

'And the colour,' said Jane shyly. 'Is it natural?'

'The colour is. But I use hot rollers sometimes.' The girl looked at Jane more closely. 'You new here?'

'Yeah. I'm in the fourth year.'

'You must know my kid brother. He's in your year. Name's Toby Green.'

Green lawns unfolding beneath a brilliant blue sky, green veins of ivy across intricate brickwork and the rich green smell of the suburbs. Jane had dreamed of this. 'I think he's in my tutor group,' she said. 'I don't know him well, mind.' The brush ran through the thick blonde hair again. Jane steeled herself to ask what had to be answered. 'You live in Preston, don't you?'

'Yeah,' said the girl. Then, with vague curiosity, 'How'd you know?'

'Maybe from Toby. I don't know.' Jane could see the girl replacing the brush in her bag, and knew there was something that had to be said before they parted. 'My name's Jane,' she said quickly. 'Jane Sullivan.'

'I'm Bev Green.' A quick darting smile, a moment of subtle embarrassment. The golden advert girl checked her hair again. 'Anyway, I'd better get going,' she said. 'Expect I'll see you around sometime.'

After she'd gone, Jane stood stock-still by the sinks and mirrors. With heightened perceptions, she saw the gleaming porcelain, the sunlight filtering through the grimy frosted glass, the clinical smell of disinfectant not quite masking something ancient and sickly. She felt that she'd reached out and touched the suburbs for the first time – a part of them now knew her name, would recognise her in a crowd. The last sentence spoken echoed in her head: 'Expect I'll see you around sometime.'

15

'But why won't you come?' asked Emma. 'I really want to see it. And you're not doing anything else this weekend.'

'I've told you already,' said Bev. 'I just don't want to. It sounds so depressing.'

It was Friday afternoon, and they were walking out of maths, which they had together. They'd been back at school almost three weeks, now. 'What do you mean, depressing?' demanded Emma. '*Mizz* said it was wicked. And *More*.'

"Oh, for God's sake, Emma. I just don't want to see it, all right?' Silence fell between them as they walked.

In the crush of the corridor, they passed a podgy brown-haired girl walking the other way. There was nothing unusual about her appearance, and Emma would have barely registered the sight of her if Bev hadn't smiled, turned and raised a hand in brief salute. 'All right, Jane?' asked Bev. 'Catch you later.' The girl mumbled a reply Emma didn't quite catch, and then she was gone.

'Who was that?' Emma asked, as they were walking out of the main doors together. 'I've never seen her around before.'

'What's it to you?' asked Bev. 'She's just someone I know, that's all.'

'Well, keep your fucking hair on. I was just asking,' Emma snapped back. 'I've got to get my bus.' She walked away from Bev fast and angry. These days, it was a relief to get away from her.

In the clamour of the bus queue, Emma stood alone, with her heartbeat hammering in her ears. The voice behind her took her by surprise. 'All right, Em? How's it going?'

She turned. It was Adele, from her geography class, who lived a few minutes' walk from her. Adele had neat brown hair and chunky thighs, and carried a reassuringly accessible world with her: the semi-detached family home, the respectable school marks, the holiday job in a beachside kiosk. Outside geography, Adele always hung out with a shy plain rich girl called Charlie and a tough pretty poor girl called Louise. Recently, Emma had started to envy their togetherness.

Emma would normally have been more discreet, but the solid anger that had built up inside her demanded release. 'Not so bad, apart from bloody Bev,' she said. 'She's driving me mad, Adele. I just can't stand her any more.'

'I thought you two were best mates.'

'We were. But she's been like a different person ever since she got back from holiday. She just bites my head off for the least little thing. I can't do anything right.'

When the bus arrived, they joined the scramble for seats. They found one near the back, and sat together. 'You know, she won't even come and see *Saving Private Ryan* with me this weekend,' said Emma. 'I really wanted to see it, and it closes at the Ritzy next week.'

'Come and see it with me and Charlie and Louise,' offered Adele. 'We're going on Sunday evening.'

'You don't think they'd mind if I tag along?' Adele shook her head, and Emma smiled. 'That'd be excellent,' she said. 'Cheers.'

'Feel free. We're going to the White Hart for a half after. They usually serve us.' Emma said she'd bring a fiver or so and, in her mind, she and her long-term best friend moved that final decisive inch apart. When she and Adele got off at their stop, they walked a while together, talking about where they'd meet up and how they'd be getting home after. In the nice safe residential area where they lived, the remnants of the afternoon sunlight were lukewarm and heavily shadowed. You could feel the chilly evening closing in like a tide, over the very end of summer.

16

Jack's Motors was open on Saturdays, and Mandy usually worked then. She had taken all the hours she could get recently. Not so much for the money. Just to see Jack. However indifferent he seemed to her now, she still needed him in her life too badly, and the further he drifted away emotionally, the more she wanted him. All that mattered was that they were still sleeping together. All that mattered was that he was still *there*.

'Mandy?' he said, poking his head round his office door. 'Could you come in here for a few minutes?'

A small thrill ran through her, and she rose from her desk. They'd made love in his office once, and she treasured the memory as the greatest excitement of her life. Maybe, she thought, he wanted to do it again. She walked through and sat down across from his desk, smiling her bright, inviting desperation as he closed the door behind her and went to sit down himself.

'Well?' she said, crossing her legs, playing with a strand of hair. 'What did you want me for?'

He didn't smile back. 'Mandy,' he said, 'I'm going to have to let you go.'

At first she couldn't take it in. It was as if she'd severed her finger while chopping carrots, and was staring at the jetting stump with leaden disbelief. '*What?*'

'You heard,' he said gently. 'I'm sorry, sweetheart, but it's the only way.'

'You can't just sack me.' She spoke slowly, tonelessly. 'I haven't done anything *wrong*.'

'Sweetheart, there's no need to make a scene. Your work just isn't coming up to scratch, that's all. It isn't personal.'

'It never has been personal. That's the whole point. There's nothing wrong with my work. You're just trying to get rid of me.'

The street noise from outside was distant; a thick oppressive silence filled the world. 'I was hoping you wouldn't take this the wrong way,' he said. 'I've been meaning to say something for a while. It's just not working out, and –'

'Bullshit. You're just tired of shagging me. Why lie?'

She saw him recoil slightly, whether from the vulgarity or the reference to their affair she couldn't tell. 'You'd better not talk about that,' he said. 'Come on, sweetheart. We can at least be discreet about it now it's over.'

'Sure. It's easier for you if I'm discreet about it, isn't it?'

'It's easier for both of us. Let's be grown-up about this, sweetheart. It's not the end of the world. You'll easily find another job.'

Her gaze panned slowly across his desk. The silver-framed family photograph smiled out at her with three dazzling sets of white teeth. It seemed to mock her. 'I'll get another job because I'm good,' she said. 'Because my work *is* coming up to scratch, and you know it is. The fuck this isn't personal. You just *admitted* it.'

'That's not true,' he said, but there was no conviction in his voice, and he sounded like he looked: evasive, shifty.

She sat across the desk and studied him for long seconds. All she'd ever really wanted was in this office, she realised – the pot-plants and the squashy leather seats, the traffic noise outside and the last of the afternoon sunlight. 'You shitbag,' she said. 'You fucking *cunt*.'

'Mandy,' he said, 'keep your voice down.'

A new wariness had entered his demeanour. Something reckless and spiteful surfaced inside Mandy and she found that his tension pleased her. 'What? You scared someone'll hear me?' she asked. 'Scared I'll go and tell people what you did?'

'You're making a fool of yourself,' he said. 'Just calm down.'

'I'll do what I want. Anything I want. You'll be sorry. You'll see. You just wait and see what I do.'

He said quietly, 'I don't like being threatened, sweetheart.'

'I don't like being used. And don't call me that. Don't you ever call me that.' Out of nowhere, she was on the edge of tears. She blinked them away savagely. 'Go to hell,' she said, 'You'll be sorry.' Then she was hurrying out of the office and down the stairs, hoping that nobody would see her as she left for the very last time.

17

On Sunday evening, after they'd eaten dinner, the air was like the air before a thunderstorm. Toby was out. Bev wished he wasn't. Even his surly presence had to be better than this strangeness.

Up in her room, she tried to read a book for her English class, but she couldn't concentrate and the whole thing seemed unreal. She felt as if she was acting. When she went downstairs to get a snack out of the fridge, the living-room door was slightly ajar and she could see her parents watching television. They sat still and expressionless as shop-window dummies, side by side but not touching, eyes fixed straight ahead. The television volume was slightly too loud. She wondered whether either of them noticed.

Something cold ran up the back of Bev's neck. Out of the fridge she took cheese and salami, then cut a slice of wholemeal bread. She picked up her plate and left the kitchen. She tiptoed past the living room without knowing why.

Back in her room, the music she'd been playing sounded all wrong, and the food on the plate looked an odd colour in the lamplight. She realised she had no appetite, after all. She laid the plate down on her desk, beside the abandoned book, and went over to the little pink Perspex phone by her bed. She dialled Emma's number. After four or five rings, a voice answered, 'Hello?'

'Hi.' Bev recognised Emma's father's voice, and was surprised he didn't seem able to recognise hers. 'Can I speak to Emma?'

'She's not in, love. Gone to the cinema with some friends. She won't be back till late.' An unseen television crackled behind him, and there was the sound of laughter from another world. 'Want to leave a message?'

Suddenly Bev didn't want to say who was calling. It unsettled her that Emma's family had forgotten who she was. 'It's okay,' she said. 'I'll see her at school tomorrow. 'Bye.'

''Bye, love,' said Emma's father absently, and then the dead buzzing tone was running through Bev's ear, and there was nothing left but the strangeness of the here and now.

After she'd put down the receiver, Bev sat at her desk and feared. Tonight she could feel things breaking down all around her. Suddenly she wanted Jane Sullivan's company with an unhealthy compulsive hunger, like a pregnancy craving for chalk or vinegar or uncooked meat. She yearned for something that saw nothing but her old perfection, something that would never look at her with eyes that knew too much, and ask her what was wrong.

18

Jane wondered what the golden advert girl was doing now. She had often wondered that recently. As she lifted her fork, the girl might be getting ready to go to a party; as she sipped her lemonade, she might be trying on a new dress. It was as if Jane slaked her thirst on salt water: her unassuageable curiosity fed off itself, and grew stronger all the time.

'Jane, dear,' said Mary, 'you haven't touched your peas.'

Over the late Sunday dinner, the kitchen seemed smaller and warmer than ever. Outside it was getting dark. 'I'm still full up,' said Jane. 'It was a big lunch at Anita's earlier.'

'We'll come and pick you up from her house next time,' said Alf. 'It's no trouble, love.'

'Oh, no, really. I'm all right getting the bus,' said Jane quickly. She looked down at her plate. That afternoon, she'd got the bus into Preston, wondering which house the golden advert girl lived in. Finally, she'd guessed it was the white Romanish house with the pillars round the door, and she'd walked back into town along the beach road. The water looked cold and grey now, and the grey-white gulls had shrieked out a welcome. 'You don't have to bother. Really.'

'Well, if you say so, dear,' said Mary, sounding affronted. 'I'm sure we wouldn't want to intrude.'

When dinner was over, Jane said she had some homework. She went up to her room, shut the door behind her, drew the curtains and dragged her eyes away from the edge of the mattress. She didn't want to see the compass point or the lighter tonight. She'd been seeing a little too much of them lately, and was disturbed by a suspicion that the ritual was going too far. Besides, she did have homework: the English essay she'd been set last week.

She was just sitting down at the dressing-table-desk when the yearning curiosity gripped her like a cramp again. Beyond the net curtain and the gathering night, in this exact instant, a golden advert girl named Beverley Green was in another world.

Jane wondered if she was sitting or standing, laughing or silent, and what she was thinking of now, and then the hopelessness of her yearning overcame her. She got her books and pencil-tin out of her bag. 'My Family,' she wrote at the top of a sheet of paper. Then her hand froze where it was. In her mind she saw Carol lying dead in the bath. She couldn't bear to think of that. Not now.

So she wrote about Anita's family. She wrote about the crowded little house and the video-boxes and the large hairy mongrel and the smell of slowly cooking meatloaf. She wrote about the trendy teenage sisters gossiping in the lounge and the sun streaming through the tiny bedroom window and the forest of pens and hair-ruffles on the bedside table. Her small untidy writing raced along the lines. She wrote about warmth and togetherness and how it had been before it had all started going wrong.

19

It had been last summer that the barrier had come crashing down between them, right after Dave had arrived. She'd been round at Anita's house, and they'd been up in her sunny little bedroom, and she'd been about to tell Anita about Dave.

It was a Saturday afternoon. How hot it was.

'What's he like?' asked Anita. They were walking down the steep narrow stairs from her room at this point. 'Is he going to be your step-dad?'

And Jane didn't smile quite as easily as she might have done. 'He's all right,' she said unwillingly, longing for Anita to ferret the truth out of her. 'I suppose he's all right.'

'You don't sound very impressed,' said Anita. They'd reached the downstairs hallway, now, and were heading for the front door. They were going down to the shop for some sweets. 'Don't you like him?'

Then the phone rang in the lounge, and Anita stopped to

listen. One of the trendy teenage sisters picked it up, and called out, 'Nita, it's for you. It's Tina.'

'Who?' Jane asked.

'My best mate at school,' said Anita. 'I've told you about her loads of times. Hang on. Won't be a minute.'

Jane stood in the living-room doorway, resentful that it had all been interrupted at the crucial moment. The teenage sisters lounged, chatting – there were only two of them, that afternoon. 'Keep it down, will you, Paula? I can't hear what Tina's saying,' complained Anita. Suddenly, Jane realised she was listening intently to the ongoing phone conversation. 'Well, I don't want to go to her party,' said Anita into the receiver. 'I think she's a stupid bitch. I don't care if she has invited me.' Jane hadn't ever heard Anita on the phone to a friend before, maybe because she usually visited Anita in the afternoon, and phone-calls from friends tended to come in the evening.

To Jane, it was chilling, and came out of nowhere. The realisation that Anita's whole way of making conversation had changed. There, in the sunlight, by the window, Anita leaned against the wall, chatting to the unseen Tina. 'You go if you want,' she said, 'but I'm not. Jessie's not, either.' How intimidating and blithely arrogant she looked and sounded, how perfect, in her cheap way. Suddenly Jane saw her life with new eyes: the trendy teenage sisters lounging disdainfully in battered leather armchairs, the big capable mother always busy in the kitchen, the aunts and uncles and cousins who came and went. For the first time, it occurred to her that maybe Michelle and Chandra and Stephanie also had paraphernalia like this in their lives, tucked out of sight as carelessly as a bra strap. And Jane experienced terror – and then she felt the pain, and then the loneliness.

When Anita got off the phone, the two of them walked to the shop together. The deepening afternoon was stickily hot, but Jane felt as if she'd been inexpertly defrosted – although she sweated and reddened, she felt icy cold inside. Long silences fell between her and Anita, and she couldn't think of any way to break them. It was awful, she thought, *awful* to walk in silence like this.

They bought sweets at the shop, and walked back to the house, where they went up to Anita's room and closed the door behind them. Sitting on the bed, Jane saw for the first time that this was how a popular girl's bedroom might look – the teddy-bears, the hair-ruffles, the stickers on the mirror. Suddenly she felt like an outsider in this sunny little room, an alien, a stranger.

'What were you going to say about your mum's new boyfriend?' asked Anita. 'You were going to say something, before we went down the shop.'

'I can't remember,' Jane lied, 'it doesn't matter.' Impossible that she'd once wanted to confide in this stranger, this girl who didn't need to lie about being accepted. It was hard to think of what to say after that, and the rest of the afternoon passed slowly. To Jane, it was almost a relief to go home, back to the shadows and the silence Carol and Dave always left behind them.

Ever since that afternoon, Jane hadn't been able to relax with Anita like she'd used to. Maybe she communicated her unease to Anita somehow. Whatever the reason, it was never quite the same between them, even before Anita had started going to Jane's school, and Carol and Dave had begun their final rows in the third-floor flat, and the world had slipped in earnest.

20

On Jack's way home from work, his car phone started ringing, and he answered while stuck at a traffic-light. 'Yeah?'

There wasn't a sound. Just dead air. He put it down to the bad reception and stared ahead, at the red light and the greying sky. Maybe five seconds later it went off again. He picked it up again. 'Hel*lo*?'

He thought he heard a receiver being replaced down the line. But nothing else. A car behind him tooted, and he saw that the lights had changed to green. He set off again. A new tension flickered round the outskirts of his thoughts. Mandy had walked out four days ago. They'd run the job ad in the *Underlyme Echo* the day before yesterday. He'd be interviewing for a new secretary next week.

He was just entering the suburbs when the ringing tone came for a third time. It sounded loud in the silent car, and jarred his nerves. 'Hello?' he snapped, and heard someone hang up, then the silence that followed it.

When he got into the kitchen, Melissa was cooking the dinner. There was no sign of Toby or Bev. 'Where are the kids?'

'Bev's in her room. Toby's gone round to a friend's for dinner.'

He sat down. Somehow it seemed quieter in here than usual. 'You went to see your father today, didn't you?' he asked.

'You know I did. I go and see him every fortnight.'

'Well. How is he?'

'How is he ever?' Her eyes moved around the kitchen restlessly, darting away from his whenever they came close. 'It's getting dark out there,' she said. 'We should eat soon. I'll go and call Bev down.'

A second after Melissa had walked out of the door, the phone rang in the downstairs hallway. Jack was about to get it, then heard her doing just that. 'Hello?' she said. 'Hello?' There was a long silence before she came back into the kitchen. 'I meant to say,' she said, 'someone keeps making silent calls. After I got back from seeing Dad it happened three times.'

'Was that a silent call?'

'Yes,' she said. 'It's quite worrying. It could be burglars.'

It was a relief to return to the normal, the dismissive, the contemptuous. 'Don't be stupid. A burglar's not going to ring us up and make an appointment.'

'That's not what I meant. Of course that's not what I meant.' Anger stirred simultaneously in her face and voice. 'I read about it. Burglars do ring a house, to see if it's empty or not. So it *could* have been burglars.'

He backed down, startled and a little alarmed. 'Okay, okay,' he said. 'You'd better go and call Bev down for dinner. I'm bloody starving.'

Melissa left the kitchen. It was like an action replay of the first time: the phone started ringing almost the second she'd walked through the door. Jack moved past her. 'It's okay,' he said, 'I'll get it.' He watched her preoccupied, nervous face turn away from him, watched her start walking up the stairs towards Bev's room. As he picked up the receiver his heart thumped in his chest. He thought about Mandy Roberts – of how she had all his personal numbers – and he heard the distant click of someone hanging up, and the dead buzz down the telephone line.

October

1

Adele called round for Emma at twenty past eight on Monday morning. With her was Louise, a pretty red-haired girl with a sarcastic sense of humour and scuffed, shabby shoes. They got the bus into school together. The morning was pale, misty and melancholy as they walked towards the main double doors. Last night, they'd all gone to the cinema again.

'Great film last night, wasn't it?' asked Adele.

'Wicked,' said Emma. As they entered the school, she grinned. 'Beats the pants off trailing round after Bev.'

Louise laughed. 'You spoken to her lately?'

'Don't even *mention* that girl to me,' said Emma, irritated. 'Jesus Christ.'

'What. She still not talking to you?' asked Adele.

'Not since the week before last. She hasn't said a word to me,' said Emma. 'God, she's like a stroppy five-year-old.'

'Does it bother you?' asked Louise.

'Not really,' said Emma. 'If she wants to play the prima donna, that's her problem.' As she spoke the words, she realised their truth, and something lightened in her eyes. 'To be honest, I'd miles rather hang out with you guys. She gets on my bloody nerves.'

Outside the assembly hall they met up with Charlie, who used to complete the set of three and now completed the set of four. Charlie only lived a few streets away from Bev, but there any resemblance ended: Charlie was dark, plump and dreamy, and wore her accountant dad and family BMW with something like embarrassment. She and Bev had never been close. 'Hiya,' she said. 'Wicked film last night, wasn't it?'

'I know,' said Louise, 'me and 'Dele and Em were just saying,' and they all set off to the cloakroom. They were taking off their coats and chatting in its sweaty, overcrowded confines when Emma saw Bev walking towards them.

2

'Hi, Bev,' said Emma, as she passed her.

Bev walked straight on without a word. She hated the sight of Emma now. The cautious, tentative sympathy in her eyes made her shrink up inside. Jane Sullivan never looked at her like that.

It was as if the memories of Florida had turned down inside Bev over the past month or so, and the rest of the world had grown deafening around them. At one time, Bradley had blocked out her parents and Emma completely, but now they competed for space in her nightmares: Emma, Adele and the others giggled in an ugly little Orlando lounge, as her parents sat in silence on the creaking plastic sofa and the atmosphere crackled like static. Darkness fought against darkness. Everywhere she looked she saw herself reflected in other people's eyes, and she saw they didn't really notice her at all.

Jane Sullivan noticed, though. Jane Sullivan always noticed.

She'd become important to Bev, the brown-haired girl in Toby's year – far more important than a casual acquaintance had any right to be. Bev saw her maybe once a day by chance, encountered in a cloakroom or a corridor, and the brief sightings were always the highlight of her day. It was as powerful as a heroin fix – far from her subtle new fear of the staring boys, something blissful and asexual that always faded into the distance far too soon. The reassurance of knowing someone who couldn't see through to the chaos inside.

In those brief moments with Jane Sullivan, the lonely, frightened girl in the bedroom didn't exist, and her life was as perfect as an advert, and she always knew exactly the right thing to say. She slept well every night, and she'd never gone further than kissing, and her home was the happiest in the world, and she had all the friends a girl could wish for. For maybe twenty seconds a day of banal conversation, she tasted the beguiling illusion of contentment as she saw herself reflected in Jane Sullivan's eyes, and knew how deeply she was admired.

If only those moments could last longer . . .

Bev walked into the classroom and sat down alone. She steeled herself for Emma's cautious glance at her as she walked past her table with Adele and the others. She looked out of the window at the misty, shadowed morning. A chill sank into her bones like claws. She hoped she'd see Jane Sullivan at some point that day. Recently Jane Sullivan was the only thing that made her days worthwhile.

3

Before registration, the crowded classroom was quiet and somehow subdued. The weather had turned in a matter of days. You could tell it wasn't the very end of summer any more.

Jane sat alone, listening to the deafening noise from the central table. It was always the focal point of her attention in the mornings. She was very aware that they might start in on her at any time, and felt a vague transient reassurance at hearing them gossiping among themselves.

'It's going to be wicked, the funfair,' Josie was saying. 'Michael's going to bring some booze down.'

'We can drink it under the pier,' said Melanie. 'You're coming, aren't you, Tobes? Your dad's not making you stay in and *do your homework*?'

Toby Green, of course. By now Jane knew Bev's brother was going out with Tiffany. The way he was included in the Melanie set intensified her loneliness and her sense of unworthiness – the golden advert girl's family were liked and accepted by people like that, as her friends would be. Not like Jane. She had nothing in common with the people who lived in the beautiful houses after all, she realised. Bev's occasional perfunctory hellos meant less than nothing. And she was on the verge of tears as the teacher came in, and she made her small contribution to the morning registration, and then they were all filing out towards Assembly.

In the assembly hall, she took her seat. Background noise came and went, echoing under the harsh, impersonal lights, and greyish light filtered through the hall's huge windows. Melanie and Tiffany sat behind her, as they always seemed to. As Assembly progressed, she became aware of them poking the back of her seat and fizzing with suppressed giggles. The impulse to cry became greater than ever – not for them, but for something beyond them that they wouldn't understand. The gulf between herself and Beverley Green: between herself and what she loved.

When Assembly was over, they were all trooping back to the cloakroom when Melanie and Tiffany and Davina pressed around her. 'She farted in Assembly!' shrieked Melanie. 'Didn't you?'

'Dirty bitch!' howled Tiffany. 'She farted right in front of us!'

She wasn't going to cry, Jane told herself, wasn't going to let them think it was *them* who'd made her cry. 'No,' she said quietly. 'No, I never.'

'Don't lie! You *farted*!'

The words repeated over and over again in Jane's head – *not going to cry, not going to cry* – but it was becoming almost impossible not to, her eyes hot and prickling, a hard uncomfortable lump in her throat. And then she saw Bev, in the distance, alone, walking over.

And she was sure that Bev had approached them to speak to Toby, or Tiffany, but she didn't. With an overwhelming sense of disbelief, Jane realised the golden advert girl was speaking to *her*.

'Hello again,' said Bev amiably. 'How's it going?'

The joy, the amazement, the knowledge that Melanie and Tiffany and Davina and the world had fallen silent, and were watching this public recognition wide-eyed. 'Oh, I – I'm all right,' she said. 'How are you?'

'Oh, not so bad,' said Bev. 'Listen, I've got to run. Catch you later, yeah?'

When Bev had dwindled to a streak of blonde hair in the uniformed crowds, the rest of them walked to the cloakroom in near silence. Jane realised she'd never felt a pride so intense in her life. It had been to *her* that Bev had spoken, she kept repeating to herself – she'd ignored her own brother and his girlfriend, but had spoken to *her* – and she knew that all eyes were upon her, without contempt, with a new and towering curiosity. And when moronic Davina tried to resurrect the fart issue in the cloakroom, it sank like a stone, and Jane tasted something like true worship: the joy of a belief that paid off in spades, the euphoria of having been blessed by a goddess.

4

Driving home from work, Jack looked at the dashboard clock, and saw that it was seven o'clock. Although the car heater was on full blast, he felt cold. It had been a bad day. The silent phone calls had started coming for him in the office.

And he knew exactly who was making them.

More terrible than anything was the knowledge that there was nothing he could do about it. Telling anyone the full story, from Melissa to the police, would inevitably produce a flood of questions (*Who do you think would do this? Have you any serious enemies?*) leading straight back to Mandy. And the truth of their affair.

So he wouldn't tell the guys at work that he was getting silent phone calls at home. And he wouldn't tell Melissa and the kids that he was getting them at work.

The weight of secret knowledge was heavy, and he'd begun to wish he'd never set eyes on Mandy fucking Roberts.

He got home, parked and let himself into the house. In the kitchen Melissa was cooking, and Bev was reading a magazine at the table. Neither looked up or spoke as he entered. A terrifying sense of invisibility gripped him, and he spoke harshly to dispel it. 'Where's Toby?'

'He's in his room,' said Melissa, stirring, tasting.

'Well, call him down,' said Jack. 'We'd better eat soon.'

For maybe three long seconds, Melissa looked at him, face frozen, lips compressed. 'Keep an eye on the potatoes, will you, Bev?' She left the kitchen without giving him another glance.

Alone with Bev, Jack was uneasy. His daughter's eyes never left her magazine, and he felt as if he was in the company of a self-possessed stranger.

'How's school going, sweetheart?' he asked, sitting down across from her. 'Got any more good marks to tell me about?' He might as well have been in a lift, making some fatuous remark about the weather. She laid down her magazine politely, and smiled a stranger's smile.

'I got an A in maths today,' she said. 'Nothing else, really.' Silence fell again. Bev's eyes strayed cautiously back to a fashion spread, and Melissa's voice drifted down from the first floor. 'Toby,' she called, 'your father says you've got to come down for dinner.' An uncharacteristic fear crept over Jack. As he heard the footsteps descending the stairs, he thought of the silver-framed family photograph in his office, and wondered if they'd had any more silent phone calls here today. He knew he wouldn't be the one to ask.

Under the bright circle of white light, Melissa dished up lamb with rosemary, new potatoes and peas, and he thought that the silence was appalling. He heard four sets of lungs taking in the air, breathing in, breathing out. The tiny click of a fork on china filled his world. Melissa finished handing round the plates and sat down, picking up her cutlery. 'Give me some more potatoes, would you, Mel?' he asked. He knew the dish was only a few inches away from his hand, but he'd never thought she minded serving him.

It shocked him to see his wife's face: it set so hard that it seemed to tremble – her mouth was a bloodless white line. For several seconds, she didn't speak, and when she did he could barely hear her voice. 'Jesus *Christ*,' she muttered. 'Why don't you just –' He thought it was like watching something come out under extraordinary pressure, a jet of steam from a boiler that was about to explode. Then her teeth pressed down on her lower lip, as if to hold the pressure inside.

Jack didn't know what to say. He told himself he hadn't meant any harm. 'Mel?' he asked. 'What's the matter?'

'*Nothing*,' she sang out brightly. She laid down her cutlery slowly and deliberately, rose from her seat, dished up his potatoes with a gentle precision that said she might have slammed them down. 'There you are, *darling*.' And Jack knew it was the voice of a good actress deliberately pretending to be a bad one, and that if she'd really wanted to fake wifely affection, she could have done it a hundred times better than that.

When Melissa returned to her seat and they all started eating, the silence fell again. It grew so thick that when Toby spoke it seemed as strange to Jack as hearing loud voices in a cathedral.

'Oh, yeah, Bev. I meant to ask. How come you know Jane Sullivan?'

'Jane who?'

'You know,' said Toby. 'That girl in my year. The one you said hi to after Assembly.'

'What's it to you?' asked Bev.

'Nothing,' said Toby. 'I just *wondered*.'

'Well, don't bother *wondering*. I'll speak to who I want. So mind your own fucking business.'

It was glaringly obvious to Jack that her penultimate word should have drawn a rebuke of some kind from Melissa, but none came. Just the silence, heavier than ever, pressing in around them and not pushing them together at all. The shrilling of the phone in the downstairs hallway cut through it. Jack rose to get it. In the tasteful shadows, where nobody was watching, he approached the receiver as if it were a poisonous snake. He wished he could believe there'd be a voice at the other end.

5

'That was Joyce. She sends her love,' said Mary, as she came back from the phone in the hallway and sat down. 'And to you, dear,' she said to Jane. 'She says she's ever so pleased to hear you've settled in at school so well.'

'Well, we all are,' said Alf. 'It isn't easy to settle in in a new place.'

'You must invite that nice friend of yours round for tea, soon,' said Mary. 'That nice Anita you always talk about.'

There was something terrible about the little kitchen now, especially in the evenings. The cold darkness outside seemed to send the four walls creeping together. It was always far too bright, far too hot, far too claustrophobic. The froth of suds glittered in the sink as it always did. Jane picked indifferently at her dinner, trying to think of something to say. 'Maybe,' she said. 'I'll ask her, and see what she says.'

'Well, I don't see what else she could say but yes,' said Mary. 'After all, you've been to her house, Jane, dear. It's high time we returned the favour.'

'Yeah. I suppose.'

'We'd be only too happy to have her over for an evening,' said Mary. 'She sounds like such a nice, well-behaved girl. Not like Carol's friends at school.'

'She never asked *them* round for tea,' said Alf.

'I wouldn't have had them in the house,' said Mary. 'Nasty little tarts, they were. I saw her with them when we had to go to the school. Not sixteen years old and they looked like common prostitutes. Teaching our girl to drink and swear and go with boys. It was all their fault when she went and got herself pregnant. If she'd taken my advice and had the abortion – but oh, no. She just ran off with that dirty little hooligan of hers, and –'

'*Mary*,' said Alf warningly. He turned to Jane, a false smile pasted on his face. 'Well, you can invite your friend over as much as you like, love,' he said. 'There'll always be a welcome for Anita, here.'

Jane smiled, and nodded. It was a great effort. She was as tense as strung elastic and longing for a release that couldn't be found here. It pulled at her senses through the floorboards upstairs, from the compass and the lighter under the mattress in her room. She cleared her plate and rose from the table, putting it and her used knife and fork in the sink. 'I'd better go on up to my room, anyway,' she said. 'I've got a lot of homework tonight.'

6

She shut her bedroom door and went over to the mattress. She pulled out the package and sat down at the dressing-table–desk. Then she peeled back the bandage, and the ritual began.

She had been doing this more and more often recently. She tried to ration herself to once a week or so, but the temptation was almost impossible to resist. A moment's escape, a moment's forgetfulness. The times she spent with the ritual were the only times she spent free of a sadder knowledge: she and the golden advert girl moved in different worlds, and the gap between them would never be truly bridged.

Impossible to express how much Beverley Green had come to mean to her. Their short, casual exchanges in corridors and hallways had effectively become the focal point of her life – the suburbs incarnate, a distant, drifting saviour who was never too perfect to be kind. Nobody else ever stopped and smiled, but the golden advert girl always did. Nobody else ever took time out from the golden advert world to ask Jane how she was.

It was as if the rest of Jane's world had begun to wither around that perfection, leaving it the only solid object. Melanie and her friends, Mary and Alf downstairs, the memories of Carol and Dave and Anita: nothing else really mattered except as background for the golden advert girl, the scenery she moved through, the velvet curtain that fell to conceal her. A charcoal-grey four-wheel-drive travelled through Jane's dreams. She thought she would see it for ever.

Jane sat at her desk and finished with the compass point. She replaced the little package under the mattress and taped tissue paper over the cut on her arm. She sat back down at her desk. Through her half-drawn curtains, the night was bleak, dark and infinite. For the thousandth time, she wondered what Beverley Green was doing at this exact second. She wondered whether Beverley Green was laughing with a friend.

7

Carol had met Dave just over a year ago, in the May of Jane's thirteenth year. Jane didn't know where or how. One day she came home from school and there he was: a tall, rangy, dark-haired young man, pallid, sneering, leather-jacketed, snake-hipped. Not bad-looking, maybe, if you liked the type. Carol did, and always had. She fell for Dave hard.

Jane was used to Carol having boyfriends, but she'd never seen her so wrapped up in one before. She'd used to have her current man round along with the rest of her friends, and they'd all sit in the lounge chatting together, but with Dave she didn't seem to want to share him like that. At first, she either had Dave round or her mates round, and then she only ever had Dave round. To Jane, there was something terrible about their slow descent into isolation – the walls moving together, the net tightening.

Jane would always remember how it had been in the evenings of last summer, when Carol and Dave had thought they were happy together. Coming home from town or Anita's, how strange it had been. A scrawled note from Carol in the kitchen, saying she and Dave had gone out somewhere and wouldn't be back till late. Overflowing ashtrays and empty beer-cans and an overwhelming sense of desolation. Silence filled the world, and the sunsets were extraordinary – hectic, unsettling sunsets that slanted across the carpet in stripes the colour of fire. It felt as if the rest of the human race had faded out of the world when she hadn't been looking, and emptiness echoed in her head. Deep inside, she could feel things preparing to go wrong.

She was right. In a matter of months, the arguments had started. Carol's fault, mainly. There was nothing sweet or submissive about her, even now that she was in love. Rather, her hard edges grew jagged and blurred, and Jane watched her eroding. She'd always been a heavy drinker, but now it was getting out of control: she got paranoid and hysterical. Late at night, she screamed at Dave that he didn't care about her, she accused him of shagging other women. He yelled back and slapped her and cracked open another can from the fridge. Jane sat up sleepless in her room, and listened, and worried.

In the January of that year, when the arguments had been building slowly to a crescendo, Carol had lost her job in the launderette. Jane asked the details and was told to mind her own fucking business, it wasn't anything to do with her. It seemed she'd tried to steal some money and they'd found her out. She didn't get another job after that, and Jane supposed she was getting her money from Dave. In her eyes, there was something nightmarish about her mother's dismissal, and the launderette took on the shape and colour of nostalgia: there was nowhere left for her to go when she wanted to pretend her life was normal, where she could run into Anita in the sweet smell of hot fabric and washing-powder and talk as equals did.

Not that she'd have wanted to run into Anita now. Anita had started at Jane's comprehensive that month, and had a big group of new friends there. It hurt to see Anita ignoring her in the playground.

She came to dread coming back from school in the evenings. When she got home, they'd be in, her mother and Dave – they'd be in and they'd be drunk and they'd be arguing furiously, and she'd sense a new, deeper darkness pressing in outside. And she came to hate the faces she passed on those long journeys home. Something raw, desperate and murderous surfaced towards the smiling, complacent faces that might have cared, and should have cared, and didn't care at all.

The compass point had come soon after.

It seemed inevitable.

8

Mandy sat at the canteen table, one of the girls, absolutely alone. She listened to the middle-aged woman called Janet talking.

'He's a dirty old sod, I can tell you,' said Janet, laughing as she flicked an inch of ash off her cigarette. 'You know what he got me for my birthday this year? You know what he got me?'

There were murmurs of interest and encouragement round the table. The secretaries always sat together for lunch. Outside, the afternoon was grey, bleak and dispiriting, and heavy black clouds threatened rain. 'He only got me all this pervy *lingery*,' continued Janet. 'All red lace and black plastic. Got it out a catalogue he sent off for out the *News of the World*. Expected me to wear it. I could have shoved it up his arse. I told him, "Steve," I said, "I've been hinting about that blender for *months*, and . . ."'

Lingery and blenders and the *News of the World* – it was like nettles on Mandy's flesh, a reminder of all she'd lost. The cheap metal ashtray on the table overflowed with lipsticked butts, and she found the sight nauseating. 'Look at her, sitting there like she knows something we don't,' said Janet, and the laughter rolled again. All eyes were on Mandy. 'I'll tell you, love, when you get to my age you'll appreciate a good blender. I'd have preferred the pervy stuff too, when I was twenty.'

The laughter that seemed to rejoice in its own ignorance, that didn't know about the Merc's powerful headlights zooming away into the night, the dreams of something else and the desperation for revenge. Suddenly amiability was as hard as the thirtieth sit-up. 'I suppose,' she said, hiding behind her brassy young smile. 'If you say so.'

'You got a boyfriend, then, Mand?' asked another woman. 'You thinking of settling down soon?'

'No,' said Mandy. 'I'm single right now. I had a great boyfriend, though. Once.'

Back in the office, in the admin department of Underlyme Council, in the boring little job she'd been lucky to find so soon after getting fired from Jack's Motors, old grey metal filing cabinets glinted dully in the thin grey afternoon light. She sat in front of her elderly Apple Mac and felt them staring at her, challenging, taunting. A couple of weeks ago, she'd thought the silent phone calls would be enough, but now she knew more: they'd begun to feel pathetically inadequate, a pinprick to an elephant, a petty, childish game. When three o'clock came, she knew what she'd do. She'd call round on his smiling blonde wife from the silver frame, and tell her about her husband's little indiscretion. Of course Mandy knew Jack's home address. She should do: after all, she'd been his secretary for almost a year.

9

For a few seconds, Jane just sat and stared at the paper in silence. It was the family essay she'd written last month, the one about Anita that she'd lost herself in for over two hours. F, it said at the bottom in a neat little circle, SEE ME.

It was a cold day, a dark day, a bleak day. Through the window, drizzle speckled the glass without energy, and the harsh yellow striplight overhead was all wrong. English was the last lesson of the day. She heard voices across the aisle – 'I can't believe I got a B!' exclaimed Tiffany, and Josie said sourly, 'Well, I got a C, that's not bad either' – and she felt the cold waters about to close over her head.

A few minutes later, the home-time bell rang out sharply. Jane was about to walk out, when the teacher called, far too loudly. 'Can you stay behind for a few minutes, Jane? I'd like a word about your essay.'

Melanie and the others swaggered out and past her. 'Now

you're in for it,' said Melanie, and Josie said, 'Probably wrote about shagging her nan. They're going to get the police round.' Then they were giggling out of the door and down the hallway, and the classroom drained empty.

Outside the windows, the rain fell interminably. Jane shuffled her feet, and stared at the patch of linoleum in front of the teacher's desk. 'Now, Jane,' said the teacher, a prim-faced, fussy woman somewhere in her thirties, 'I don't think you quite understood what I was asking for, hmm? I wanted a short factual essay. Not a short story.'

'I'm sorry,' said Jane.

'Oh, goodness, Jane, I'm not telling you off. But if you want to pass your GCSE, you're going to have to *listen.*' She spoke again, more gently. 'Now, I'm not going to ask you to write it again. That wouldn't be fair. But I want you to promise me, next time, you'll pay attention when I set an essay topic. Not just drift off into a daydream. I've seen you in class, sometimes. You look like you're in a little world of your own.'

'I promise,' said Jane, then, again, 'I'm sorry.'

'Well, then. Let's say no more about it. Run along, Jane. You'll be late home for tea.' When Jane reached the doorway, the teacher spoke again. 'And I hate to say this, Jane, but you really should invest in a dictionary. Your spelling's appalling.'

Outside, the hallway was almost deserted. The corridors stirred with the afternoon's last stragglers. Jane leaned against the wall and fished her family essay out of her bag. It was no good, the golden advert girl's friends would be brainy and college-bound – in spite of that one perfect morning, her kindness must be no more than an extension of pity, after all. In that second, Jane saw the gulf between them more deeply than ever, and tears pricked the backs of her eyes. Then she walked through the main double doors and out into the cold.

10

Bev had hated coming home from school lately. She always delayed it as long as she could, lingering in classrooms and corridors and toilets where she could see the immediate future far too clearly. A silence as unbearable as a physical cramp, glances that never quite met across the kitchen table. The thunderstorm atmosphere not only unrelieved but gathering in on itself till the air was still and heavy, and you rehearsed words over and over in your head before you let them leave your mouth. That was how it always was at home, these days, and it was why Bev never wanted to go back there.

She walked down the hallway alone. Her fellow pupils had almost all gone home, and her footsteps rang out under the sallow striplights. Through the windows, she saw deepening rain across a bleak landscape. She didn't want to go out there, but of course she had to. So she buttoned her coat and left by the main double doors.

Outside the afternoon was cold, dark and forbidding. She put up her umbrella, and felt the rain coming down all around her. She remembered how the world had looked that summer. Back then, she'd longed for an end to pretending, she thought, and a huge sense of loss overcame her just before she noticed Jane Sullivan.

She was walking maybe twenty metres ahead of Bev, along the path that led out of school. She hadn't seen her. She carried no umbrella and walked with her head down, her hair clinging wetly to her scalp. Another fifteen seconds, and she'd be out of the gates, at the bus-stop, travelling home.

In that moment, a two-way junction loomed in Bev's mind. Something deep inside her knew that this was the point where their relationship could change for good, far from the noisy, chattering corridors and the crowds of laughing strangers, a bleak and rainy afternoon where they could talk in private, as friends did. Here was their place and time. Finding something in the thought unsettling. Bev didn't know whether to call to Jane or not. Then she remembered the tense silences awaiting her back home, and how Toby would be round at a friend's, and how she couldn't call Emma any more, and she saw that Jane Sullivan was approaching the gates now, and she saw that there was no more time to lose.

'Hey, Jane!' she called. 'Jane! Wait up!'

11

Impossible to think that a second ago she'd been thinking of nothing but the compass and the lighter, and the possibility of using them that night. Dizzy with hope, Jane turned and waited for the golden advert girl to catch her up. They fell into step together.

'How's it going, then?' asked Bev casually.

'Oh, I – I'm all right. How about you?'

'Not so bad. Listen, you fancy coming into town with me? We can get the bus just up the road.'

The subtle enormity of the request hit Jane hard. They'd never walked anywhere together before, much less shared an afternoon, as friends did. 'Sure,' she said at once, then, shyly, 'You getting anything?'

'Don't think so. Just a look-round, really.' Bev extended her umbrella slightly, and Jane pressed in under it. The golden advert girl's fresh citrus perfume filled her mind. 'They've got some wicked new sweaters in Next,' said Bev. 'I might try one on.'

They waited in silence at the bus-stop, and the rain blurred the oncoming bus like a heat-haze. They got on and sat down together near the back. Jane looked at Bev out of the corner of her eye. What she saw entranced her. 'What do your mum and dad do?' she asked.

'My dad owns a car-lot. My mum's . . . just a mum, I suppose.' Bev's eyes met Jane's. 'Why d'you ask?'

'I don't know. I don't know anyone else who lives in Preston.'

Jane could have gone further, but fear of displaying her naked yearning drove her to change the subject, in the clumsiest way possible. 'My mum used to work in a launderette,' she said. 'But she's dead now. She died in the summer.'

'Oh, no,' said Bev. 'What happened?'

'She was in a car accident,' lied Jane quickly. 'I live with my nan and grandad now. It's all right. They're all right.'

'That's such a shame. I'm really sorry.' Seconds passed slowly and took the unease with them. Sympathy faded in Bev's eyes, and was replaced by camaraderie. 'Here's town, anyway,' she said, as bright lights flashed outside the window. 'You're going to love those sweaters.'

So they went into Next, and the light and warmth inside swam through the drizzling evening like a hallucination. The aloof yet beguiling smells of polish and new fabric seduced Jane as instantly as the suburbs had, and she touched cashmere and cotton and pure wool with tentative wonderment. 'I've never been in here before,' she said. 'It's ever so nice.'

'I like it,' said Bev absently. 'Oh, here's the sweaters I was talking about. What do you think?'

Jane looked. She saw a rack of soft fluffy jumpers in various colours, with big multicoloured diamonds on the front. 'They're well wicked,' she said, in a tone and an idiom not her own. 'You going to try one on?'

'Think I will,' said Bev, then, 'You should, too. The red one'd suit you.'

In the changing room next door to Bev's, Jane took off her school sweater and shirt, and slipped the suburbs over her head. Her heart was pounding harder and faster than she'd ever known it to. Bev called out to her from outside the drawn curtain. 'You tried it on yet, Jane?'

'Yeah. Just coming out.' She pulled back the curtain, and saw Bev reflected in the big mirror outside the cubicles. She was studying herself critically. 'Oh, wow,' said Jane. 'You look ever so nice.'

'I like it,' said Bev thoughtfully. 'I might get it.' Jane was silent. Bev had always been the golden advert girl to her, but never more so than now – beautiful and preoccupied in this glossy shop – and a combination of adoration and loneliness swept over her under the bright lights and the muted music, as if she was alone here with her dreams. She noticed Bev staring at her. 'Hey,' said Bev, 'what've you done to your arm?'

Jane's heart skipped a beat. She looked down, and saw the bandage was showing. She pulled her sleeve down quickly. 'I hurt myself the other night,' she said. 'It doesn't matter, it's okay.' Fearing further questioning, she spoke too fast. 'It doesn't look right on me, this sweater,' she said. 'I'll change back.'

In the cubicle, she removed the sweater she could never have afforded in a million years with a kind of regret – also, a sense that she'd narrowly escaped a terrible unmasking. The golden advert girl wouldn't understand about the ritual. Pain didn't exist in the suburbs. She changed back into her school shirt and sweater, and walked back out into the shop. Bev was dressed and ready, waiting by the shelves.

'I'll ask Mum to get it for me on Saturday,' said Bev, as they left the shop and the umbrella went up again. 'There's a Next in Bournemouth. We're going shopping there together.'

In that single second, the power of the evening came together for Jane, and overwhelmed her. She found a kind of bleak majesty in the cold lights and the lethargic downpour, and felt the joy and pathos as a single emotion, walking beside something perfect and amiable and utterly unattainable that would soon drift out of reach once more. She knew that Bev would check her watch soon, and spoke too loudly, emboldened by desperation. 'I've had a wicked afternoon,' she said. 'We could go there again, some time.'

'Well, I'm mostly out with the others in my year,' said Bev, and Jane's heart plummeted, but then Bev smiled, and Jane's heart leaped. 'Tell you what,' said Bev. 'Give me your number. I'll give you a call some time.'

They stood in a brightly lit shop doorway, and Jane fumbled in her bag for a pen and paper, wrote down her name and number on a scrap of A4. Bev took it, and folded it into her neat, perfect wallet. 'Well, see you later, Jane,' said Bev. 'I'll give you a call.' And then she was gone.

At the bus-stop, Jane waited for a long time. It didn't seem to matter. Around her, empty streets gleamed black with rain. Deep in her mind, fireworks exploded.

12

Melissa sat in the neat, stylish little Bournemouth café, with two of the neat, stylish, convenient friends who didn't know a thing about her. Outside the window, the day was cold and bleak, and the sky looked like a sheet of dull steel. 'Well, of course, it's Kate and Tony's anniversary next month,' Betty was saying. 'I was only talking to her yesterday, and she says . . .' And Melissa smiled and nodded as Trisha did, trying far too hard to look interested. She could feel the hours ahead of her slipping through her hands like a greased rope – they'd finish their coffee and she'd drive back to Underlyme, where she'd start cooking the dinner, and wait for Jack to come home.

A sense of nightmare nibbled at the edge of her mind. It crept and rustled beyond the bright lights and the polite, smiling banalities, something dark and real. 'I expect they'll be throwing a party,' said Trisha, 'to mark the occasion, you know.' Melissa smiled, and raised her cup of cappuccino to her lips. She saw that Betty was giving her an odd look. 'Why, Melissa, dear,' said Betty, 'you're shaking like a leaf. Are you all right?' Melissa noticed the cup juddering in her hand. She laid it down on the saucer, and heard the brief chatter of china on china. 'It's nothing to worry about,' she said. 'Honestly. I'm fine.'

When the bill had come and been paid and they'd all air-kissed their bright, meaningless goodbyes, Melissa's sense of nightmare deepened. The shadowy streets had the feel of *film noir*, and the cold wind tore and stung. She didn't want to go home, but there was nowhere else to go.

Behind the wheel of the Mitsubishi Shogun, terror came and

113

went in waves and she drove erratically – a collision with a battered Transit van was narrowly averted by its driver, who wound his window down, furious-eyed: 'Why don't you look where you're going,' he yelled, 'you stupid bitch?' The words meant nothing to her. She completed the rest of the journey on autopilot, dreading the silence in the kitchen, the ticking clock, the slow approach of yet another unbearable night.

When she let herself into the house, it was almost four o'clock. She hung up her coat in the hallway, and went into the kitchen. The air was still and oppressive, and the neat lawn through the french windows had a sombre look under the bleak grey sky. It was too early to make a start on dinner, so she polished the already gleaming table for the sake of something to do. It felt like cleaning an instrument of torture.

It was getting to be so much of an effort to keep her temper, her tongue and her hatred under control. So much of an effort –

The sound of the knocker at the door cut through her thoughts. She laid aside the cloth and the polish, and walked out to answer it. Behind the frosted-glass panel set into the front door, she saw a face she didn't recognise, distorted and ghostly, framed in red.

13

Melissa couldn't think of anything to say. The stranger on the doorstep just stood there, young and hard-faced and pretty, apparently comfortable with the ambiguous silence and the air of confrontation. It came to the point where there was only one question left in the world. 'What do you want?' asked Melissa.

'I want to talk to you,' said the girl. 'Can I come in?'

There didn't seem to be any way of denying the terse request: Melissa stood aside, and watched the girl's back as she walked in. Hard, purposeful eyes moved this way and that. 'Great house,' said the girl. 'It's what I'd have expected.'

It was like some surreal dream, where strangers came in and

commented on your hallway décor in the voice of a hanging judge. 'What do you mean?' asked Melissa, then, again, 'What do you want?'

'I just wanted to talk to you,' said the girl. 'I know your husband.'

Something suddenly changed in the atmosphere between them and the way they stood. 'We'd better go and sit down,' said Melissa. 'We can discuss this in the kitchen.'

In the kitchen, the smell of polish hung heavily, and the table shone. Melissa sat down; the girl did too. Melissa faced her like an interviewer. 'How do you know Jack?' she asked.

'I thought maybe he'd have told you,' said the girl. 'I used to work for the bastard. I was his secretary.' Her small beringed hand rose to her mouth, and she sniggered as if she'd just seen the point of a dirty joke. 'And his mistress,' she said. 'He was knocking me off on the side, Mrs Green. For *months*.'

For a long time, Melissa just sat in silence. She wondered why she didn't feel surprised, but a part of her knew – she'd always sensed it would come to this, one day. Arrogant, insecure Jack, with his desperate need to prove himself. 'I might have known,' she said quietly.

The girl's look betrayed brief bewilderment. When she returned to character, it was as if she was overacting in a bad mini-series – she smirked and sneered, cold-eyed reptilian. 'You wouldn't think it, would you? Not of your perfect husband. Shagging me in the Merc on his way back here. Such a lovely house. Such a lovely tasteful family.' It was Alexis Colby in a red velour jacket, confronting a Krystle Carrington who didn't seem to care. 'He got fed up with me, though. Sacked me over it. That's why I thought I'd better have a little word. Tell you what your perfect husband's really like.'

'I know what he's really like,' said Melissa. 'Better than you do.' There was something almost desperate in the girl's eyes – as if they scanned the wings for an absent prompter. 'Those silent phone calls,' said Melissa. 'Was that you?'

'Sure,' said the girl. 'How did he explain all *that*? Burglars?'

'He didn't explain a thing. He never does.' There was a long silence. Melissa's hands lay on the table-top, and didn't move. 'I don't know why you came here,' she said eventually. 'I don't know what you want.'

'I wanted to. I wanted you to see that. He's not what he seems. Your nice happy perfect family. It's all a fucking *lie*.' It occurred to Melissa that the girl had come here to loot and vandalise only to find the shop windows broken and the shelves stripped bare: her eyes held the ultimate anticlimax of realising there was nothing left to destroy. 'It's all *fake*,' she said furiously. 'It's all *bullshit*.'

'I've known that for years,' said Melissa. 'I think you should go now. You can't tell me anything I don't know. Not about Jack.'

The red-haired girl rose slowly from the table. Melissa barely noticed. So it had come to this, she thought. The tense silences at the dinner table had exploded into the ultimate put-down, the ultimate indiscretion, the ultimate betrayal. 'Do what you like to him,' she said quietly. 'Tell who you like about him. I don't care *what* happens to the bastard any more.' And as the red-haired girl hurried out, Melissa sat and gazed into space, seeing a thousand resentful submissions blossom into a hatred beyond the world.

14

At five o'clock, she opened the door to Toby, who always forgot his key. This evening, he was in the company of a spotty teenage Goliath who shuffled huge feet awkwardly on the doorstep and didn't meet her eyes. 'We can't stop, Mum,' said Toby. 'Remember? It's the funfair tonight. I'm staying round at Craig's.' He grabbed the sports bag with his day clothes in it from the hallway alcove. 'See you tomorrow, yeah?' Then he was gone, he and the surly Craig mooching back up the drive.

A few minutes later, she heard Bev let herself in and walk into the kitchen. Sitting at the table, Melissa didn't dare look up for fear of what Bev might see in her eyes. She gazed through the french windows at the lawn beyond. 'Hey,' said Bev, sounding slightly bewildered, 'aren't you cooking tonight?'

'I don't think so. Get something out of the fridge, if you're hungry.' Melissa could feel Bev's eyes on the bare surfaces, the dearth of bubbling pans and drifting cooking smells.

'You and Dad eating out tonight?' Bev asked.

'No.' The darkening garden held Melissa hypnotised – the things that had always been there, that she'd never been able to bring herself to recognise. 'We never do anything when it's just the two of us.'

Bev approached Melissa slowly, and sat down at the table. 'Hey,' she said, 'what's the matter?'

'It's nothing. You don't have to worry.' Melissa tried to keep her voice quiet and normal, but a part of her knew that Bev must see through it. 'Your brother's gone to the funfair,' she said. 'Are you going to the funfair tonight?'

'No. What's the matter?' Bev repeated. Her voice sounded plaintive and accusing.

Melissa ignored her. 'You should go out tonight,' she said. 'It's not a night to stay in. You should go out with Emma, to the funfair.'

'What's the *matter*?' asked Bev again, but it was the way you asked a question when you didn't really want to know the answer. Already, she was backing away to the door with fear in her eyes. 'I don't want to go out,' she said in the doorway, 'I don't like Emma any more,' and then she was hurrying out of sight, up the stairs.

Melissa sat at the kitchen table. She looked out into the gathering night, at the garden and the swimming-pool and the meandering stone path. Slow fury ticked in her ears. It wasn't really about Jack's affair, or even the strong new suspicion that he'd had a lot more than one – the hard vengeful little redhead had simply lit the fuse. She'd been ready to explode for a long time. She sat up in the cold creeping evening, and waited for her husband to come home.

15

Jack drove home from work with the radio on. He felt in a tolerably good mood. For the last few days there hadn't been any silent phone calls for him at work or in the evening, and he guessed that that Mandy bitch had finally lost interest in the whole thing. Besides, he'd found an apparently efficient and well-balanced new secretary, and business was booming.

When he got in, he couldn't work out at first what was wrong. Then he could. There were no voices from the kitchen, no beguiling smells of roasting meat and fresh-chopped herbs lingering on the air. The house was dark and silent and unscented. He walked into the kitchen. Melissa was sitting with her back to him, framed by a circle of bright white light, looking out of the french windows at the floodlit patio. A new bewilderment overcame him, and he fought to dispel it with prosaic irritation. 'Haven't you even started the dinner yet?' he demanded. 'What the hell's the matter *now*?'

Slowly, she turned to face him. He couldn't make sense of her expression. 'You've got a bloody nerve talking to me like that,' she said quietly. 'I had a visitor today. You should have been here. We could have made up a little party.'

He took a step back, his heart slowly picking up speed. 'What do you mean?' he asked. 'Who?'

'I didn't catch her name. But I think you'd have recognised her,' said Melissa. 'Just a young girl, no more than twenty or so. Good-looking, in a nasty sort of way. Red hair.' Recognition dawned on his face. She smiled tightly. 'I thought you'd remember her,' she said. 'She certainly remembers *you*.'

'*That* bitch.' Cold horror hit him out of nowhere. He'd begun to think Mandy was harmless and meaningless after all, that she'd disappeared back into nothing with a flick of his wrist. 'What did she say?'

'You *shit*,' said Melissa. For the first time in their marriage, he heard real fury trembling in her voice. 'You're covering your bets even now, aren't you? See how much your little slag told me before you admit a thing. But I think I know just about all of it, Jack. Let's see, now.' She sat back, and started counting off facts on her fingers. 'You were screwing her for months. *Months*. She was your secretary. You fired her. Because you were bored. And that's pretty fucking low, Jack. Even for you.'

'Melissa –' he said. It terrified him to see the perfection of his life breaking down like this but, knowing he was irretrievably in the wrong, he fumbled for righteous rage. '*Melissa* –'

'Oh, and I almost forgot,' Melissa interrupted. 'She's the one who's been making all those silent phone calls. The ones we've all been so worried about. As if you didn't know. Pretending you were just as baffled as us. When me and the kids were so scared. You *shit*.'

He didn't know what to say. 'Melissa,' he said again. 'I didn't –'

'Didn't what? Didn't care? Didn't want to get found out? Are you honestly telling me you didn't *know* who'd have a grudge against you?' She broke off, and took a long deep breath. 'I hate you,' she said. '*I hate you*.'

'You've got no right to say that. You've got no reason. You're just upset. Hysterical. She didn't mean a thing. Melissa. *Melissa*.' He felt helpless and trapped and appallingly culpable. He'd played with matches, he thought, and was watching his carefully constructed world go down in flames – the carefully constructed fiction of her love. 'I've always been good to you and the kids,' he said. 'You know I've always been good to you. The holidays. The house. When you calm down, you'll see that. Your father –'

'Oh, that's right. Trot my father out. What would you do without him?' Melissa's smile was savage. 'Get on to your family next, why don't you? How much you've sacrificed. How much I owe you. Jesus Christ.'

'You don't know what you're talking about. That's not fair.' Her accusing, hating silence drove him on to say more. 'They wouldn't have come round. You don't know what they were like.'

'You're a liar,' she said. 'A bloody liar.'

'The fuck I am!' It enraged him that she could speak like this, that it was all his own stupid fault she now felt able to. 'They'd never have accepted you, even if –'

'If you'd tried to talk them round? If you'd stayed in touch? They weren't so callous that they'd lose their own son just because he got engaged to a Catholic girl. If you'd tried a bit harder to make it up to them. But, oh, no. You did everything short of beg me to take you back to Underlyme with me. " What about your family?" I said, and you said, "To hell with them". Your exact words. And ever since then, it's been "Look what I did for you, look how much I lost for your sake". You think you're some kind of tragic hero. I'll tell you what you are. You're an arsehole.'

'I didn't want to break with them.' But it came out as weak and feeble, knowing that she'd always sensed the truth – how ashamed he'd always been of the tacky terrace back in Manchester, of his loud, embarrassing mother and his father's shitty little grocery store, how he'd jumped at any opportunity to sever ties and escape. 'I loved my family,' he lied.

'Yeah. Like you love me and the kids,' said Melissa. 'Look how good you've been to us. I'm a nervous wreck the second you step in the door. Toby's terrified of you. Bev hardly speaks to you from one week to the next.' There was a long silence. 'I'm sick of you,' she said eventually. 'I hate you. I want a divorce.'

16

Bev sat at her desk and put down her pen – she couldn't even pretend to concentrate on her history assignment any more. The voices from the kitchen downstairs filled her mind. Although she couldn't quite make out the words, she could somehow chart the sound patterns: a terrible quiet tension occasionally rising to an even more chilling rage. In a way, she wanted to know what her parents were saying, but the idea of creeping downstairs to eavesdrop was somehow even worse than the uncertainty.

She sat and listened and pretended not to hear. Her breath came slow and hard. She tried to think about something else, but it was like burrowing through layer upon layer of solid darkness. Retreating from the quiet murmur in the kitchen, she discovered Emma and Adele and the others giggling together in French and seeming not to notice her. Retreating from them, she came upon an ugly little flat in Orlando, the taste of the joint and a squashy plastic sofa. 'Ah, come on, honey,' murmured Bradley in her ear, 'just relax, let it happen,' and she jerked away from the memory and back to the here and now, and the voices from the kitchen filled her mind all over again. There was nowhere else to go, she thought, not tonight, not ever.

Toby would be at the funfair now, with the big group of friends their father didn't approve of. The idea of them all laughing together touched Bev deep inside with inexpressible loneliness. Something pulled at her through the window; a noisy, colourful night out on the pier, the wheeling lights against the black sky and the pounding music. 'It's not a night to stay in,' her mother had said earlier, and Bev realised that she'd been right: it wasn't a night to sit in your room, to feel small and lost and alone, to listen to your parents arguing as they never argued, and wonder when it had all started going out of control. It wasn't a night to be afraid.

On the very last night of the Underlyme funfair, you were supposed to have a good time. She'd always gone with Emma before. She'd always had a kind of fun.

Bev sat at her desk, and wondered and worried and listened. Then something clicked into place in her mind. She saw the trendy little pink Perspex phone by her bed with new eyes. She rose from her seat, and got a folded piece of paper out of the wallet in her schoolbag. She went to the phone, picked up the receiver and started dialling.

17

When the phone rang downstairs, Jane knew it was going to be the golden advert girl. She always knew it was going to be her lately, and this sureness was beginning to feel more and more like desperation. That afternoon in town couldn't have been unimportant after all – the golden advert girl must have intended to call her, soon.

Jane sat in her room and turned the volume on her radio right down. She craned to hear every word as Mary picked up the receiver. A tiny part of her braced herself for the familiar, paralysing disappointment – Mary's questioning voice settling into an easy flow of chat. In the lamplight, near-silence pressed in all around her, and she realised she was holding her breath.

'Jane, dear!' Mary called up the stairs. 'Phone for you!'

The joy, the disbelief that she hadn't been forgotten. She pounded downstairs, and took the receiver without even looking at the hovering Mary. She spoke slightly breathlessly. 'Hello? Bev?'

'You must be psychic.' Jane heard her laughing down the line. 'How'd you know it was me?'

Impossible to explain that nobody else cared enough to dial her number, that there was a kindness you only found in the suburbs. 'I don't know,' Jane said stupidly, then, 'How's it going?'

'Oh, I'm fine. Just fine.' Jane pictured her as she must be now: lounging in a beautiful pastel-coloured bedroom with Preston through the windows, her hair loose around her shoulders. How perfectly happy she sounded. 'Listen, I just called to ask. Fancy coming to the funfair in town tonight?'

A thrilling excitement hit Jane out of nowhere. This was more than an impromptu shopping trip – she'd heard about the funfair endlessly at school. Melanie and her friends were all going tonight. To think the golden advert girl was inviting *her*. For a second, she couldn't think of anything to say. 'Sure,' she said eventually, 'I'd love to.'

'Great,' said Bev. 'So? When shall we meet up?'

Mary had gone back into the lounge, closing the door behind her. Jane stood in the neat polished respectable hallway, alone. 'I – I don't know,' she said. 'When d'you want to?'

'In about an hour or so? That'd be good for me.'

What was she doing now? Jane wondered. She envisaged those perfect French-manicured nails idly pulling the kinks out of the phone cord, those blue-blue eyes flicking over an unheard television. 'Sure,' she heard herself saying. 'That'd be wicked.'

'Cool,' said Bev. 'Meet outside the Menzies in town, at half seven?'

Jane fumbled for the pen and paper by the phone. 'Okay,' she said, as she wrote, 'okay. I'll be there.'

'Well, I'll see you, then,' said Bev, and laughed her unreachable laugh. 'Don't be late.'

For a few seconds, Jane stood, umoving, with the dialling tone running through her mind. Then the lounge door opened, and Mary stepped out. 'Who was that, dear?' she asked, as Jane put down the receiver. 'Was that Anita?'

'No,' said Jane. 'It was Beverley. She's my best friend now.' She paused for a second, trying to put something vast into words. 'You'd really like her. She's miles nicer than Anita.'

18

'You want me to go,' said Jack. 'So I'll go.'

'Get out, then,' said Melissa. 'Just get out.'

'So I will,' he said. 'I'll be back for some clothes tomorrow. Give you time to think about it. How it'd be if you divorced me. All you've got to lose.'

'I haven't got anything left to lose. You and your empty threats. You make me sick.'

'I'll let you sleep on it,' he said. 'I'll be back in the morning.'

'Just get out,' she ground out slowly, and she turned away

from him. There had been nobody to watch his big dramatic exit and he couldn't tell whether or not she'd been impressed by his hard, decisive door-slam.

Behind the wheel of the Merc, fury fought with bewilderment. How wrong and unfair she'd been, how much she'd miss him if she really filed for divorce. And the kids would miss him, too. He'd always been good to them, always been there for them. Distant unwelcome images stirred in his mind – the silence at the kitchen table, Toby's scared eyes – and he held them at bay with the immediacy of a problem that could be solved by action and anger. That bitch Mandy Roberts. How dare she come round and turn Melissa against him and make Melissa say things she didn't mean? They'd all been so happy before.

He remembered where Mandy lived. In the beginning of their meaningless affair, he'd driven her back there sometimes after work. He drove until the streets became familiar – shabby little red-brick terraces stared down at him on both sides. He got out of the car, and walked maybe three steps up a narrow strip of concrete path, and pressed down hard on the doorbell for maybe four seconds, fury hammering at his temples. He'd tell her what was what.

A window flew open above him and Mandy's hard, set face poked out. 'Fuck off,' she called. 'Go on. Just fuck off.'

'Answer the fucking *door*!' he shouted, and pressed the bell again. He could hear it ring inside the house. 'I'm warning you, Mandy –'

He heard female voices from behind Mandy's face and torso. 'What's up, Mand?' asked one, and another asked, 'Who's that screaming out there?'

Mandy turned to them. 'It's nothing,' she said. 'This cunt just keeps hassling me.' She turned back. 'Bothering my fucking housemates,' she yelled, 'you've got a right nerve. Just *fuck off!*'

'Not till you tell me what you were playing at,' he yelled back. 'Coming to my house. Telling my wife. What the hell did you think you were doing?'

'What do you think I was doing, you stupid sack of shit? It's called *revenge*. Kiss my arse.'

Christ, he thought, it was like some grotesque parody of *Romeo and Juliet*.

She bellowed down from the window with hatred in her eyes, 'Now fuck off, or I'm calling the police.'

'*Mandy*,' he yelled, and pressed the doorbell for a third time.

'That's *it*,' she said at the open window, and turned away. 'You just . . .' but he didn't catch the rest. He heard voluble female murmurs from inside the house. Something inexorable and heroic took hold of him. He deserved a proper apology, he thought. Even if she called the police, he wouldn't leave without one. And he was standing and pressing the doorbell with new iron in his soul when a rush of freezing water hit him out of nowhere, and he looked up, shocked, blinking, dripping.

She was standing at the window with an upturned plastic bucket in her hands. 'Do you want the police next?' she yelled. 'I can get you the police next.' Jack looked around him, and saw that the dramatic spotlight had snapped into a well-lit stage. His audience consisted of an elderly lady with a small dog on a lead, two snickering teenage girls tricked out for a big night, a middle-aged man who looked shocked. Embarrassment turned out to be stronger than fury, after all. He gave up. He turned and walked over to the parked Merc.

'That's right,' Mandy called after him. 'Fuck off. And don't come back.'

Behind the wheel, he drove, shivering, his clothes wrapped around him like a cold wet towel, his hair dripping into his eyes. He turned the Merc's powerful headlights up full blast. New uncertainties tormented him. More than anything he wanted to go home, but he knew he couldn't. After his grand exit it would look pathetic if he slunk back in as he was, sheepish, wet, humiliated. He'd have to find a hotel or something for the night, he thought. He'd sort out something more sensible in the morning. For the first time in his life, he yearned for a close friend to turn to. Feeling like a king in exile, Jack drove without purpose. He saw the empty black sky, the tiny wheeling colourful lights from somewhere far away. He wondered what the kids were doing tonight. He wondered if they were out there.

Bev's taxi dropped her off opposite the promenade, and she hurried on to the Menzies in the pedestrianised shopping precinct. Jane was waiting outside, as Bev had known she would be.

'Sorry I'm late,' she said, as she and Jane fell into step together. 'I got held up.'

'It's all right,' said Jane. 'I don't mind.'

'Good,' said Bev. 'Let's get a move on, shall we? I want to go on the rides.'

Together, they walked through dimly lit streets that stirred with families and teenagers and couples on their way to the funfair. Bev fought to recapture a cheerful camaraderie that seemed very far away tonight. 'You like big rides?'

'Yeah,' said Jane shyly. 'I suppose. Do you?'

'Yeah.' To her own ears, her voice sounded too bright and oddly false. She was pretending to be happy, she thought, and remembered the furious voices in the kitchen. I'm just out with a friend, she told herself fiercely. I'm all right, everything's all right. 'We can go on the Rattlesnake,' she said, 'and the Wall of Death. We'll have a really good time.'

Out of the shopping precinct, they turned back on to the promenade and headed through the cold electric night towards the crowds. Soon they were at the funfair, walking through the squashed raffle tickets that lay like confetti in the puddles underfoot, through the wheeling lights and the shrieking music and the delicious greasy smells that drifted from the hot-dog stand. 'You should have been here last year,' said Bev. 'It was great last year.' The edgy malaise was still muttering in her mind when she saw her brother and his friends out of the corner of her eye, approaching them.

In maybe an eighth of a second, Jane's sudden apprehension snapped into an equally sudden relief: a sixth sense told her that Melanie and the others wouldn't giggle about her nan tonight. She was right. As the two groups came closer together, she saw they were smiling like friends – reassuring, approachable, matey.

'All right, Bev?' asked Toby Green, and Melanie and her friends nodded at Bev like cocky, awed wannabes backstage after a stadium concert, before turning their attention to Jane – the manager, perhaps, the bass guitarist. 'All right, Jane?' asked Melanie. 'Have a good evening, yeah, guys?' Then, the big, noisy teenage group was swaggering away into the crowded distance.

So this was how it felt to be inside. Jane had thought she knew how it felt, but nothing she'd ever experienced had come close to this – pretending to do a radio show with Anita in her shabby little room, walking to the shop on a Sunday afternoon and buying blue drinks in plastic cartons. To think she'd thought of that as being *inside.* Now she saw and tasted the real thing, all around her: the frantic shrieking camaraderie and the music from the rides, the joy of the suburbs and the golden advert girl walking beside her. This was happiness. This was heaven.

'Let's have a go on the raffle,' Bev said, and they had a go on the raffle.

The raffle was one of many little booths dotted round the funfair. A cornucopia of leering baby dolls and garish soft toys stared down from makeshift shelves. You paid a pound and dipped your hand in the barrel the man held out for you, and if the number on it ended in a 6 you won a prize. Jane got 57, Bev got 266. 'Well done, love,' the man said to Bev, smiling at her as people always did, 'you've won a prize,' and he extended a three-foot-tall blue-and-white teddy bear that stared blindly at the night through button eyes.

'Do you want it?' Bev asked Jane, as they were walking away from the booth.

'Oh, no,' said Jane, slightly aghast. 'Really. You keep it.'

'No, *really*,' said Bev. 'It's all right. You can have it.'

'But it's your *prize*.'

'Well, it's *your* prize, now,' said Bev, laughing as she pushed the teddy into Jane's unresisting hands. 'Think of it as an early Christmas present, if it makes you feel better.'

A Christmas present. Never in Jane's life had she got one that meant half as much to her as this, that she knew she'd keep for ever. She hugged it in her arms, her wide, dazed eyes staring over the top of its head. 'It's lovely. Thanks ever so much.'

'It's nothing. Shall we get a hot-dog? I'm starving.'

They bought hot-dogs smothered in ketchup and fried onions from the stall, and stood around eating them. Jane watched the people come and go with something like love. How nice they all seemed tonight. 'What time you got to be home?' Bev asked abruptly.

'Oh, you know. Any time, really,' said Jane, who'd promised Mary she'd be in by half nine at the latest. 'Whenever you want to go.'

'Great,' said Bev. 'I don't have to be in till late, either. We can stay and watch the fireworks.' They threw away their greasy napkins, and went on the Waltzer, and the Rattlesnake, and deafening chart music pounded through the swooping, shrieking bliss of the Wall of Death.

At half nine, the fireworks started off the pier, and Jane and Bev trooped down to watch them with everyone else. Colours exploded and faded then exploded again; *oohs* and *aahs* rose and fell in time to the colours. Crowds pressed in easily, with unselfconscious good-fellowship. Out of the corner of her eye, Jane looked at Bev gazing up at the fireworks; reflected light swam red and orange and green over an upturned face that was curiously impassive now nobody was talking. In its serenity, Jane thought it looked more than ever like the face of a goddess – a face you could pray to, and know someone was listening.

When the last of the fireworks had died away, Bev showed no sign of moving on with the crowds, and Jane felt reluctant to disturb her reverie. The two of them stood there for some time, people draining away around them, staring into a black empty sky – black swirling water glinted like oil far below. 'Well,' said Bev finally, 'that's that, then. Suppose we'd better be getting off home.'

21

There were a lot of taxis out by the seafront. As they neared them, Bev turned to Jane. 'Do you want to share a cab home?' she asked. 'I don't mind sharing.'

Jane didn't want Bev to know that she didn't have the money for a taxi, that the ten pounds Mary had given her had almost all been spent keeping up with Bev and doing what Bev did. 'Oh, no,' she said. 'Really. I'll get another one.'

'Well,' said Bev, 'if you're sure . . .' She smiled at the driver at the front of the line, and opened the taxi's back door. 'I'll see you in school on Monday, then,' she said. ''Bye.' She shut the door behind her, and Jane saw her mouth moving in unheard directions to the driver, and powerful rear lights shot away into the night.

When the taxi had gone, Jane turned back, and began the long walk home. After the noise of the funfair and the fireworks, there was something unearthly about the silent town centre, the dead black nothing behind the window displays and her footsteps echoing under the streetlights. Out by the harbour, she passed a fist-fight – a dozen or so teenagers she didn't recognise standing in hushed reverence around a scene of violence. She heard quiet ragged sobbing – 'that's it, you cunt,' a young voice snarled. 'I'm gonna –' Jane walked on, faster, trying not to see the bone-white boats bobbing on the harbour's dark glinting water, or the distant towering buildings, or the spire of the little church the colour of soot. She didn't want to acknowledge the shadows. She was happy with the lights and music in her head.

Checking her watch under a streetlight, she saw it was almost half ten. She'd be in trouble when she got back, she thought, and realised that she didn't care. In the most literal sense, the suburbs had become her friend and ally: they walked beside her in the darkness of the night and blocked out fear. It didn't even matter that Melanie and the others had smiled at her without malice, not now. Suddenly nothing mattered but the blue-and-white teddy-bear in her arms, the phone ringing in the hallway downstairs, the way the reflected lights moved across the golden advert girl's upturned face. There was nothing beyond that in the world. At all. Ever.

She passed the shabby little furniture shop with the letter still missing from its sign, and the second-hand-clothes shop. The still-open newsagent looked like a lighthouse in the darkness – the thin glow behind curtained windows and the locked doors and the plaster gnomes smiling out into the starless night. Two teenagers snogging in a glass bus shelter broke off and watched her pass with offended eyes. Jane barely noticed them. Orange sodium lights stared down at her rapture all the way home. When the neat little terrace came into view, it was five to eleven.

22

Sitting in the back of the taxi, Bev saw home approaching too fast. No lights were on in the windows, and the bright coach-lights by the gates and door looked cold and impersonal. 'Right, then, love,' said the cabbie, 'that'll be four pounds twenty.' Bev paid. 'Thanks,' she said. ''Bye, then.' She got out and walked across the gravel driveway to the front door, got her key out of her bag and let herself in.

Inside, the silence was absolute, and she moved through the moonlit hallway as through an empty cathedral – her slow deliberate footsteps sounded much too loud. She remembered her mother's terse responses in the kitchen, earlier.

'Hello?' she said quietly. 'Hello?' There was no sound. She walked up the stairs with her heart in her mouth. She touched the door-handle of her parents' bedroom as though scared of an electric shock, then steeled herself and pushed it open.

Her mother lay in the familiar double bed, alone, making the small restless movements of uneasy sleep. Her parents *always* shared a bed.

It was what she'd been afraid of.

Bev closed the door as quietly as she'd opened it. Blood pounded in her ears. She went into her room, switched on the light and went through the motions of preparing herself for bed. Lying awake between the sheets, she wondered where her father was and what had happened in her absence. More than anything, she wanted to be back with Jane, out in the wheeling lights and the music, reliving the Perfect Greens like something that had happened a long time ago.

She didn't think that sleep would come to her at all that night. But it did. Eventually.

November

1

When the bell went for lunch, Jane swung her bag over her shoulder, left the classroom and went into the girls' toilets by the hallway. She never used the ones by the changing rooms any more. There was nothing to hide from now.

Inside, Tiffany and Josie were adjusting their hair and spraying on perfume in front of the mirrors. They glanced over as Jane came in, and smiled. 'All right, Jane?' asked Tiffany.

Extraordinary to think that these girls had once mattered to her. She held them up against Beverley Green, and felt them disintegrate. 'Yeah,' she said, offhanded. 'You?'

'Yeah,' said Josie. 'We saw you with Beverley, right after assembly.' Jane leaned back against the tiles; their alert faces watched her in the mirror. 'You're really good mates now, aren't you?'

How deeply she'd been blessed, Jane thought. These girls adored the golden advert girl as she did, but she and not they had been chosen. She felt shabby and unworthy and ecstatic. 'Yeah,' she said. 'I suppose.'

Neither Tiffany nor Josie quite knew what to make of the situation. You could see it in their eyes. 'She's so cool,' said Tiffany eventually. 'You been round her house yet?'

'No. Not yet.'

'You wait. It's wicked,' said Tiffany. 'I'm going out with Tobes, you know. Went round there the other day. Like something out of a movie or something. They've only got a swimming-pool.'

'Wow,' said Jane, but of course, she'd known that much for months – the rolling green lawns, the wrought-iron gates that tantalised the eye with what they concealed. She'd loved Beverley Green before she'd ever met her. 'It sounds amazing.'

'You're just after Tobes for his money,' said Josie, turning on Tiffany with the airy nonchalance that had once chilled Jane's soul. 'I'm going to tell him you're just going out with him because he's *rich.*' Their laughter rang out. Tiffany tossed her hair back in the mirror and Josie picked up her bag. 'Well, see you later, Jane,' said Josie, and the two of them went chatting out of the door, leaving a strong smell of hairspray and cheap perfume, and watchful new respect.

When they'd gone, Jane went to the toilet, came out and washed her hands. Recently, the dark scabbed lines beneath the hidden bandage had repelled her. She never did the ritual any more. She was unworthy of the golden advert girl as it was. Adoration and creeping self-doubt had become her only emotions. The time she spent without Beverley Green had become time spent in limbo, and she lived for nothing but their meetings.

Jane checked her reflection in the mirror one last time. She didn't really see herself at all. She saw the girl Beverley Green phoned in the evenings, who went into town with Beverley Green at weekends, who was meeting Beverley Green outside the assembly hall in ten minutes' time for lunch. Dark worship looked back from her eyes. She felt complete.

2

'Sorry I'm late,' said Bev. 'I ran into someone.'

'It doesn't matter,' said Jane. 'I don't mind.'

'Great. Shall we get going to the shop?'

Out of the main double doors, a dry frozen chill stung the nose and cheeks, and the sky was pale and empty – a faded sign in the newsagent's window announced that fireworks could be bought inside.

'What've you got to get?' asked Jane.

'Just a magazine,' said Bev. 'We can go to the park, after. I don't feel like sitting in the canteen all lunch-time. It's so stuffy.'

The little newsagent was quite crowded. Jane saw the colourless fair-haired girl from her English class lurking round the magazine racks with a couple of mousy others, talking in a listless, perfunctory way – the girl nodded at Jane, and Jane nodded back with a kind of pity. They were denied the joy of the golden advert world, she realised, the world that had let her inside, that had rescued her.

'Let's get off to the park,' said Bev, when she came back from the till, and the fair-haired girl and her friends stood and watched them leave.

In the little park a few minutes' walk away, they went to the swings and ate their sandwiches and crisps, swinging idly, in companionable munching silence. The rhythmic creak of chains filled the world. 'I saw Tiffany Morris and Josie Wheeler in the toilets earlier,' Jane said. 'They think you're really cool.'

'Oh, Toby's friends. Well, that's nice, I suppose.'

It was what Bev often said when she was neither interested nor actively bored. Jane felt she should go further. 'They said you've got a swimming-pool. Have you really?'

'Yeah. You can come over and see it some time, if you like,' said Bev, and smiled. 'It's not that amazing, you know. It doesn't really matter.'

'I think it's amazing.' Jane spoke without thinking, her voice quiet and reflective on the near-silence. 'I walked through Preston a couple of times, you know. When it was sunny and that. It looked so beautiful.'

'I suppose everywhere's nice in the summer,' said Bev idly, and they carried on eating and swinging for a while without speaking.

'It's my birthday, the Monday after next,' said Jane eventually, shyly. 'I'm going to be fourteen.'

'That's nice. You having a party?'

'My nan wants me to have some mates round for tea. I don't know, really. You want to come over?'

'Who else are you asking?'

'Well, nobody, really. Unless you want me to.'

'God, no. Don't worry about it. Sure. I'd love to come over.'

A dizzy sense of gratitude overcame Jane. She spoke quickly, as if to reassure. 'It'll be ever so nice, Bev. It'll be *wicked*. There'll be music and everything. And loads of food.'

'Cool,' said Bev. 'You can come round to my house some time, too. We can watch a video or something.'

'That'd be great,' said Jane. Something quivered in her voice when she spoke again. 'It's wicked going round with you. Everything looks so different.'

'Well, I suppose that's nice,' said Bev, but it seemed to Jane almost as if Bev was looking at something else, beyond her – as if Bev looked and talked without really seeing her at all. 'I suppose it is pretty cool, having a swimming-pool,' Bev said. 'I never really thought of it before.'

3

When the alarm woke Jack at ten to seven, he couldn't place where he was. Then he could. The four-room flat close to the town centre: the neat impersonal little stop-gap he'd been living in for the past fortnight. Underlyme's more elegant properties were largely for families only, and the flat had all the idiosyncratic charm of a Holiday Inn room. He got out of bed, and stepped into the dark raw morning, showered and shaved, and tried not to think about anything.

He left for work even earlier than usual, and the roads were practically deserted. Pale streetlights stared down on empty black tarmac. Behind the wheel of the Merc, he drove fast. He parked and went into the building where he walked through empty corridors and straight to the gents'. His own reflection stared out at him from the mirrors, tired and yellowish in the artificial light. He went into one of the toilet cubicles, and locked the world out.

He was just pulling his pants up when he heard two loud

laddish voices come in and settle by the urinals. Recognising them as belonging to Tim and Evan, he was about to call out with a semblance of bonhomie, when something Evan said stopped him.

'And have you heard about Mandy?' asked Evan.

'Our Mandy?' asked Tim. 'The one Jack fired?'

'That's right. I ran into one of her housemates, last night. You'll never believe it. It's fucking *hilarious*.'

'What is?'

'It's a real story.' Jack heard Evan snicker. 'Jack was only shagging her all the time she worked here. Then she started giving him all this commitment shit, so he bottled it and fired her. Well, she was not a happy bunny. So get this. She storms right over to his house and tells his wife the whole story.'

'Fucking hell,' said Tim. 'Is that why his wife's chucked him out?'

'No shit, Sherlock,' said Evan impatiently. '*Anyway*. What he does then, right, he drives right down Mandy's to have a go. And she won't let him in. So they're screaming at each other through the window, right, and she tells him to fuck off, and the wanker's just standing there on the doorstep like he thinks he's John fucking Wayne or something. And Mandy, right, she goes and fills this bucket up with water, and –'

'*No.*' Tim burst out laughing.

'Yeah. All over the twat. Her housemates were behind her, laughing their arses off. So he just stands there dripping water all over the shop, right, then he turns round and legs it back to his car like Linford Christie. It's fucking *hilarious*. Just wish I'd been there.'

'Me and all,' said Tim. 'Serves him right, pompous little twat. How he treated Mandy, that just sucks.'

'His wife's going to take him to the fucking *cleaners*. I heard him on the phone to his lawyer, the other day,' and then the voices moved away, and the door creaked open and shut, and they were gone.

Jack stood in the cubicle for several minutes, his heart pounding. When he was sure Tim and Evan wouldn't still be lingering in the corridor, he slipped out fast. Back in his office, Melissa and the kids stared out of the silver frame. On a sudden impulse, he picked up the phone and dialled the familiar home number. The ringing tone echoed endlessly on the silence until he gave up.

4

'You're early,' her father said. 'You don't normally come till later.'

'I know,' she said. 'I just had to tell you. I'm not going to be with Jack for much longer. We're getting a divorce.'

Melissa sat across from her father in the retirement home's little common room. Outside the window, the day was chilly and dispiriting. 'What do you mean?' he asked. 'What did you do to upset him?'

It was what she'd expected, Melissa told herself. She'd known in advance what she'd find. 'I'm leaving him,' she said, with weary patience. 'You don't understand. *I'm* leaving *him.*'

He might as well not have heard her. 'He might come back. You've got to try and make him come back.'

'*No,*' said Melissa, too sharply. 'I don't want him to. *Really.* I feel better. I feel *good.*'

'You're being selfish,' he said. 'What about *me?* What'll happen to *me?* He's a good man, he's been good to you, Melissa. What more do you expect?'

'Anything,' she said. She remembered the hard-working holidays, the hatred and the apprehension that had become her constant companions over the years. How strange it felt to wake up without them. 'Dad, you don't have to worry. I've talked to our solicitor. Money's not going to be a problem.'

'It's easy for you to just say it like that,' he said, accusingly, fearfully. 'What about *me?*'

'Look, if you won't believe me, what am I supposed to say?' Melissa broke off for a few seconds, taking a long, deep breath.

'Our solicitor knows what he's talking about. I'll almost certainly keep the house. And the kids. That's a foregone conclusion.'

'It'll ruin *them*. Ruin their lives.' There was something both contemptible and sad in the way he tried to hide behind a deeper moral tragedy; his naked attempts at manipulation moved her with sympathy and revulsion. 'Ruin their *lives*, Melissa. Don't you even care about your children?'

'You don't know what they think about anything. I know the kids. You should see them now. Toby's so much more talkative. And Bev seems happier.' Melissa looked out of the window, and saw near-naked branches flailing in the wind. 'I might start looking for work soon,' she said. 'Not for money. Just . . . I don't know. The kids aren't really kids any more. Just something to do.'

'You can't do anything.' He stared straight ahead at the telly. 'You didn't even pass your O levels.'

'I can learn,' she said quietly. She gathered up the last remnants of triumphant joy with her car-keys and handbag. 'Anyway, I'd better go, Dad. Don't worry. Nothing's going to change. You'll be all right.'

Melissa walked out of the common room and down the corridor. The nurse she often spoke to was walking the other way with a stack of folded sheets in her arms. 'Hello, Mrs Green,' she said, stopping. 'How's your dad this morning?'

'Not good. You know how it is. I think I've upset him.'

'Oh dear,' said the nurse. 'Why?'

'Something's happened at home,' said Melissa. 'I don't know why I told him about it. I don't know why I thought he'd be interested.'

The nurse looked cautious and sympathetic. 'Good news?'

Melissa glanced through the open main door and felt an overwhelming sense of freedom and relief touch her. It didn't look quite as bright or straightforward as it did in the movies, but she supposed real emotions never did. 'You could say that,' she said, and realised with a shock that she was smiling.

5

The atmosphere was strange in the kitchen that night, Bev thought. Long silences fell, but without the tension, and she couldn't tell if it was contentment or shell-shock that had taken the edge off. When the phone rang in the hallway, Melissa went to get it.

Bev spoke. 'It seems weird without Dad here.'

Toby looked at her with vague surprise. 'Yeah,' he said. 'I think so.'

There was a short silence. Melissa's voice drifted in through the door. 'Well, okay,' she was saying, 'that should be fine.'

Unexpectedly, Toby said, 'You miss him?'

'I don't know. What about you?'

'You've got to be taking the piss. I'm just hoping Mum won't take him back.' The raw certainty in his voice shocked Bev despite herself, and they sat, fidgeting, for a few seconds.

'You told your mates at school yet?' Bev asked.

'No.' Toby sounded unwilling. 'I know it's a bit sad, but . . . you know, out in Florida and stuff, we always had to look happy. When people were watching.'

'I know. I haven't told anyone either. Not at school.'

Bev felt as if they'd moved a step closer together, like enemy troops she'd read about stopping their guns on Christmas Day. They weighed each other up in their eyes.

'I'm going out with Tiffany Morris, you know,' said Toby. 'Maybe I'll tell her about Dad and stuff soon.' He held out his news like a tentative cigarette, and she took it awkwardly. Neither spoke another word before Melissa came back into the room.

'That was your father,' she said, sitting down at the table. 'We're going out for dinner on Saturday evening.' Bev saw Toby's face freeze. 'It's just to talk about the divorce,' said Melissa hastily, and Bev saw Toby's face return to normal just before their mother spoke again. 'It must be hard for you both,' she said. 'I'm sorry.'

'It's all right, Mum,' said Bev. 'Really. We're all right.'

'You must miss him being around all the time,' said Melissa. 'He's your father, after all.'

Toby's shoulders rose and fell. 'Yeah. I suppose.'

Melissa looked at him. 'You don't sound very convinced.'

'I dunno,' said Toby. 'I don't reckon I miss him at all.'

'You shouldn't say that, Toby. Not about your father.' But Bev thought her mother spoke for form's sake, and that Melissa's eyes betrayed her agreement. 'He wants you both to come on Saturday evening,' said Melissa. 'He says he misses you.'

'We only saw him last Sunday,' said Toby, 'when he took me and Bev for lunch at the Harvester. He just talked about GCSEs the whole time. It sucked.' When he spoke again, it was with unmistakable relief. 'Anyway, I can't, I'm going to Pete's party on Saturday night. You remember. I asked if I could go and you said yeah.'

'Well,' said Melissa, 'you know I wouldn't force you, Toby. What about you, Bev?'

'I can't,' Bev said. 'I'm going out Saturday night, too. I'm meeting a friend.'

'Oh, well,' said Melissa, 'I suppose it wouldn't be right for teenagers, anyway.' They finished eating, and Bev helped her mother clear away the plates. Then she went up to her room, did a bit of homework and got ready for bed.

6

She was sleeping better now. Her state of mind had lightened in almost imperceptible stages. For a month or so the solid blackness of Bradley and Orlando had been in retreat, now it was at the edge of her thoughts. She didn't feel dirty or secret any more. And the atmosphere at home was better than she'd ever known it.

Still, she was not what she had been. She knew that for a fact. She'd never see the boys at school in quite the same comfortable, contemptuous light, for one thing – in that area, she suspected she'd been scarred for life. And she couldn't come to terms with the way life in Preston had changed. A part of her needed to believe in the Perfect Greens as it had never believed before: in her head a family photograph framed in silver, Jack smiling paternally beside Melissa, she and Toby the happiest kids in the world. Even though the change was profoundly positive, some superficial part of her couldn't deal with it – she couldn't help wishing that her family looked as it always had to outsiders, ultimately happy, ultimately blessed.

In these areas, Bev still needed a crutch, and that crutch was provided by her ongoing friendship with Jane Sullivan. Jane never giggled about horny boys, as Emma had. Jane didn't know about her parents' divorce. Jane believed in the Perfect Greens as deeply as anyone had ever believed in anything.

She didn't need Jane as she had a month ago, but still, she needed her.

When she came down from her room on Saturday, it was a quarter to eleven and Toby wasn't in. Melissa was tidying the kitchen. She looked round as Bev entered. 'Hello, darling,' she said. 'Have a nice lie-in?'

'Yeah. Slept like a log.' Bev sat down at the table. 'What time are you going to meet Dad this evening?'

'About half five. We're not going to be out too late.' Melissa looked at Bev closely. 'Why? Changed your mind about coming with us?'

'No. I just thought I could invite my mate round,' said Bev. 'She said she'd like to see the pool.'

'I thought you were going out tonight. Or did you just say that because you didn't want to come?'

'It's not that. I just wanted to have my mate round.'

'Well, I'm sure it's your decision,' said Melissa. 'You know, you look like a different person recently, Bev. So much happier. I was getting quite worried about you, after Orlando.'

Bev rose from her seat. 'Thanks,' she said. 'Listen, Mum, I'd better get going. I'm meeting my mate in town. She should have gone by the time you get back.'

'Well, there's no need for *secrecy*.' Melissa laughed. 'You sound as if you're ashamed of her.'

Bev smiled, but it didn't come quite as easily as it should have. As she closed the front door behind her and set off down the drive, her mother's words haunted her, and she was aware of her ambivalent feelings towards her new friend. It wasn't true, she told herself, she wasn't ashamed of Jane. They were mates, pure and simple, and she was going to invite Jane back to her house that afternoon.

7

It was what Jane had been waiting for. What she'd dreamed of.

'I thought you wanted to go and see the bonfires on the beach,' she said.

'I hate bonfires,' said Bev. 'Don't you want to see my house?'

'Of course I do. You know I do.'

'Well, then, let's get the bus into Preston.'

It was almost half five, and the town centre was busy and bustling on Bonfire night. They'd passed a pleasant, undemanding afternoon together, trailing round the shops and talking about nothing in particular. Now, in the gathering darkness and the early Christmas lights, Bev's request had come out of nowhere. Jane walked beside her, and couldn't quite believe she was being invited back to her house.

'Your mum and dad going to be in?' she asked at the bus-stop.

'No,' said Bev. 'It's their anniversary. They've gone out to celebrate.'

On the bus, Jane felt both eager and frightened. She wiped steam off the window with the sleeve of her anorak, and stared out into the neon-lit shadows. It got dark so early, these days. The black sky reflected Bev's profile beside her as clearly as a mirror, a face in the window imprinted on landmarks Jane had seen before. 'Well,' said Bev, at last, 'here we are. This is the stop.'

As they got off, Bev explained that Jane could get her bus back from right across the road when she headed on home. Jane barely heard her. She looked, and saw that the suburbs were even more beautiful than they'd been in the summer, that this new darkness suited them more than anything. Overhead, formless clouds moved like smoke and distant doorways glowed with a happiness that had once seemed unreachable. She spoke haltingly. 'Can you see all this through your bedroom window?'

'All what?'

The cold majesty, the lights against the darkness, the rosily lit windows that promised a life beyond life. It amazed Jane that Bev might not be able to see it. 'I don't know,' she said, as they passed the house she'd once thought might be Bev's and she realised it wasn't. 'That funny white house. The one with the pillars.'

'Not really. Just our front garden,' said Bev, and laughed. 'I wouldn't want to look at someone else's house all night, would I?' And then they turned down a driveway, and were there.

8

The joy of recognition almost stopped Jane's heart. It was more perfect than even she'd dreamed of, the three-storey mock-Tudor house with the long, sloping drive and the detached garage. To think it had been Beverley Green's swimming-pool that she'd seen glittering round the back, as she'd walked and dreamed her way through summer. They'd been destined to meet, she thought, even then. 'It's so beautiful,' she said quietly.

'Thanks,' said Bev, as she unlocked the front door. 'Come on, let's get inside. I'm freezing.'

The burglar alarm shrilled *meep-meep-meep* and Bev opened a cupboard door to turn it off. 'Come on,' she muttered crossly, 'come on, you little sod.'

Jane stood in the hallway, and stared. Even the shadowed half-light couldn't conceal a beauty this intense – the oak-panelled walls, the smells of polish and perfume and heaven. The reality of the suburbs overwhelmed her. 'God,' she said quietly, almost inaudibly. 'Oh, God.'

'That fucking thing. It does my head in,' said Bev, as the interminable *meeping* finally ended and she closed the cupboard door. 'Come on into the kitchen. You can see the pool from there.'

For Jane, Bev's brief guided tour passed in a lightning-fast succession of images – glinting dark water behind a floodlit patio, a dream kitchen that gleamed with polished marble, an oak-panelled, leatherbound lounge that reminded her of things she'd never known. She longed to linger, but Bev hurried her on. 'Let's go on up to my room,' said Bev. 'We can watch TV up there.' Jane followed her up the wide, curving staircase, hastening through paradise before Bev opened a door, switched a light on.

There were no surprises. By now, Jane's eyes had grown inured to wonder. If anything, she felt a remote, complacent pride that she'd been right, that her imaginary Bev had moved and chattered in the right stage-set, after all. She'd known that the golden advert girl's room would be a pastel-coloured light-trap, all padded pink and pine – she'd seen the gold-framed ballet prints in her dreams, the little pink, plastic phone by the bed, the draped, frilled canopy over the pillow end. There was nothing here that wasn't exactly as she'd imagined. 'It's so cool,' she said quietly. 'I knew it would be. I knew it.'

'Thanks. We might as well stay up here. I'll just go and get us some Cokes and munchies from the kitchen. Won't be a sec.'

When Bev left the room, Jane went over to the window. She drew the pink-striped curtain aside, and raised the fluffy net meringue behind it. Night and the suburbs looked back at her – the tall tree in the weedless front garden, the luminous windows of other houses, far away. It was amazing how different it all looked when you were inside. How small. How reassuring.

Jane lowered the curtain and stepped back. She glanced briefly into drawers and cupboards, listening for footsteps on the stairs. Nothing she saw told her anything she didn't know already: there was nothing here that wasn't perfect, nothing that you could ever be anything but proud to own. The neat corners of pale fabric and the subtle smell of pot-pourri merely affirmed a belief she'd have staked her life on. She sat down on the padded window-seat and waited for Bev to return. She felt blessed.

9

She was blessed. She felt it the following Monday when she met Bev before school and at lunch-time, and the two of them walked out of the gates and down to the shop together, talking about Jane's imminent birthday party. She'd explored deep inside the golden advert world, and found that it cared after all, that it was every bit as beautiful seen up close. A new security warmed her deep inside. However unworthy she might be, Beverley Green had publicly chosen her as a friend, and there was nothing insecure or impermanent about their togetherness now.

After lunch-time was over and she'd said goodbye to Bev, Jane walked to her last lesson of the day. She sat down and watched the people around her with a kind of pity. They hadn't been to Beverley Green's house that weekend, or looked out of Beverley Green's window, or invited Beverley Green round for their birthdays and heard her say she'd come. Jane had never felt this infinitely privileged before – as if she had something other people didn't, that they'd envy her beyond words if they could see.

When the bell rang for the end of lessons, the teacher held them behind for a few minutes to explain a point of grammar they'd mostly all got wrong in a recent test. Jane could feel the rest of the class shifting and muttering impatiently all around her, but couldn't find it in herself to be irritated by the small delay. Her rapture reached out to embrace the whole world – the teacher's earrings, the buzzing striplight, the greasy-haired boy who sat in front of her – and, when the class was finally allowed to go, she left the classroom smiling.

Outside, the end-of-school rush was almost over, and the corridors were practically empty as Jane walked. Noticing that her shoelace had come undone, she ducked into an alcove, and crouched to refasten it. She was still there when she heard the quiet confidential voices approaching down the corridor, and recognised them at once as Melanie's and Tiffany's.

'I can't believe Tobes didn't tell the rest of us,' said Melanie. 'Like, we're all his mates. He never said a word to me about his mum and dad getting divorced.'

'Well, I'm going out with him,' said Tiffany, 'and he only told me the other evening.'

Jane could hear the two of them stopping by the noticeboards, delaying the inevitable steps out into the cold. 'You sure it's true?' asked Melanie.

'Course I'm sure,' said Tiffany. 'Toby's not exactly going to lie about something like that. His mum kicked his dad out last month. He says he reckons his dad was having an affair.'

'That's so weird,' said Melanie. 'Like, you know, Toby and Beverley and all. I always thought their mum and dad were like *that*.'

'Me, too,' said Tiffany. 'Look, you mustn't tell anyone else, mind, Mel. I promised Toby I wouldn't say a word.'

'Don't worry,' said Melanie. 'Come on, let's get out of here.' The main double doors creaked their exit, and Jane became aware of the pins and needles in her feet. She left the building and walked to the bus-stop. The bus back to the Darlington Estate arrived almost instantly.

Back in the bright little kitchen, Mary was cooking the dinner. She glanced up, as Jane came in through the back door. 'How was your day at school, then, dear?'

'It was all right,' said Jane absently, taking off her coat. 'It was fine.'

'Only a couple of weeks till your birthday, now. We'll be getting you a lovely present, dear. You know I didn't mean what I said when you went and worried your grandad sick coming back so late that night. You can choose something out of the catalogue tonight. Anything you like.'

'Okay, Nan,' said Jane. 'Thanks.'

'Now, Jane, dear, you know there's no need to thank me. You know we're not like your mother, God rest her soul. You'll have a lovely birthday with us.' Mary chopped busily. 'Your grandad and me are looking forward to meeting that nice Beverley you always talk about. What about Anita? Can't she come, too?'

'I've asked her,' said Jane. 'She says she's busy. It doesn't matter, though. Beverley's coming.'

Up in her room, Jane changed out of her school uniform and hung it up in her wardrobe. Her thoughts swarmed around the conversation she'd overheard at school. She thought she knew why Bev hadn't told her about her parents splitting up. Bev hadn't thought she'd really understand, Jane thought – Bev hadn't thought she knew what it felt like.

It was wonderful, this new emotion. Not admiration or awe or even gratitude, but real empathy, the emotion one felt for a genuine soul-mate. For the first time since she'd met Bev, Jane saw her as something more than *the golden advert girl*. A link between her own world and that of the suburbs finally became clear. She could talk to Bev about the unspoken terrors surrounding Bev's parents' breakup, and Bev would be thrilled and amazed at how completely she understood. She should understand. She'd been there herself.

To think that a goddess had listened to the furious voices, too.

10

Beyond the window, the May afternoon was beautiful. Jane had just got home from the comprehensive. She sat on the bed with her heart hammering in her ears, and listened to the voices through the wall.

'You're a crazy bitch,' said Dave. 'I didn't touch her! Didn't even go near the slag!'

'Don't lie to me! I saw you kissing her. You don't give a fuck,' said Carol. 'You don't give a fuck about me! You're like every other prick – you're like that fucking bastard got me pregnant! You're like my fucking mum! You don't give a fuck if I live or die!'

The words should have been moving but, even through the wall, Jane recoiled from the violence in her mother's voice. She heard the sounds of a scuffle – a hand cracking hard on flesh, a thud, a grunt of pain. 'You bitch,' said Dave slowly, in an odd strangled voice. 'You *kicked* me. You crazy fucking bitch.'

'You don't even care.' Carol wept. 'Not if I live or die. You don't even care.'

'You need help. You know that? Mental help,' said Dave. He sounded like something had sobered him up in a second – he spoke with the caution of a banker in a back alley. 'I don't need this, Carol,' he said. 'You want to get help. You're all fucked up.'

'Fuck off, then.' Carol wept. 'You don't give a fuck about me, anyway. Go on. Fuck off back to Lorraine.'

'I'm going,' Dave said, 'I don't need this,' and then the front door slammed hard behind him, and he was gone.

A new silence filled the world. Slowly, Jane rose from the bed and walked into the lounge. Carol was slumped on the sofa with her head in her hands. Tears trickled through her fingers. As Jane came in, Carol screamed at her to fuck off, go on, fuck off, and Jane scuttled back to her room, and changed for bed, and hid from her fear under the blankets. In the long hours of the night, a kind of hope overcame her. If Dave had really gone, maybe it could all go back to how it had been in the old days, she thought – and she remembered the launderette and the loud, raucous laughter with something like love.

But although Dave didn't come back, things didn't return to how they'd used to be. Rather, they got worse. Weeks passed, and Carol took on a hollow-eyed look; she veered erratically between inexplicable silences and equally inexplicable fury, and her drinking became worse than ever. And she said such odd things. 'Nobody's ever wanted me,' she said once, in a conversational way. 'They never gave me a chance.' It was at that point that Jane's fears took on a new dimension, and, on the bus rides home from school, she felt a terror so intense that it made her want to throw up.

She never quite knew what she'd find at home, these days. Sometimes, Carol was out, and Jane didn't know where she was, and she sat up, and waited, and wondered what would happen if she never came back. Sometimes Carol was in. In a way that was even worse. At first, she never talked to Jane beyond the issuing of simple commands – pick that up, don't do that – but soon even that become a memory, and she mostly just sat. It was awful to see her there, in the shabby living room, not moving, not speaking. And her eyes were all wrong.

Although Jane wanted more than anything to confide in someone, she knew it was impossible. The little group of losers she tagged round after in school were as remote as her fellow residents in the apartment block. Carol's former friends were ghosts. Anita was a memory turned sour. Coming home from school in the evenings, Jane hated more than ever the gossiping strangers she passed, knowing they were going home to happiness, knowing she herself was not. There was nothing left to look forward to back at the third-floor flat.

Except the compass-point. There was always the compass-point.

Maybe a month after Dave had left Carol got into the way of going out for walks on her own, late at night. Jane didn't dare try to stop her. This wasn't the hard confident figure from her childhood, but fear and admiration were hard habits to break – Jane simply didn't know where else to look for certainties. She told herself it might turn out okay after all. When the compass-point was over, she lay and worried, and couldn't get to sleep till Carol returned. She didn't like to think of Carol stumbling drunk round the streets with a mind full of Dave – didn't like to think of the things that could happen out there in the dark.

One night, exhaustion overcame fear, and knocked her out like an anaesthetic before Carol got home. When she woke, the clock by her bed said it was three a.m., and music from the lounge was pounding through the wall. It was impossible to place the tune – something repetitive and hypnotic that ricocheted through her mind. She got out of bed and barefooted her way into the hall. The lounge door was shut. She looked at it for a long time. Then she turned like a sleepwalker and went back to bed. She lay there, motionless, her open eyes staring into darkness, the music hammering through the wall like jungle drums. In her mouth, she tasted terror.

11

The following day was a Tuesday. Jane went to meet Bev outside the assembly hall when the bell had rung for lunch.

'Let's go down the shop,' said Bev. 'I want to get a magazine.'

Outside, the afternoon was bitterly cold, and the wind howled and wailed. They didn't talk much on the way to the newsagent. Jane barely noticed. She was preoccupied with thoughts of comfort and honesty and togetherness – the final seal upon this wonderful friendship, something that would unite her and Bev for ever.

In the newsagent, Bev got a magazine off the shelf and went to pay. Jane stood by the racks. She looked at the beautiful cover-girls and the words that screamed from glossy front pages. 'I SLEPT WITH MY FATHER'; 'TORTURED BY A GIRL GANG'; SOLD INTO SLAVERY – ONE WOMAN'S STORY'. A deeper darkness shone out from the polite banalities, and Jane saw it for the first time, and found that it warmed her.

'Let's go,' said Bev, and they went.

They were walking back into the school grounds and Bev had just finished talking about some jacket her mum was getting her, when Jane stopped dead in her tracks. Bev walked on a few steps before noticing, and turned in vague surprise. 'What's the matter?'

To Jane, stopping felt like the last step on a high-diving board. They were standing on an isolated pathway, and chill denuded greenery faced them on both sides. Far away, a flock of birds took off. 'I heard about your mum and dad,' said Jane.

'What do you mean?' asked Bev sharply.

'About them splitting up. Honest, Bev, you should've told me. I know what it feels like. I understand.'

'What are you talking about?' demanded Bev. Then, on the heels of that question, 'How do you know? Who told you?'

'I just heard Melanie Dyer and that talking about it. It's all right, Bev. I understand.'

'That bloody Toby,' said Bev quietly. 'I should've known he'd end up telling everyone.'

'Listen, *Bev*,' said Jane. 'You can talk to me about it. *Really*. My dad walked out on my mum when I was little. Don't worry. I know how it feels.'

For long slow seconds, Bev just looked at her. The damp smell of earth filled Jane's senses. 'You know how it feels,' said Bev, and her voice held no tone whatsoever.

'I know it hurts,' said Jane. 'Really, you don't have to be embarrassed talking to me about it. I understand.'

'I don't *want* to talk about it.' Bev started walking again.

Suddenly, Jane was full of an awful foreboding – she couldn't understand why Bev had sounded so cold, almost hostile. She hurried to catch Bev up. Her face was half hidden by her hair, and Jane couldn't make sense of its expression. Desperately, Jane fumbled for her trump card. 'Look, Bev, I haven't told you this, but – after my dad walked out, my mum met this other man. Almost my step-dad, really. Then he walked out, too. What I said about a car-crash that time – it wasn't true. My mum killed herself over it. She cut her wrists in the bath with a razor-blade and –'

'I said I don't want to talk about it. Are you deaf?'

Something in the voice and the posture cut Jane dead. She didn't know exactly what, but it was unmissable – as if they'd been talking on the phone and Bev had slammed down the receiver. Bev hadn't ever sounded like that before, hadn't ever walked in silence looking straight ahead. For endlessly protracted minutes, Jane trotted along beside her, trying to think of something to say. But there didn't seem to be anything. The silence was unbroken till they arrived at school, and then Bev turned to look at Jane. She was smiling, but it didn't look like her usual smile, and her eyes were like a stranger's. 'I'd better go,' she said. 'I'll be late for registration. See you later.'

Jane was about to say something, but Bev was already walking away. Jane stood and watched her go. She couldn't understand what had just happened. That afternoon had been supposed to bring them closer together.

Bev turned a corner, and was gone.

12

To Bev, the afternoon's lessons passed impossibly slowly. She kept looking at her watch and being amazed it wasn't later. Although her rational mind knew it was pathetic, she felt like a small hurt animal. She wanted her room, her den, a place where she could cower safely and lick her wounds in peace.

Across the room from her, Emma sat with Adele. Their murmured conversation was almost inaudible behind the teacher's loud voice, but Bev heard them with paranoid clarity. They were talking about some film they'd seen. God, thought Bev, what if they start talking about me next? What if I hear them? And she felt an appalling helplessness. More than anything, she wanted to turn and run, but the strong arms of convention held her down in her seat.

Jane Sullivan, of course. It was Jane Sullivan who'd made her feel like this. To think that Jane Sullivan knew about her parents' divorce. The sudden wave of pure dislike she felt was shocking. She'd never felt this kind of dislike for Jane Sullivan before.

Because she'd never really seen Jane Sullivan at all. It was, she realised, as if Jane had carried some huge magic mirror that hid her completely and showed nothing but the reflection she'd wanted most to see. In as much as she'd thought of Jane, it had been as no more than a set of passport statistics: average height, brown hair, going on fourteen.

But now it was different. The words Jane had spoken had spoiled it all, changed it all.

It had been like something clammy crawling over Bev's bare skin – Jane's earnest eyes and sympathetic voice. To think that, in this one area, Jane could see past Bev of the Perfect Greens to the dark, unspoken truth. The thought destroyed everything that had gone before – the afternoons round town, the night at the funfair, the evening drinking Coke and eating munchies in Bev's room. In a split second the magic mirror was broken, and there was nothing left to see but the girl who'd been carrying it.

And the sight of her was somehow repulsive, hot on the heels of the false reflection: her skin unhealthily pale as something that lived under a rock and never saw the sunlight, her hair greasy and lank. Even her voice: a sort of insidious whine, that wheedled without hope of alluring. It chased after Bev deep in her head, whining terrible words that echoed and rebounded. *My mum killed herself over it. Cut her wrists in the bath with a razor-blade. Listen, Bev. I understand –*

Bev knew she should have felt sympathy, and that, if she'd read Jane's family story in a paper or a magazine, she'd have sympathised – but in the here and now, it felt far too immediate for sympathy, too entangled with her own instinctive mental recoil. In Jane's inarticulate words, she saw a strange, rancid world staring out at her, and it appalled her that Jane thought she might share it.

Bev looked across the classroom at Emma and Adele. Suddenly their intimacy looked like an unattainable daydream, something clean and solid that you'd never be ashamed of in the cold light of day. She thought of the lank hair, the complexion as smooth and sunless as a plump puffball. She sat at her desk and listened to the teacher talking. She wanted to run.

13

'Mind if I sit here?'

So far Emma's day had passed predictably enough. Thursday-morning breakfast had given way to Thursday-morning gossip with Charlie and Louise, which had given way to Thursday-morning registration. Now it was maths, the first lesson of the day. Adele, who she usually sat with, was off school with flu, and Emma had been using the first few teacherless minutes to check over her homework. The voice above her snapped her out of her reverie. She looked up. It was Bev.

There were too many things to say – Emma didn't know how to begin. She felt awkward as she glanced at the empty seat beside her. 'Sure,' she said. 'Go for it.'

Bev sat down, and got her pencil-tin and books out of her bag. For a few seconds, they sat in confused silence. Bev looked ill-at-ease, but was the first to speak. 'Look, Em,' she said. 'I'm really sorry.'

'What do you mean?'

'You know. The whole term, really. I'm not surprised you got pissed off with me. I was acting like a real bitch.' Bev's eyes moved up and fixed on Emma's, their expression both frank and vulnerable. 'I've been having some problems at home. You've probably heard.'

Emma felt wrong-footed, her sharp suspicions rapidly draining away. Bev looked just the same, but sounded like a different person. 'I heard about your mum and dad splitting up,' she said. 'I heard some people talking about it.'

'Yeah,' said Bev. 'That's what I mean.'

Looking at Bev, Emma tried to define the nature of the change in her, but it was difficult to pinpoint, everywhere and nowhere both at once. Her snappish nastiness was gone without a trace, but there was more to it than that: the cool, careless arrogance Emma had grown resigned to over the years of their friendship seemed to have disappeared with it. Suddenly Emma felt guilty about the way she'd been criticising Bev to Adele and the others. 'I'm really sorry,' she said. 'I wanted to talk to you when I heard about it. But I didn't think you'd want me to.'

Bev's shoulders rose and fell. 'It's been a bad term for me, so far,' she said simply. 'What about you? What've you been getting up to lately?'

'Oh, you know. Just the usual, really,' said Emma. 'Been working hard. Exams next year.'

'Tell me about it,' said Bev. 'I think about them a lot.'

The teacher's entrance didn't cut off their conversation, just turned it down. Remembering something she'd often wanted to ask, Emma asked it in a whisper: 'What's the story with you and that girl in Toby's year? I keep seeing you with her.'

'Oh, Jane Sullivan,' said Bev. 'She was a bit lonely. I felt sorry for her. She's a nice girl, really.'

'So she's not a good mate of yours?'

'God, no,' said Bev. 'I was just sort of looking out for her, that's all.'

Ten minutes ago, Emma wouldn't have dreamed of saying what she said next, but now she sensed it would be different: Bev wouldn't invade, she'd emigrate and learn the language, the customs.

'Why don't you come round with me and Adele and Charlie and Louise?' she asked. 'Me and Louise are going down the shop at lunch-time. Why don't you come with us?'

'You wouldn't mind?'

Emma felt the change in Bev inspire something close to tenderness within her, a gruff, self-conscious affection.

'Yeah, Bev, of course I mind,' she said, 'you're not to come with us, I forbid it.' It wasn't funny, but, in its wonderful descent from tension, it was hilarious, and they both burst out laughing till the teacher hushed them with a cross look and a sarcastic remark. After that, they stopped whispering together and paid attention. It was easy to pay attention now, thought Emma. Perhaps Bev felt the same way.

When the lesson was over and they were walking out, Jane Sullivan was standing outside the classroom, waiting for Bev.

14

'Where were you yesterday lunchtime?'

'I had things to do,' said Bev. 'I was busy.'

'I looked for you,' said Jane. 'I couldn't find you anywhere.'

Bev walked beside Jane, past the assembly hall and the lengthening queue for lunch, out into the frosty afternoon. Outside maths, she'd apologised to Emma – she'd said that she couldn't go to the shop with her and Louise after all, that she'd give Emma a call that evening. It terrified her to think of Jane trailing round after her and the others, to think of the others seeing Jane properly. Occasionally Bev got a breath of something from Jane that faintly revolted her. She thought that Jane smelt of old clothes and stale biscuits. 'Well, don't blame me,' she said. 'I never asked you to look for me.'

'I know,' said Jane. 'I'm sorry.'

The humility that had once reassured Bev now unsettled her. She saw Jane as some small repulsive animal that twined ingratiatingly around her ankles, loyal as a flea. 'Well, then,' she said, 'if I'm not around, just do something else. Find someone else to hang out with.'

'I don't know anyone else. I thought you didn't want me to.'

'So you were wrong,' said Bev. 'I do.'

For a few minutes, they walked in silence, past the long field by the playground that was crisp with frost. 'You are still coming to my party on Monday, aren't you?' asked Jane. 'You said you'd come.'

For a second, she couldn't think of anything to say – she longed for a valid excuse, but could find none. Beside her, Jane was still talking. Her words came faster and faster, now sounding distinctly panicky.

'You see, I told my nan you'd come, and her and Grandad are really looking forward to it, they've bought the cake and everything special. It'll be really nice. There'll be snacks and everything. You are still coming, aren't you, Bev? You said you'd come.'

Bev imagined a kindly old woman fussing over jelly in a mould, a gruff old man for whom Jane's so-called party would be one of the social highlights of the year. She felt the pathos and the fear as a single emotion, driving her on to something she couldn't see. 'Yeah. Sure,' she said. 'I'm still coming.'

'Oh, that's wicked! We'll have the best evening, Bev. There'll be music and everything. And you'll really like Nan and Grandad –'

A kind of desperation made Bev cut in, 'I won't be able to stay long. I'll have to get my mum to pick me up about nine.'

'It doesn't matter,' said Jane. 'Don't worry. We'll have a wicked time, anyway.'

'Well,' said Bev, 'I'll come, I suppose. I suppose I have to.'

Her tone of voice expressed a lot, she knew – the subtle resentment of having been forced by weakness, by pity. But she didn't think Jane noticed. As they walked aimlessly through the school grounds, Jane chattered blithely about the following Monday evening and what it would hold. Beside her, Bev walked with her eyes fixed straight ahead. She didn't know quite why, but she didn't want to go to Jane's party. At all.

15

She was being abandoned. The knowledge followed her through her dreams. When she closed her eyes, she saw lifeboats drifting away, rescue planes growing smaller in the sky. She prayed to the suburbs, and there was no answer.

'Happy birthday, dear,' said Mary in the kitchen, kissing Jane on the cheek. 'To think of it, you're fourteen years old today.'

'Almost a grown-up,' said Alf. 'Many happy returns, love.'

'You can open your present when you get home. Right before your friend comes round for tea,' said Mary. 'What's the matter, Jane, dear? You're looking a bit peaky.'

'It's nothing, Nan,' said Jane. 'Listen, I'd better get on. I'll miss the bus.'

On the bus, she sat alone, voices shrieking around her like bats. 'She gave him a blow-job,' someone was giggling, 'at Matt's party, on Saturday.' And Jane listened without interest, and looked out of the window into the empty morning, and waited for school to arrive.

That day, the world played on in her head like a song in the wrong key. Everywhere she looked she saw a small, sordid ugliness she hadn't noticed before – Melanie's hair stiff and crusted with gel, a bluebottle beating itself to death against a window, crudely coloured pictures carelessly pinned to the noticeboards. Once upon a time she'd walked through Preston, and the smell of cut grass had filled her nostrils. It was unthinkable that she could be abandoned to this nothing. *It was unthinkable.*

When the bell rang for lunch, she walked down to the pretty little park she and Bev had once swung and chatted in, and she found peeling metal fixtures desolate with discarded fag-ends, and overgrown bushes crowding in on all sides. She turned away with an overwhelming sense of loss and began the long walk back to school.

Jane got in just as the bell was ringing out the end of lunch, and the noise hit her hard as she came through the main double doors. She quickened her step. She was walking down the dingy, overcrowded little corridor towards 10H when she saw Bev approaching her and not seeing her at all, in the centre of a laughing group of girls.

In that second, Jane tasted true terror. Down the hallway, she saw the golden advert girl exactly as she'd seen her on that first fateful afternoon – carefree, perfect, remote – yet now Bev's sunny beauty was almost too painful to look at. To Jane, her brightness accentuated the monochrome nothing around her, and she realised Beverley Green hadn't ever seemed so essential to her life, or so inaccessible. She stopped in her tracks and watched Bev move closer; the bounce of the golden hair, the approach of the fresh citrus perfume, the dawning of ill-concealed dismay as Bev registered Jane, and saw Jane, and tried to pretend she hadn't noticed Jane.

Jane didn't want to be the one to stop and speak, but the idea of Bev walking past her with a curt passing nod was far too plausible.

'All right, Bev?' she said. 'You're still coming to my party later, yeah?' It was the confidence of raw desperation. She saw Bev's perfunctory bus-queue smile, her chilly, distracted, irritated eyes.

'Sure,' said Bev dismissively. 'I'll be over about sevenish, yeah?' She walked away with her friends, and didn't look back.

Standing in the crowded corridor, Jane watched Bev fading round a corner. A silvery peal of laughter rang out in the distance before the group of girls was gone. People passed Jane and jostled her, and she heard them mutter briefly at her stillness, and she couldn't have cared less. It wasn't over yet, she told herself desperately, it was not as it had been with Anita. There was still the possibility of a last-minute reprieve. There was still that night.

16

It was confusing to remember the end of her friendship with Anita. It had coincided with so much else. It had been January when Anita had started at the Clapham comprehensive, just as the bloom had been fading off the rose for Carol and Dave – at a time when the real arguments were only just threatening to begin. To Jane, it sometimes felt as if Anita's arrival at school had precipitated an avalanche.

'I'm going to be starting at your school next term,' Anita had said at Christmas. 'My dad says St Joe's is crap.'

They were sitting in Anita's bedroom, which didn't feel quite the same as it had once. Listening to her, Jane felt a huge apprehension. Even though she and Anita were nowhere near as close as they used to be, their friendship still meant far too much to her – a meeting every two or three weeks, a single, private corner of her life where nobody else could go. In Jane's mind, Anita represented those too-short moments when she could forget about Dave, and Michelle and Chandra and Stephanie, and her so-called friends who paid her no attention – a little place to escape to when things got too bad, a kind of refuge.

But, in January, Anita started at the Clapham comprehensive. And all that came to an end.

They'd seemed to drag out for ever, those long, creeping days and weeks and months after Anita'd arrived in the year below Jane. It was just how Jane had known it would be. In the shrieking crowds of the corridors and hallways, a kind of caste system kicked into place: Anita giggled in the centre of a trendy little group while Jane trailed along behind a sad herd of aspiring bitches. By the time three weeks had passed, the differences between them were set in stone, and it was impossible to think they'd ever been close. At first, Anita made a point of always stopping to say hi, but her friends always fidgeted and giggled beside her when she did, and soon Jane didn't have the heart to watch her helpless embarrassment. She turned down corridors and ducked into doorways when she saw Anita and her friends approaching, and felt edgy and frightened till she was sure they'd gone. It was as if they had in some way outgrown childish things and moved into a more heartless state of being – equality belonged to another time and place, to a sunny little bedroom that used to look like home.

One time, Jane saw Anita walking through the playground with Chandra. One time, she saw Anita walking hand in hand with a boy she didn't recognise. One time, she was eating her lunch alone on a bench, and saw out of the corner of her eye that Anita and her friends were giggling at her, and she glanced round sharply. It hurt more than anything to see that Anita still retained the decency to look ashamed. Her guilty eyes said what she'd never conceded out loud – that they'd been real friends, true friends, once.

When you needed someone so much that they were all you had left in the world, it was terrible to watch them drift away like that. But that was how it had been for Jane that January, that spring, throughout the tense months leading up to Carol's death in July.

Time passed too quickly. It terrified her.

17

This was her last chance. She sensed it deep inside, with something beyond rationality. If their friendship wasn't re-kindled that night, it never would be.

'Well, go on, love,' said Alf, smiling in the lounge. 'Open your card from us.'

She tore it open with hands that shook slightly. A pink skunklike creature peered out at her beneath raised gold writing – she opened it, and read the message written in ink. 'It's lovely,' she said, tension pounding deep in her head. 'Thanks ever so much.'

'Aren't you going to open your present, dear?' asked Mary.

'Oh, sure,' said Jane, who'd forgotten it existed. 'I'll open it now,' and she tore absently at something squashy and formless, at shiny paper adorned by further pink skunks.

There were no surprises – she'd known it would be the dress she'd picked out from Mary's catalogue in what now seemed another life, when she'd been friends with Beverley Green. She held the dress up against herself, and tried to look as if she felt like she'd felt then. 'What do you think, love?' asked Alf. 'Isn't that what you wanted?'

'It's just what I wanted,' said Jane. 'I'm going to wear it when Bev comes round. Thanks ever so much.' Their indulgent smiling faces alienated her. She experienced a fresh wave of terror. 'I'd best go and have a bath and get changed,' she said. 'I want to be ready when Bev comes round.'

In the bathroom, wreaths of drifting steam blurred her reflection, and the too-sweet smell of pink bubble-bath seemed to thicken in the heat while the icy black night pressed in outside the small window. Her heart hammered in her chest as she soaped herself. Then she rose from the bath, and wrapped a towel round herself, and went back into her room. She could not be abandoned by the suburbs. Not now.

It felt like walking into a dressing room on an all-important first night. Her costume hung neatly from the wardrobe door – a flowered blue cotton dress with long sleeves and a demurely scooped neckline that Jane had thought very pretty when she'd seen it in the catalogue. She switched the radio on to banish the terrible near-silence and the busyness downstairs, and slipped the dress tentatively over her head. She'd been afraid it wouldn't fit, but it was all right, it did. Even over the bandage.

Jane stood in her pretty new dress and stared into the mirror. The siren lure from under the mattress was louder than ever in her ears. She fought to ignore it. She sat down at the dressing-table and felt something narrowing to a final point. In the mirror, her face was hungry, determined, desperate.

18

Bev brushed her hair in front of the dressing-table mirror, trying to replace the apprehension in her eyes with prosaic dutiful irritation. She was just tying her hair back in a lace scrunchie when the phone went by her bed, and she jumped up to get it. 'Hello?'

'Hi, Bev. It's me, Charlie. Haven't called at a bad moment, have I?'

The relief of blessed normality, the escape from the prospect of Jane Sullivan. 'No. I was just getting ready for that girl's party. You know.'

'Jane Whatshername? I didn't think you were really going to go.'

'Haven't got much choice, to be honest.' Bev was amazed at how business-as-usual she sounded – she could have been referring to double maths or clearing up her room. 'I sort of promised her I'd go, worse luck.'

'Poor you. She seems a bit weird.'

The casual remark brushed Bev up like an electric shock – she remembered the whining voice, the pallid moon-face that had a way of appearing out of nowhere when you least expected it. 'Oh, she's all right,' she said quickly. 'Just a bit boring, that's all.

Anyway, I'll just be putting in a showing. I won't be staying long.'

'Well, have a good time,' said Charlie, then, 'Oh, I remember what I rang for, now. Have you made a start on your French assignment yet?' They discussed perfect tenses and feminine plurals and their bitch of a teacher for over ten minutes before Bev said she'd have to go.

After she'd hung up, Bev changed into Levi's and a sweater, and put on a bit of lip-gloss. She felt a sudden ridiculous affection for Charlie, as she did for the others in their group – her nice new set of clean-cut friends bolted a door against the darkness of Jane Sullivan. Sarcastic, boy-mad Louise; pleasant, responsible Adele, who was getting engaged to her boyfriend next year; timid, sweet-faced Charlie, who lived in the suburbs like she did. And Emma, who'd always just be Emma as she always had been. Their neat smooth edges warmed her. She wished she didn't have to go to Jane's party tonight.

Downstairs Melissa was talking on the phone in the hall, and nodded a smiling be-with-you-soon at Bev, and Bev went into the kitchen to wait. Toby and Tiffany were talking at the table. 'He just keeps hassling her,' Toby was saying, in a hushed, furious voice, 'it's just pathetic. She's not going to take him back.'

Bev sat down beside them. 'That Dad on the phone?'

'What do you think?' Toby took a deep breath. 'We're all going out for lunch with him on Saturday. I heard Mum saying just now. To Poole Tower Park. We've got to go *bowling* after.'

'Look, Toby, stop worrying. They're not going to get back together,' said Bev. 'He just wants to see us. It's not a crime.'

Tiffany's face said she was out of her emotional depth – you could see the relief in her eyes as she found a way to change the subject. 'You look really nice,' she said to Bev. 'Where you going?'

'Nowhere special,' said Bev. 'Just some stupid party. I won't be staying long.'

Tiffany was asking Bev how she got her hair to go like that when Melissa came in from the hall, and asked Bev if she was ready to go.

'That was your father on the phone,' said Melissa, when they were belted into the Shogun and pulling out of the drive.

'I know,' said Bev. 'Toby said.'

'I told him we'd all go out to Poole Tower Park on Saturday,' said Melissa, with a kind of apologetic determination. 'He thought it would be nice to go bowling after.'

'Toby said that, too. It's all right. I don't mind.'

'Well, I don't want to come between you and your father. Just because we're not together any more, it doesn't mean you can't stay close.'

'We never have been close,' said Bev. 'But it's all right. Really.' She looked out of the window and watched the street signs. 'Oh, hang on,' she said, 'here we are. That's Spring Lane, down there.'

Melissa stopped the car outside a neat, respectable little terrace. 'What time do you want me to pick you up?'

'Early. About nineish. I don't want to stay long.'

'You can if you like, darling. I don't mind.'

'No, Mum, *really*. I don't want to stay long.'

'Oh, well. If you say so. Have a lovely evening, anyway. I'll pick you up at nine.'

'See you, then, Mum.' Subtle fear overcame Bev as she saw the front door opening an Advent calendar of light against the darkness, and saw Jane's eager unsettling smile in the doorway. ''Bye.' And she got out of the car, and walked out into the night, towards whatever it might contain.

19

The little lounge was far too hot, and the central heating was on full blast. Bev's first impressions were of a room crammed almost solid with furniture, surfaces crammed almost solid with tacky brass and ceramic and porcelain knick-knacks, a life crammed almost solid with hot artificial air that left the visitor fighting for breath. A coffee-table was pulled up in the middle of the carpet, and snacks and a birthday-cake were arranged on top of it. Bev had no appetite for any of it.

She hadn't seen the dress Jane was wearing before, and its wrongness was towering – it looked as if it might have been worn to church in the height of a nineteenth-century summer. And she thought Jane's grandparents' joviality also struck a wrong note. They were slightly too eager to please her, and there was something worrying about their attentiveness.

'Are you in Jane's class at school, love?' asked Alf.

'No, I'm fifteen,' said Bev, trying far too hard to smile. 'I'm in the year above.'

'Oh, really?' asked Mary. 'Have some more lemonade, dear. We've got lots left.'

'Thanks,' said Bev. 'I'll do that. No, it's all right, Mrs Sullivan. I can pour it.'

She poured herself another glass of lemonade, and saw that they were all looking at her somehow hungrily – the elderly, too-amiable couple, the suet-faced teenager in the anachronistic summer dress. She felt as if the walls were closing in on her. She saw china dogs leaning out from the overcrowded sideboard, and their fixed idiot smiles made her feel cold inside. 'Well,' she said stupidly, 'thanks for inviting me this evening. It's really nice.'

'The pleasure's all ours, dear,' said Mary. 'We hardly ever get to meet Jane's friends. Well, never, to be honest.'

'Except Anita,' said Alf.

'Don't be silly, Alf, we've never met Anita,' said Mary. 'I don't know if you know Anita, Beverley, dear. She's a friend of Jane's, at school.'

'Lives in Preston,' said Alf. 'Rich family.'

'But Jane's never had her round for tea,' said Mary. 'Never once.'

'Hey, Nan,' said Jane quickly, 'you don't mind if we go up to my room for a bit, do you? We can listen to some music or something up there, Bev.'

'Well, of course we don't mind, dear,' said Mary. 'I'm sure you'd like to be on your own, to gossip about school and things.'

Suddenly Bev didn't want to go up to Jane's room – more than anything she didn't want to be alone with her. But of course she couldn't say that. As she walked up the stairs behind Jane, her mind lingered and hurried like a rat in a maze. She knew all the girls at school who lived in her area. She'd never heard of anyone called Anita.

20

When they got into Jane's room, the first thing Bev noticed was the teddy-bear on the bed. It was blue and white, and sat as on a throne, dominating everything. She didn't want to mention it, but somehow had to. 'That's the one I gave you at the fair, isn't it?'

'Yeah,' said Jane, as she flicked the side lamp on. Then she went to the wall switch and turned off the harsh centre bulb. 'Thanks ever so much, Bev.'

'I can't believe you kept it. It's *horrible*.'

'Don't say that. Don't ever say that. It's *yours*.'

There was something all wrong in Jane's voice, something passionate and chilling that didn't belong in this tacky little room. It hit Bev like a punch out of nowhere. In a moment of stark realisation, she understood that Jane had used that self-same tone before, maybe many times before, and she simply hadn't noticed. It was like waking up to find you'd been sleepwalking through a minefield – immediacy flashed into her mind and, for a second, she thought she might black out.

They stood in the middle of the room, facing each other, and the lamplight cast too many shadows.

'It's too quiet,' said Jane. 'I'll put some music on.' She went to the little radio on her dressing-table-desk, and turned to switch it on. The silence lasted a second too long before she noticed it stretching out behind her. 'Bev, what's wrong?' she asked, as the radio came on. 'What's the matter?'

'Who's Anita?' Bev asked quietly.

A cool classic Simply Red track strolled urbanely round the

room. Jane's expression betrayed sudden guilt. 'What do you mean?' she asked, too quickly. 'I don't understand.'

'You know what I mean. What your nan said. Your friend at school.' Bev didn't know exactly what she was afraid of, or even the exact nature of her accusation. She only knew it was the worst thing in the world. 'I never saw you with anyone,' she said. 'Not in the toilets. Not in the corridors. I thought you said you didn't know anyone else who lived in Preston.'

Jane spoke fearfully. 'It's okay, Bev. I can explain. It doesn't matter. You'll understand, Bev. You just don't know all this stuff about me. Not yet.'

'Not ever,' said Bev deliberately. She sat down on the bed, and her knuckles clenched white in her lap. 'I think we should stop hanging out together, Jane. It's all wrong.'

For a second, Jane just stared at her blankly. 'What?'

'I've been meaning to say something for a while. But I didn't want to spoil the run-up to your birthday. I mean, we don't have that much in common, and –'

'But that's the whole *point*,' said Jane. Her voice trembled. 'That's always been the point.'

'No, it's not. You must know that much.'

'It is,' said Jane. 'It's why we first started talking. It's why *everything*.'

'Look, we're not even in the same year,' said Bev. 'You should find some other friends of your own age.'

'You don't understand. I don't want friends of my age. It doesn't matter that you're older. We can still talk about stuff,' said Jane. 'I don't mind. I don't mind. I *don't mind*.' Her voice grew a little louder with each repetition.

She was furious and on the edge of tears both at once. Bev could read it in her face. Her own profound unease combined with a crawling revulsion – she felt the imminence of graceless snot-clogged sobbing, and knew she couldn't stand the embarrassment of watching Jane break down.

'Come on,' she said quietly. 'It's not the end of the world.'

'It *is*,' Jane howled. 'You don't understand. It *is*.'

Bev felt something tighten in the pit of her stomach. 'It's not.

You'll soon get over it. But I don't think we should hang out together any more. Come on. Let's go back down.'

Bev descended the stairs at a near-trot. Jane trailed behind her like a tin can. Suddenly Bev couldn't wait for her mother to arrive and collect her. The image of the blue-and-white teddy on the bed screamed in her mind.

21

Melissa was sitting at the kitchen table, filling in the application form for the computer course she'd been thinking about doing to brush up her secretarial skills, when the phone rang. She got up to get it. She thought it might be Jack.

'Hello?'

'Hello? Mel?' said her sister's agitated voice down the line. 'It's me, Katie.'

'Oh, hi, Katie.' Her heart sank. She'd been avoiding all four of her sisters for some time. 'What's up?'

'I just had to call you. I don't even think I should believe this.' Katie sounded flustered and breathless, as if she'd called Melissa right after a strenuous run. 'I heard from Dad that you and Jack are getting divorced.'

'Oh, God.' It was the call Melissa had been dreading. Her hand tightened on the receiver. 'I know I should have told you and the girls sooner. But I've been so busy, Katie. I feel as if I've spent my whole life in that bloody solicitor's office lately.'

'It's true, then. Jesus. When I got the letter from Dad, I thought he'd lost it completely.'

'No. It's true. It's all true.'

'But – I don't know what to say. *Why*, for Christ's sake?'

'He was having an affair. There's more to it than that, but that's the official reason.'

'Did he – has he left you for her?'

'I'm not sure he even knew her surname,' said Melissa. 'I threw him out.'

'Well, *shit*, Melissa,' said Katie. 'I mean, one affair. Don't you think you're overreacting?'

'No,' said Melissa. Deep inside, she braced herself for the shame of confession. 'Look, Katie, you don't know the full story. I never told you and the girls. But it's been a long time coming. It's for the best. We were having a lot of problems.'

'You mean you *argued*?' asked Katie, in a voice of utter disbelief.

'Believe it,' said Melissa. 'Even here in the suburbs.'

'But I don't *understand*,' said Katie. 'You always seemed so *happy*. The perfect couple. We all envied you and Jack so much.'

'Maybe that was the problem.' It was what Melissa had dreaded, and she was amazed to find it liberating beyond words – the Perfect Greens on the bonfire, a final symbolic destruction of the cosy old lies. 'There wasn't ever anything behind that. I'm happier now. I think the kids are, too.'

'And Jack?' asked Katie. 'What about Jack?'

'Fuck Jack,' said Melissa calmly. 'I've been working for Jack for the past sixteen years, Katie. I think I deserve a life of my own, now.'

'*Melissa.*' Her sister sounded shocked, lost, plaintive. 'I don't know what to say.'

'You don't have to say anything. It's all right. Listen, I'm going to have to go now. I've got to pick Bev up from a party. I'll give you a ring tomorrow.'

Melissa replaced the receiver. She went into the living room and told Toby she'd only be half an hour or so. Then she walked to the garage and started the car. On the long drive to the Darlington Estate, tiny lights twinkled out of the darkness. Soon it would be Christmas.

22

The big shiny car made the houses look somehow unreal, robbed of life. Jane stood in the doorway, and watched the suburbs drain the last drops of hope from the world she lived in.

The beautiful blonde woman behind the wheel beamed welcome to the golden advert girl as she walked over and got in, and Jane caught the hint of perfect mouths moving around the language of the blessed. Then the passenger door closed, the engine purred, and rear lights shot away into blackness. It was over. They had gone.

Jane turned away from the empty road. She saw gaudy streamers and china dogs in the hallway. Empty eyes mocked her agony like a crown of thorns. 'What's the matter, Jane, dear?' asked Mary, as she closed the door. 'We didn't like to say anything in front of your friend, but you were in ever such a funny mood when you came down from your bedroom.'

'It was all very uncomfortable,' said Alf. 'What's the matter, love? You two fall out over something?'

In the hallway's bright overhead light, Jane saw her grandparents with awful clarity – Alf's bloodshot eyes, Mary's smudged coral lipstick. They were ordinary and accessible and repulsive, and suddenly Jane hated them for ruining what was wonderful. 'You told her about Anita,' she said quietly. 'Why did you do that?'

'Well, we didn't know it was a secret, dear,' said Mary. 'What's secret about that?'

Jane's eyes were hot and hating. 'I didn't want her to know about Anita!' she said. 'You've ruined everything! *Everything!*'

'Jane,' said Mary, 'what on earth's got into you tonight?' But Jane was pounding up the stairs into her bedroom, where she leaned back on the door to stop the following Mary from coming in. 'It's all right,' she screamed, as the inevitable knock came. 'I'm just going to bed. Leave me alone, can't you?'

Jane stood, breathing raggedly, eyes closed tightly, tears squeezing through the lids. She could still smell Bev's perfume on the air. She realised it would have faded in an hour or less and would never be replaced here. It was all someone else's fault. Her grandparents', or someone she couldn't see yet. The suburbs had liked her, and they had invited her in, and then someone had said something that might or might not have been about Anita, and then the door had slammed shut in her face.

Yes. Someone had lied to the golden advert girl about her. Even if a part of Jane realised that this explanation was untrue, she wanted to believe in it so badly that it became its own proof. Beyond that, there was nothing but nothing. She couldn't understand why it had all gone so wrong, why she and Beverley Green were no longer friends.

She would find out who had lied to Beverley Green. She could do that much, at least . . .

She listened out for footsteps on the stairs and heard none. She went to the mattress and got out the lighter and the compass. She sat down at the dressing-table–desk and rolled back the sleeve of her pretty new dress and peeled back the greying bandage and held the compass point steady in the flame. She slashed her arm like paper with a knife, and the blood soaked through wadded tissue in less than a minute.

December

1

'You went to see your dad the other day, didn't you?' asked Emma.

It was late on Saturday afternoon, and Emma and Bev and Louise were sitting in a quiet little town-centre café that smelt of cake and coffee, drinking cappuccino and eating chips dipped in the relish-tray. Outside it was dark, and long streaks of rain lashed the glass. 'Yeah,' said Bev. 'He took me and Toby out to some Italian place in Bournemouth. Mancini's, or something.'

'What was it like?' asked Emma.

'Oh, you know. It was OK. The usual, really.'

'Well, that just says it all,' said Louise. 'Just another three-course Italian dinner in Bournemouth. How *boring*.'

It was amazing, how things had changed. Just a few weeks ago, the remark would have been either sycophantic or bitter, and Bev would have purred or snarled accordingly. But now, it was just a harmlessly sarcastic bit of fun, and she laughed with Emma and Louise. 'Yeah, *right*,' she said, 'you think it *sounds* exciting. You should have *been* there.'

'Couldn't make it, I'm afraid. So many premières, so little time,' Louise said airily. 'Oh, yeah, I meant to say. Me and Adele had a thought about Christmas Eve the other day.'

'What?' asked Emma, sipping her cappuccino.

'Well, we can't exactly stay *in*, can we? We are almost sixteen now. So me and Adele thought we could all go to the fancy-dress party at Maxine's.'

'Yeah, right,' said Emma. 'We'll never get in. Since when have we been eighteen?'

'Since they served us last Sunday in the pub,' retorted Louise.

'Anyway, since when's Maxine's given a toss about ID? I even sounded out Charlie. She thinks it's a great idea.'

'You really think we'll all pass as eighteen?' asked Bev.

'In fancy-dress? Sure.' A thoughtful silence fell. Louise's confident eyes looked round the table. 'Hey, Emma, Bev. Speak to me. What do you think?'

'Well . . .' Emma's voice tailed off longingly before the practicalities broke in. 'What'd we tell our parents?'

'There's an under-sixteens Christmas do at Charlie Brown's,' said Louise. 'Why don't we just tell them we're going to that?'

'They're not exactly going to mind *that*,' said Bev. 'How could they?'

'And it'd make it miles easier if all our stories matched,' said Louise. 'That way, if our mums call each other and stuff, they still won't know what we're up to.'

'It's a good idea,' said Bev, and they arranged to ask their parents when they got home that evening if they could go to Charlie Brown's, and Louise said she'd ring Maxine's and find out about getting the tickets. They finished their coffee, and lingered chattering over the dregs till the waitress came over with a bill that told them to sod off home.

Outside, the rain had abated slightly, and reflected Christmas lights spilled red and white and green across the wet pavement. The three of them walked together through the busy town centre, towards the bus-stops. Bev glanced round, and did a double-take. 'Oh, God. That's my bus coming,' she said. 'Listen, I'd better run. See you in school on Monday, yeah?'

'Yeah. See you, Bev,' said Emma and Louise, then Bev was racing into the distance.

2

Bev paid her fare, and went to sit down at the back. Gazing out of the window as the bus started off, she saw bustling crowds and well-lit shop windows and Christmas lights and darkness, and she found something both reassuring and evocative in the sight. As the bus left the town centre, a neon Santa winked at her through a haze of rain.

It was impossible to pinpoint the exact nature of the change she felt. In a way, it was the change Emma had noticed last month but, at the same time, there was far more to it than that. Emma and Louise and the others would never know all she'd been going through – she'd never tell them about the sleepless nights, about the terror, about Bradley in Orlando. But, to some extent, Bev had come to terms with it herself. Even when Emma and the others occasionally talked about horny boys and who'd got off with who, her loneliness felt infinitely less painful than it had once – a moment of revulsion, and nothing more than that. The point was that it was over. She'd found a real escape from the Perfect Greens, right here in Underlyme, a new contentment, a kind of honesty.

Whatever didn't kill you made you stronger. Bev had heard the saying somewhere, and suddenly recognised its unsentimental truth. All that had happened hadn't eroded her, after all. She stepped out of its awful shadow scarred with memories, but stronger than she had ever been. She didn't need to be the invulnerable princess to be happy or loved, after all. She hadn't ever felt a lasting contentment like this before – not brittle hilarity but something silent and reflective that was every bit as potent when she was alone.

She knew what had driven her to seek out comfortable equality among her peers, to abandon the old lies for good. Not her parents' breakup, or her edgy new friendship with Toby, or even the infinitely improved atmosphere at home. They were all good, but good like side-effects could be. The main agenda lay far from home. Jane Sullivan. Of course.

Like a pregnancy scare might stop you sleeping around, Jane Sullivan had stopped Bev taking refuge in a past that wasn't there any more. Bev had thought it was just a harmless way to feel good again – but then she'd found out more. She remembered a hideous blue-and-white teddy she'd given to Jane as carelessly as she might have thrown a chocolate wrapper in the bin – a hideous blue-and-white teddy that now held pride of place in Jane's room. The chilling worship in Jane's eyes and voice, and a girl called Anita who'd never lived in Preston. To Bev, Jane was inextricably allied to the perfect illusions, and as Jane became terrible in her eyes, so did they. How could she ever have sought out this false, unsettling world, this disturbed and loathsome little creature that stood whining at its gates? It was as if Bev had found a lock of her own hair framed on Jane's wall. Something brushed her deep inside with a sense of nightmare.

By contrast, truth and reality both seemed impossibly sweet. Her mother calling, 'Hi, Bev,' when she got home from school in the evenings; Toby and Tiffany watching telly in the living-room; Emma and the others calling her on her bedroom phone. How clean and open and normal it all seemed now, Bev thought. She was amazed at how the world seemed to take this sort of thing for granted – it was wonderful, it was where she belonged, after all.

Now, sitting on the bus home, Bev felt her new happiness at the same time as she felt the one thing that could threaten it. It was something she tried her utmost not to think about, that she turned her back on each time it leaped up in her mind. And it wasn't the rape in Florida, or the memory of how scared she'd been when her parents had just broken up. The wheel of her thoughts had come full circle. It was Jane Sullivan. Again.

.

3

When Bev had been very young, she'd read a fairytale whose title she couldn't quite remember. She hadn't been a particularly imaginative child, but it had disturbed her all the same. Even its happy ending hadn't diminished its power and darkness.

The fairytale had revolved around a beautiful princess who lived in an ivory palace. The king and queen adored her, and suitors fought for her hand. But the princess was silly and frivolous, and liked nothing better than to play where she wasn't meant to, with the golden ball that was her favourite toy in the world.

One day, when the princess was playing with her golden ball in some distant garden, she threw it too far. She raced to get it. To her horror, she saw it had fallen into a deep pond where she'd never be able to get it out. A repulsive warty frog saw her staring into the water. 'I'll get it out for you,' said the frog, 'but, if I do, you must treat me as your friend. For ever.'

And the princess, who could see no further than the loss of her prized golden ball, agreed at once, without thinking. The frog retrieved it, and the princess took it. She was about to walk away, when the frog stopped her. 'Have you forgotten your promise? Take me back to the palace with you. Now, you must treat me as your friend . . .'

And finally, the princess saw how her careless promise bound her to an unthinkable future. She had to take the frog to the palace ball, to let it sleep beside her at night, the stench of it clouding her dreams. And the frog's demands were never-ending, orders behind a grotesque façade of cringing humility. 'Where are you going?' asked the frog, when the princess tried to sneak away from it. 'Have you forgotten your promise? You must treat me as your friend . . .'

In the end, the frog, of course, had turned into a prince, and the princess had fallen instantly in love with the handsome young man. But somehow, that last bit hadn't rung true to the young Bev: it had looked like something inexpertly tacked on for the sake of a happy ending. In her own mind, the middle part of the fairytale looked like the *real* ending. The princess doomed to lug the horrible little creature around on a silk pillow, the frog's demands becoming ever more arbitrary and brutal. That was how they all lived ever after, Bev had thought, and not *happily* at all.

In the here and now, the parallels with her own life were unavoidable. She'd turned her back on the frog called Jane, and heard its whining voice chase after her through the darkness of the palace grounds. Amidst her contentment, it was like a spectre at a feast – the frog with the golden ball.

Often, at school, she'd see Jane watching her. She didn't wait for Bev or approach her any more. Just watched her. Somehow that was worse than anything, the way it always took Bev by surprise. She'd be walking and chatting with Emma and Adele and Charlie and Louise – happy conversation as in the café earlier, talk of GCSEs and Christmas presents and parties they should go to. And then she'd see Jane Sullivan leaning on a wall, standing in a corridor, stock-still, dead-eyed. Watching her. None of the others noticed, but Bev was terrified that they would. The idea of their noticing scared her every bit as badly as the recollected darkness in Jane's eyes, Jane's voice.

Because it was probably nothing. And if nobody else saw it, it might not be there at all. Bev closed her mind and told herself she couldn't see Jane Sullivan watching her. She dreaded others corroborating the creeping fears that spoiled the look of the new contentment and complicated the happy ending. She'd never tell a soul that she was worried.

Bev got off at the bus-stop, and started walking towards Goldcroft Drive. Like someone changing the tape on a Walkman, she inserted new thoughts in her mind. As she walked, she saw colourful windows cut out of the drizzling evening, and thought of honesty and normality and true happiness – dinner in the kitchen, Christmas Eve at Maxine's nightclub.

4

The three of them were eating dinner under the bright circle of light, but now there wasn't anything terrible in the silence at all – just that none of them had anything much to say. 'I heard from the college this morning, you know,' Melissa said eventually. 'I'll be going on that computer course in January.'

'You'll be the oldest person on it,' said Toby callously. 'They'll all be eighteen and nineteen and stuff.'

'*Toby*,' said Bev. 'How long's it last for?'

'Ten days,' said Melissa. 'It's all day-time classes, so it's not as if you'll be fending for yourselves when you get in from school. And I'm quite looking forward to it, to be honest. It'll be nice, doing something new.'

'It should be great,' said Bev. 'Oh, yeah, Mum. Can I go to the under-sixteens' party at Charlie Brown's on Christmas Eve?'

'Well . . . I suppose so. Are Emma and the others going?'

'Of course they are going,' said Bev. 'I'm not exactly going to go on my own.'

'Well, in that case . . .' said Melissa. 'I'll want to know what time you'll be back and everything, mind. Remember, you're not sixteen for another two months.'

'But I can go?' pressed Bev. 'You don't mind?'

'I don't see how I can mind, really. There won't be any drink or anything at an under-sixteens' party,' said Melissa. 'All right, all right. You can go.' Another short, easy silence fell, and cutlery clinked on china. 'Your father phoned this afternoon,' said Melissa, mainly to Bev. 'I don't want to ruin the surprise but he says he's still going to be buying you that iMac.'

'I don't mind if he does or not,' said Bev. 'I suppose it's nice, but . . . you know . . . it's not like I'm *living* for it.' And she saw her mother looking comfortable and relaxed, and Toby not looking jealous, and the three of them finished their dinner talking about Christmas.

Upstairs in the bathroom, Bev washed her hair and wrapped a towel round her head and returned to her room. She was about to plug in her hairdryer when the phone rang by her bed, and she walked to get it. 'Hello?'

'Hi, Bev. It's me,' said Emma. 'You ask your mum if you can go on Christmas Eve?'

'Yeah. She says it's fine,' said Bev. 'What about you?'

'Ditto,' said Emma. 'This is too cool.'

'Tell me about it,' said Bev. She squeezed the receiver between her ear and her shoulder, and went to draw the curtains. 'God, I can't *wait*.' At the window, she saw her room clearly reflected in the mullioned glass – the towel round her head and the pastel-striped wallpaper – and then she pulled the curtain across, and the view was gone, and it was just her talking to Emma, in the warmth of Goldcroft Drive.

5

At first, Jane thought that Bev was wearing a turban, but then she realised it was just a towel. For long seconds, she stared at the tiny Bev in the well-lit window, and wondered if Bev was seeing her, too. A thrill crawled over her skin at the thought – maybe she wasn't quite invisible to this perfect world, after all – and then the pink-striped curtain pulled across, and shut her out.

Jane stood by the gatepost at the end of the sloping drive. A coachlight burned white beside her. She stood in the gathering night and watched the house.

She often came here after school now. She was always touched with a kind of relief when she turned the corner and saw Bev's house towering against the sky – the comfort of knowing that something beautiful still existed in the world, that the lights still went on inside each night, that the people in the suburbs still laughed, and loved, and were happy. There was such distant kindness in those windows, before the curtains were drawn to lock her out. There was such perfection.

But now the final curtain had been drawn, and the windows expressed nothing, and it was time to go home.

Jane turned, and started walking back towards the bus-stop. It was almost half seven, and the winter night was rainy and forbidding. Under the empty black sky, the houses she passed seemed icily inviolate – dark castles, with their drawbridges pulled up against the night. There would be no cheerful family barbecues tonight. Distant streetlights held tiny flames against the darkness, and the sound of her own breathing filled her ears. She remembered how different it had all looked from Bev's bedroom window, and experienced a tragedy beyond tears.

She wanted more than anything to walk down to the beach road, but she knew she couldn't. Her grandparents would be waiting for her with dinner. At the stop, the bus arrived in a spray of puddles and was more than half empty. Jane sat in the anaemic light of the top deck, and watched the suburbs fading. She saw the ugly graffiti on the seat-back in front of her. She waited for home to arrive.

6

She never snapped at her grandparents any more. There was no point. With a deepening obsession that felt almost like perspective, she now knew it hadn't been their fault Bev had gone. It would have taken more power than theirs to alienate the suburbs. At home, Jane said what they expected her to, and acted as she always had, and locked up the chaos in her head where nobody else could see. Her grandparents seemed to have written off the row after her birthday as a freak temper storm. They hadn't alluded to it since.

In the kitchen, the brightness was all wrong. Suds glittered in the sink with an unforgiving cosiness.

'Hello, dear,' said Mary. 'Have a nice time at Beverley's?'

'Yeah,' said Jane. 'It was wicked.'

'That's nice,' said Mary. 'I half thought you two'd fallen out for good. You know. At your party.'

'Oh, no,' said Jane. 'It was just a little row. About Anita. She didn't want me to hang out with Anita.'

Mary's forehead corrugated. 'Doesn't she like Anita, then?'

'She didn't used to,' said Jane. 'She does now. Anita was round tonight, and we all drank Cokes up in Bev's room. It was wicked.' Jane's eyes were bright and distracted. 'It's all right now. I can be friends with both of them.'

'Oh, that's nice, dear. Well, I daresay we'd better eat, now you're home,' and Mary called Alf in from the lounge, and they ate.

After dinner was over, Jane said she had some homework to finish, and hurried up the stairs. She shut her bedroom door and got out the compass and lighter from under the mattress. She sat down at the dressing-table and found that the much-needed high was over far too quickly. She tried not to look too closely at her bared arm. Recently the sight had started to disturb her.

She sat there for a long time, in the too-thin, too-bright lamplight, listening to the distant mutter of the television and her heartbeat hammering in her ears. She thought about Beverley Green, and how things used to be.

That night, she had a very bad dream.

7

She was woken up by music at some point in the night, a non-specific rhythmic beat, like jungle drums pounding through the wall. She rubbed her eyes and got out of bed. She went into the bathroom and snapped on the light. She saw Carol lying naked in a bath of blood that smelt like pink bubble-bath, and the dead flesh was reflected in the spotless wall mirror, and she was just about to scream when Carol's blue eyelids snapped open, and Carol spoke.

'Nobody's ever wanted me,' she said. 'They never gave me a chance. Fuck off. I'm not drunk. I'm going out.' And Jane saw her bloody hands closing on the sides of the bath, and realised that Carol was trying to climb out, and the deafening music hammered on and on and on as she tried to block the doorway, and naked dead Carol rose from the bath, and struggled with Jane to escape.

'Jane's got crabs,' a childish voice whispered solemnly behind her, 'she caught them off her mum.' And Jane saw with horror but no real surprise that it wasn't the shadowed hallway in the Darlington Estate at all: it was the girls' toilets back at the Clapham comprehensive. Michelle and Chandra and Stephanie faced her squarely, cold-eyed. And Carol pushed past her and out into the toilets, and the three girls smiled welcome at the dead woman. 'You coming to my party tonight, Carol?' Michelle asked, 'Anita's going to be there, we can walk down the shop' – and Jane's eyes were swivelling wildly from side to side when she saw Beverley Green come in, and points of glitter on her clothes caught the light as she moved.

Beverley Green stopped in front of the mirrors and started to brush her hair. Her face was the serene face of a goddess. Jane realised Bev alone could save her, that Michelle and Carol and the others meant to kill her here. Trapped in the doorway by the ring of laughing girls, she shrieked at Bev to save her, to see her, to notice. But Bev didn't seem to see anything in the mirrors except her own reflection, and she pushed her hair back and replaced the brush in her bag, and in the seconds before she left, Jane had time to see that the brush was perfect, and the bag was perfect, and she was a golden advert girl, after all.

Jane's eyes snapped open to the charcoal shadows of her room. At first, the terror was so immense that she couldn't place what was still wrong. Then she could. The music. She could still hear it.

But she knew she was awake, now.

She sat up. Her heartbeat was a pendulum tick and the music was deafening. Muffled, as if by a thick wall, but so *loud* – inhuman and mindless and grotesquely catchy – its savage beats evoked nothing but fear. It was impossible that her grandparents couldn't hear it. *It was impossible.*

Slowly, Jane got out of bed. The carpet felt oddly metallic beneath her bare feet, and told her that this wasn't a dream any more. She went to her grandparents' room, and pushed open the door quietly. It was what she'd dreaded. They were both fast asleep. Somehow she could hear her grandfather's loud snoring even above the music.

In the bathroom, she steeled herself and switched on the light. But the gleaming empty tub held no secrets, and the familiar respectable clutter stared down from the shelves – deodorant, shaving-foam, bubble-bath, toothpaste. Everything was as it should be. Except for the music, which followed her all the way down the moonlit stairs, hammering in her head like the voices of madness, pounding in from another world.

She stood in the silent shadows of the lounge for a long time. Then she turned and tiptoed up to bed. Between the sheets, she clung to the blue-and-white teddy. She lay awake, and listened to the music, and yearned for an oblivion that simply wouldn't come.

8

Somebody had lied to Beverley Green. That was all that mattered. Someone had lied to the suburbs incarnate, and had made them go away.

The thoughts thudded over and over again in Jane's mind, combining with her exhaustion. She sat on the bus and looked out of the window. The faces and voices around her seemed somehow unreal. It was a Monday morning, and she'd had no sleep the night before.

When the bus stopped at the school gates, it felt as if the trees and bushes and laughing crowds were flowing around her and she wasn't moving. Her senses operated with a new and dreadful clarity, and tiny things overwhelmed her everywhere she looked. The dark green smell of winter foliage, the squashed Ribena carton on the path, the shriek of gulls. Disinterested terror kicked deep in her guts. She'd never experienced anything like this before. She didn't know what was happening to her.

The golden advert girl. Someone had lied to Beverley Green.

Through the main double doors, terror grew and blossomed. Her peripheral vision had drained to monotonous shades of orange and black, and darkness throbbed at its furthest edges. The loud squealing voices around her seemed to echo in her ears. She walked past the noticeboards and down the hallway, moving without conscious volition away from the noisy crowds, towards the girls' toilets by the changing rooms, where she'd first met Beverley Green.

Inside, the silence was squalid and desolate, and the cubicle doors all stood open. A part of her had hoped to see Bev reflected

188

in the mirrors but she saw nothing but herself. Loneliness overcame her, and eclipsed even the fear. She realised she was reaching into her bag. Without real surprise, her fingertips registered the familiar outlines of a small package. She supposed she must have taken it out from under the mattress that morning. She couldn't really remember. It didn't matter. Now the ritual was the only thing she'd ever needed – a drug under the striplight in this strange dark morning, the reassurance of a familiar face.

She went into a cubicle and bolted the door behind her. She leaned against the wall, unwrapped the package and held the compass point steady in the flame. As she peeled back the bandage round her arm, she saw the crude phallus that had been carved into the back of the door, and observed it without interest. For the hundredth time, she wondered who'd turned Beverley Green against her – how they had lied about her, exactly what they'd said.

9

Morning registration. The windows showed not charcoal shadows but thick black ink, and it felt like one of her nightmares, in which she was in school at midnight. The yellowish striplights had a lot of work to do.

She sat alone at a table, feeling the classroom filling up around her, staring at her hands, listening to the teacher come in. It seemed to her that Melanie and the others had begun to look at her from the central table – speculative glances flickering restlessly between her and one another, occasional giggles that cut off when she turned her head. Perhaps they were preparing to pick on her again. She weighed up the prospect in her mind, and found that she didn't care. They didn't matter. Nothing mattered any more but Bev. Then registration was over, and they were filing out towards Assembly.

In the assembly hall, Jane sat a few rows back from the front, hearing coughs and sniffles echoing in quadrophonic stereo behind the headmaster's voice: ' . . . and I'm pleased to be able to tell you,' he was saying, 'that the new science lab's going to be . . .' Her strange drugged terror came and went in huge rolling waves. Something was terribly wrong, she thought, something was going terribly wrong. Incomprehensible syllables caught and rebounded in her head, and the bright lights and the oracular voice from the front of the hall meant nothing to her. And even when she heard Tiffany giggling behind her she was far too engrossed in her own unease to pay the sound any real attention.

When Assembly ended, the front rows were the first to file out of the hall, and the corridors moved again. The world was flowing around Jane like water when a beringed hand on her shoulder spun her round. Laughter greeted her as she turned. It was Melanie and her friends.

'What's the matter, Sullivan?' asked Melanie. 'Lost your friend from the fifth year today?'

There was nothing else she could have said that would have had the same effect. Jane spoke slowly. 'What do you mean?'

Tiffany, Josie and Davina giggled. Melanie took the stage. 'Doesn't seem to want to hang out with you any more, does she?' she asked. 'Wonder why not.'

Jane thought of Beverley brushing her hair in the mirrors and not seeing her, the pink-striped curtain drawing across the bedroom window – the beautiful and perfect suburbs moving slowly out of sight. And these four anonymous wolves knew all about it. Suddenly Jane was full of conviction: they'd been the ones who'd lied and plotted, who'd wrenched Bev's friendship out of her reach.

'What did you say to her?' she demanded. 'I have to know what you said to her!'

'Oh, we just had a little word in her ear,' said Melanie airily. 'Told her it was spoiling her reputation and all, hanging out with an ugly fat slag like you. She listens to us, Sullivan. Everyone listens to us.'

An iron fist clenched down on Jane's guts and twisted hard. 'You didn't,' she said slowly. 'You *couldn't.*'

'We did,' Melanie mimicked, 'we *could*. You'd better believe it, Sullivan. Beverley hates you now.'

In that second, Jane stared into the heart of hatred. This stupid, shadowy girl, with her chorus of meaningless sycophants giggling behind her. This – *nonentity* – had stolen the golden advert girl, the pink-and-white bedroom, the life beyond life. In that second, Jane felt her mind quiver. She flew at Melanie like a wildcat, and the giggles snapped into screaming around her.

10

The little ante-room outside the headmaster's office was plain and sparsely decorated. A door led on to the school secretary's office, and Jane could hear the muffled *clickety-click* of her typing at the computer. It didn't matter. She hadn't told them about Beverley Green and how Melanie and the others had tried to steal her. That was all that mattered.

The door to the headmaster's office was ajar. If she craned, she could just about make out the words from inside. They'd called her grandparents into the school. They'd been talking with the headmaster for a long time. Her form tutor was in there, too.

'I can't understand it,' twittered Mary feebly, on the edge of tears. 'She's always been such a good girl, Mr Martin. Never the slightest trouble at home.

'Well, Mrs Sullivan,' Jane's form tutor sounded cautious, 'it certainly wasn't an unprovoked attack. I've had a long talk with Jane, and with some of her other teachers. It seems Melanie and her friends had been picking on Jane for quite some time.'

'You mean they've been bullying her?' asked Alf. 'Oh, no. Jane's always seemed so happy at school.'

'Well, that can happen,' said the form tutor. 'My impression of Jane is that she's rather a vulnerable girl, and that she's extremely sorry for what she's done. *Extremely* sorry. She was in tears when I spoke to her.'

'Well, I should hope so,' said Mary, gathering herself together with an effort. 'I'm sure she's properly ashamed of herself, Mr Jones. I can promise you, she won't be in any more trouble, if –'

'But you won't be expelling her, will you?' Alf interrupted anxiously. 'I mean, it's not all Jane's fault. Not if they were bullying her.'

'Well,' said the headmaster, 'I've talked to Jane's teachers, and we all feel expulsion would be too severe, under the circumstances. As it is, we've decided that two weeks suspension would be altogether more appropriate. You can see that we have to take some action, Mr Sullivan. There'd be an uproar if we did nothing.'

'Oh, I can understand that, Mr Martin,' said Mary, melting with relief. 'Of course she has to be punished somehow. But we're ever so pleased you're giving her another chance. She's a good girl really, and –'

Jane sat in the little ante-room outside the headmaster's office, and looked out of the window at the darkening afternoon. The secretary was still typing. It was all right, she realised, they suspected nothing, couldn't see how the world had started to fade around her. She hid the scars beneath her bandage like a weapon. She had won, she was safe, they knew nothing.

She sat on a squashy plastic chair and listened to the voices through the wall. Around her, she saw tiny things: the ratty-looking red tinsel pinned around the functional cork-board, the worn linoleum, a white patch on the wall where someone had taken a picture down. She thought about the golden advert girl, and let the fresh clean smell of citrus perfume fill her mind, and when a nearby bell rang out for the end of lessons, she hardly heard it at all.

11

When the bell rang out for the end of lessons, Bev and Emma left the classroom together. 'I can't believe we've got *another* science assignment,' Emma was complaining. 'You'd think we were doing a medicine degree or something. I've never worked this hard in my *life.*'

'Tell me about it. God, I can't wait for the holidays.'

'Not long to go till we break up. Just less than a fortnight.'

'And then Maxine's,' said Bev, and Emma laughed and said, sure, and, as they came out into the dark cold afternoon, Bev experienced something as comforting as a cup of hot cocoa – she warmed her hands against the easy banal chitter-chatter till their paths separated at the bus-stop. ''Bye, Bev,' called Emma, 'see you tomorrow.'

Back at Goldcroft Drive, the sense of contentment grew. Melissa was making mince pies in the kitchen, and Bev changed into jeans and a T-shirt, and came downstairs to help her. 'Your father's coming over for dinner tomorrow,' said Melissa. 'It's ridiculous, you and Toby going out to restaurants every time you want to see him.'

'We don't,' said Bev, but without real rancour – she had a shrewd suspicion that her father wouldn't ask her mother for this or that or the other tomorrow night. 'Still, it'll be nice, I suppose.'

'I haven't told him about my computer course yet,' said Melissa. 'Maybe tomorrow.'

'Do you want to?'

'No,' said Melissa, and bit her lip. There was something at once awkward, guilty and humorous in her eyes. 'Maybe I won't.'

'I wouldn't, if I was you,' said Bev, reaching for the mincemeat. The front door opened to a murmur of voices. 'Looks like Toby's home.'

Toby came into the kitchen with Tiffany. 'It's freezing out there,' he said. 'You don't mind if Tiffany stays to dinner, do you, Mum?'

'Of course not,' said Melissa. 'You know you're always welcome, Tiffany. Pass over that mincemeat, will you, Bev?'

'What a day !' exclaimed Tiffany, addressing herself directly to Bev. 'You heard about it yet?'

Bev was moulding the edges of a pastry case together with neat little nips of her fingers, and didn't look round. 'Heard about what?'

'You know that Jane Sullivan in our year – that you used to keep an eye out for?'

Bev's fingers froze where they were. 'What about her?'

'Well,' said Tiffany, 'right after Assembly today she only beat up Mel Dyer.'

'You're joking,' said Bev.

'Cross my heart,' said Tiffany. Then, with reverential breathlessness, 'Right after Assembly this morning. I was there. Mel just went up to her, you know, she was just taking the mick a bit, she didn't mean any harm. And Jane Sullivan just went for her. Like a mad dog or something. It was terrible. She punched Mel right in the mouth.'

'The poor girl,' said Melissa. 'Is she all right?'

'Not really,' said Tiffany. 'Jane Sullivan knocked one of her front teeth out. And split her lip. Her mouth was pouring blood. It took two teachers to drag Jane Sullivan off of her. Davina went with her down the hospital. She's had to have two stitches in her lower lip. And she's going to have to have a cap put in where her tooth was.' For a couple of seconds, Tiffany just sat beside Toby at the kitchen table, savouring the silence and the spotlight. 'Jane Sullivan's in real trouble, mind. They had her up in front of the head all afternoon. Josie says she's been suspended for the rest of term.'

'That's terrible,' said Melissa absently. 'You don't expect that sort of thing in Underlyme. Not in a good school like yours.'

'Everyone in our year's been talking about it all day,' said Tiffany. 'They say Jane's going to be let back in after the holidays. It's so unfair. Me and Josie and Davina reckon they should just expel her.'

'Well, this Jane sounds like a very disturbed girl,' said Melissa. 'You don't know her well, do you, Bev?' But Bev was staring into the middle distance, and didn't seem to hear her mother's question.

12

'Are you listening to me, Jane?'

They were eating dinner in the bright little kitchen. Jane chewed at a potato that didn't taste of anything in particular, and dragged herself away from her thoughts with a great effort. 'Yes, Nan,' she said. 'What did you say?'

'I said, I can't think what possessed you. It's like something Carol would have done. That poor girl. The headmaster said she needed stitches.'

'I know,' Jane said dully. 'I'm sorry.'

'It's those friends of yours,' said Mary. 'They're a bad influence. Leading you into bad ways. Like your mother all over again. I'd never have thought it, Jane. Not of you.'

'Steady on, Mary,' said Alf. 'They *were* bullying her, you know. And that Beverley seems like such a nice girl.'

'She is,' Jane said quickly. 'It's not Beverley. Anita, maybe. But not Beverley.'

'Well, that's as may be,' said Mary. 'But I'm not happy, Jane. That was a terrible thing you did. You should be ashamed.'

'But Beverley?' asked Jane. 'I can still see Beverley?'

'Oh, let her keep her friend, Mary, love,' said Alf. 'She seems like such a nice girl, that Beverley. You've seen her. She wouldn't lead Jane astray.'

'Well, I daresay it's not her fault,' said Mary. 'But still. But *really.*'

'But I'm not grounded?' Jane pressed. 'I can still go and see Beverley?'

'Oh, let her, love,' said Alf. 'We can't keep a young girl cooped up in the house all day. It's not natural.'

'Well, of course you can still see her,' said Mary crossly. 'I wouldn't dream of keeping you apart. But I'm not happy with you, mind, Jane. To think of what you did. Just to think of it.'

They finished their dinner in silence. When it was finally over, Mary tidied the plates away and started washing up. Jane sat at the kitchen table – she could hear Alf switching the telly on in the lounge. 'Can I go up to my room now, Nan?' she asked. 'I'd better get on with my homework.'

'Homework. I like that,' said Mary. 'You're not going to have any homework for a long time. If you'd only told us you were being bullied. If you'd only told your teachers.'

'It's not homework. Just. It's just.' For a protracted second, Jane couldn't think of anything to say. Cold sweat broke out on her forehead; the world pressed in around her like a tight, itchy sweater. 'It's just the bathroom,' she heard herself saying as if in a dream, and horror drifted over her. That had been all wrong, she thought, Mary would notice, would ask her what was the matter. But Mary was bent over the washing-up, not meeting Jane's eyes. 'Well, I'm sure you can have a bath if you want to,' she said. 'Your grandad and I would hardly grudge you a bath, Jane. Whatever you did.'

A small relief overcame Jane, and she hurried up the stairs. Of course, she didn't go into the bathroom. It scared her so badly now. She went into her room and shut the door behind her. When it had closed, the world looked different. It didn't matter that she'd been suspended, or that for several seconds she'd been incapable of making normal conversation, or even that she'd finally got a kind of revenge on Melanie. All that mattered was Beverley Green. They'd told the golden advert girl lies about her, she thought – that was why she'd gone away like that.

She would have to tell Bev that it had all been a mistake. That Melanie and the others had lied.

Jane sat at her dressing-table–desk and felt the night coming down outside her bedroom window. The prospect of telling Bev the truth shadowed her tangled thoughts with an intolerable tension. She'd felt it once before. It was a bad omen.

13

When Jane woke up, the golden rays of a perfect July morning were slanting through the bedroom window. Anxiety flooded her mind the moment her eyes opened. No school today. It was the summer holidays. They'd broken up over two weeks ago.

She got out of bed, and tiptoed into Carol's room. She saw the jumbled chaos with familiar apprehension, realising that it was getting worse and worse – a pot of powder spilled and not brushed away on the carpet, a long dark stain on the duvet cover, a stale unpleasant smell of cheap perfume and old wine. The idea of acknowledging the sheer wrongness of the situation by cleaning her mother's room frightened Jane worse than anything. But it looked so horrible in the clean light of a summer morning. It made her want to run.

In the tangled bed that hadn't been properly made for months, Carol was asleep, snoring thickly. Jane had hoped she would be, and didn't wake her. Carol scared her so much, these days. One time she'd come home in the small hours of the morning, and she'd still been drinking in the lounge when Jane had got up to brush her teeth. One time, Jane had come home to find her passed out on the kitchen floor, and she'd lugged the limp body to the bedroom like a sack of grain. Jane was full of an agonising awareness that she should call someone, but she didn't know who to call, and she didn't know what to say when they answered.

She kept seeing brown envelopes on the hallway mat in the mornings. One time she'd gone to the drawer where she knew they were kept, and she'd peeked inside one, and Carol had come in unexpectedly and shrieked at her to leave her fucking things alone. The madness in that sound had chilled Jane's blood. Before the paper had been torn out of her hand, Jane had seen rows of figures, and she'd had the impression of something practical and hostile and unforgiving. She didn't know what Carol was doing for money. Still, it seemed safe to assume they wouldn't have enough to live on for much longer.

Now, however, it was a beautiful July morning, and it seemed best just to let her mother lie.

Jane went back into her bedroom, and changed into jeans and a T-shirt. She didn't dare put the radio on, for fear of waking Carol, and stillness filled the flat. The only sound was her mother's muffled snoring, like hearing a sleeping monster through the wall, Jane thought – only pity and concern and even love combined uneasily with the fear, and made it worse. She felt as if she was suffocating. She knew that she had to get out.

In the living room, the air was thick with stale smoke. Jane moved across to the drawer where the brown envelopes were kept. Carol always put money in there, and Jane plundered it when she couldn't face solitary beans on toast in the silent kitchen. Today there were three ten-pound notes and nothing else. Jane didn't want to take a whole tenner, but had no choice. She told herself she'd put the change back later. In the second before she closed the drawer, the brown envelopes stared out at her, and she averted her eyes and slammed it shut.

When the front door closed on the sound of Carol's snoring, Jane hurried down the stairs, and felt that she'd narrowly escaped something awful.

The summer morning was so beautiful, so perfect. Slim elegant girls who looked like Anita's sisters strolled in threes and fours and shorts and crop-tops, and the sun blazed down from a cloudless sky. A gaggle of black guys in a scarlet Batmobile eased at a red light with music pounding from the stereo. Jane walked for a long time before her feet began to hurt. On Streatham High Street she bought a cold blue drink in a plastic carton, and poked the thin red straw through the top, and tasted an aching nostalgia. Things had been good once, and they were good on the bus into Brixton, and in the McDonald's where she spent part of Carol's tenner on a cheeseburger and chips. She sat and munched and watched the people come and go until the last chip was gone, and then she went to the public library, and the minutes ticked away in the shadowed, muttering teenage section.

She read about the Wakefield twins in Sweet Valley High for long hours, as the sun blazed down outside and dust motes danced in streaks of light, about the split-level house in the suburbs and the country club, about cashmere sweaters and the cheerleading squad until she glanced up and saw that the shadows had lengthened across the floor. She checked her watch. It was almost five o'clock, she saw. It was time to go home.

Outside the library, it was calmer and cooling. People strolled hand in hand, and drank pints outside pubs, and talked about things that had nothing to do with the third-floor flat. The world's indifference overwhelmed Jane all over again. A ghastly foreboding shadowed her journey home, and she was far too relieved when her key turned in the door to silence. Carol's open bedroom door showed an empty tangle of sheets, and the dressing-table mirror reflected nothing. She'd gone out, Jane realised. The world was safe for a little while longer.

Suddenly the quiet evening wasn't terrible at all. In the kitchen, Jane opened a window to get rid of the stale air, and put the radio on, and heated up ravioli from the cupboard, and ate it out of the can with a fork. She wondered vaguely when Carol would be back. When she'd finished eating, she turned off the radio and washed up her fork and went into the living room. She put five pounds back in the drawer with the brown envelopes, curled up on the sofa and watched *Neighbours* and the news as the sunset slanted red and orange stripes across the carpet. Half-way through an item about Russia, she needed the toilet. She rose from the sofa, walked down to the little bathroom at the end of the hallway and opened the door.

The bathtub was an abattoir. Her mother lay in the red water, whiter than white, shockingly naked. Raw tendon showed dark red through the pale flesh of her wrists. A razor-blade winked up from the dank carpet, and Carol's closed eyelids looked blue.

Jane stood in the doorway and screamed. She was still screaming when the man next door started banging on the wall and yelled that he was calling the police.

14

'You get your ticket yesterday?' Adele asked Charlie. People always fussed around Charlie like that. Bev had an idea it got on Charlie's nerves.

'Course I did,' said Charlie – waspishly, Bev thought. 'I wasn't exactly going to forget, was I?'

They were all walking out of school together after the last lesson of the day. Down the corridors, institutional tinsel winked out from notice boards with austere bonhomie, and striplights buzzed before they came out into the dark, drizzling afternoon. 'We've all got our tickets, then,' said Emma. 'God, I can't *wait*.'

'I think I'll go as a St Trinian's girl,' said Bev. 'I know it's not that original but at least it's easy to do.'

'I might go as a gangster,' said Adele. 'I've got a gangster hat knocking round my room somewhere. You remember, Louise? I wore it to that fancy-dress do last New Year's Eve.'

'It doesn't look like a gangster hat,' said Louise. 'Everyone thought you were supposed to be *Michael Jackson*,' and Adele hit out at her playfully, and Louise laughed, and ducked and weaved like a boxer. 'You know Michael Jackson's new single?' she asked, ' "Don't Let Your Son Go Down On Me",' and a dizzy sense of imminent fun filled the rainy shadows with euphoria, and they all cracked up and clutched at each other. 'I can't believe we're all going to *Maxine's*,' squealed Charlie. 'On *Christmas Eve*. My dad'd kill me if he found out.'

'So make sure he doesn't find out,' said Louise. They were walking up the bush-lined path that led out of school, approaching the gates. 'Just stick to the alibi, kiddo, and –'

'Bev?'

The voice was small and uncertain by the gates. As Bev turned, horror hit her out of nowhere. It was Jane Sullivan. In the shadowy half-light cast by a nearby streetlamp, she looked paler than ever, with an unhealthy greyish undertint to her complexion. The deep shadows under her eyes could only have been caused by lack of sleep, and her face shone with rain that looked like sweat. Suddenly Bev was terrified that the others would see how ill Jane looked. She turned back for a second. 'Go on, guys,' she said. 'I'll see you in school tomorrow.'

Bev stood by the gates with Jane, in the flickering drizzle and the streetlight's orange glow, and watched the others move on. When she was sure they were out of earshot, she spoke harshly. 'What the fuck do you think you're doing? Have you been *waiting* for me?'

'I knew you often came out of school this way,' said Jane. 'I'm sorry. I just had to. I don't know what they said, but it wasn't true. You have to believe me, Bev. *They're lying.*'

There was an almost hysterical urgency to her voice. Bev recoiled inside as from a snake. 'What are you talking about?' she demanded. 'Who's *they*?'

'All of them. Melanie and Tiffany and Josie and Davina. What they said to you about me. I promise you, Bev. *They were lying.*'

'They haven't said anything to me. Not about you,' said Bev. Hideous new suspicions surfaced in her mind. 'She's had to have two stitches in her lower lip,' said Tiffany, and Bev spoke faster, louder. 'Anything at all.'

'Then why aren't you talking to me any more?' asked Jane.

Bev ignored her. Her mind was full of a different question, almost too unnerving to put into words. 'Is that why you beat up Melanie Dyer?' she asked slowly. 'Because you thought she'd lied to me about you?'

'Yes. No. I don't know any more,' said Jane. 'I just wanted to see you again. Please, Bev. I'm frightened.'

The silence was broken only by the sound of passing cars; headlights splashed red and white in puddles.

'What of?' Bev almost shouted. 'Why won't you leave me alone?'

'I can't sleep,' said Jane. After Bev's anger, her words were almost inaudible. 'There's music. It wakes me up late at night. I – I – The bathroom. I keep thinking I'll see something in the bathroom.' Bev started to turn away, and Jane spoke with frantic speed. 'Please don't go. I'm so frightened. I hurt myself. Look.'

At first, Bev thought Jane was reaching for something, then

realised she was rolling up her sleeve, peeling back the bandage Bev had noticed once before. It was a great effort to speak. 'What are you *doing*?'

Jane thrust out her bared forearm, the single word catching on a sob. '*Look.*'

At first, Bev couldn't take in what she saw: white flesh that wasn't white flesh any more, a grotesque palimpsest of dark scabs and raw red meat. The sound of her own breathing filled her ears. *I hurt myself.* Jane had done this to herself. She stepped back. 'Go away,' she said numbly. 'Just go away.'

'*Please,*' said Jane. '*Please* don't leave me. Nothing's the same any more. Please, Bev. Can't we be friends again?'

There was a tension around Bev's heart. 'We were never friends,' she said. 'I don't want to see you ever again. All I want you to do is go away.'

'I can't,' said Jane. 'Don't you understand? I *can't*.'

'You can,' said Bev. 'You *will*. If you don't, I'll tell my parents. The police. Go back where you came from. I never want to see you again as long as I live.' She turned and started walking. At first she dreaded hurrying footsteps behind her, but none came. On the bus, her hands clenched white in her lap. She looked out of the window and saw well-lit windows sparkling with tinsel, and the darkness beyond them, and the deepening rain that fell interminably through the night. She waited for home to arrive.

15

Abandoned. She'd been abandoned by what she loved more than anything. The shock was appalling, the sudden cataclysmic realisation that it simply wasn't there any more, it had disappeared like mist.

And – behind that – a deeper and more awful knowledge. There had been no kindness in those blue-blue eyes. None at all.

Through the colourful crowded town centre, Jane walked. Walked until her eyes stung with cold rain and hot tears, until her mind and senses were dazzled by the laughter and the falsity and the Christmas lights. She felt lost and disorientated. And it was impossible to come to terms all at once with the change inside her. As much as she'd loved the golden advert girl an hour ago, that was how much she now hated her.

To think that nobody had lied to Beverley Green, that she'd arbitrarily decided to end their friendship herself. Her glacial indifference had cut Jane far deeper than the compass point ever had. 'They haven't said anything to me,' she'd said, 'not about you.' She had looked straight at Jane's desperation and seen nothing. And – looking at Bev – Jane saw the pink-striped curtain pulling across for the very last time, and a tiny slice of light from the golden advert world now disappearing for good.

And then the hatred.

There was no kindness in the suburbs after all. Jane knew it as surely as she knew her own name. A memory of beautiful rooms became taunting and cruel in her mind – laughing eyes that looked straight through her, an elegant changing room, a smooth untouchable heartlessness with a swimming-pool glittering round the back. To think how she'd dreamed of its kindness. She had been tricked.

It was like a sacred object falling from a height and shattering into pieces. It was the darkest revelation of all.

Jane walked through the town centre and turned on to the deserted promenade. Rain lashed in the darkness, and white-capped waves crashed down on the beach. She saw the panorama of lights as she walked towards the beach road, and felt a bench facing out to sea awaiting her arrival. She thought of the words she'd heard by the school gates, as the voices had drawn closer. 'I can't believe we're going to Maxine's,' one of them had said, 'on Christmas Eve.' Behind the pounding agony, Jane turned the words over and over. She tried to work out why they suddenly seemed so important.

16

When she got home, the time was almost half nine. She'd spent a long time crying on the beach road. There was no way of hiding her bloodshot eyes.

'Oh, Jane, dear. There, dear.' Mary twittered in the hallway, peeling off Jane's sodden anorak. Sweet rose perfume came and went in nauseating gusts. 'We've been worried sick. We didn't mean to drive you away, dear. Oh, Jane, dear. You've been crying.'

Jane stood dumbly, not understanding, not caring. 'I'm sorry,' she said mechanically. 'I'm sorry.'

'Oh, Jane, dear, you don't have to be sorry. As if it was your fault. When they were bullying you all that time.' Mary fussed around Jane like an anxious mother hen in the neat bright respectability. Her hands smoothed Jane's wet hair. 'If we were cross with you earlier, we didn't mean it, dear. You'd never be like your mother. So worried. We've been ever so worried, me and your grandad.'

'Thank God you're all right,' said Alf, in the lounge doorway. 'We were about to call the police, Jane, love.'

Jane let herself be dried and fed and cosseted. Vaguely she remembered angry words before she'd left the house to meet Bev. To think they imagined she'd been crying over *that*. It meant nothing to her any more, but she fetched up a watery smile from the depths of her betrayal, and tried to look as if she was pleased they'd stopped being angry. 'And you'll be going back to school next term,' said Mary soothingly, as she washed Jane's plate. 'It'll be just as if nothing ever happened, Jane, love. A nice new start.'

As if Beverley Green had never happened, as if she'd never known the suburbs, or the adoration, or the towering hatred. It was impossible. 'I suppose,' Jane said. 'I suppose so.'

'And we'll have a nice Christmas together, love,' said Alf, 'get you a nice present. We'll be putting the tree up tomorrow.' Jane thought of the tall beautiful houses that wouldn't hold any comfort any more, and realised that she was crying helplessly, and then Mary was cuddling her again and Alf was patting her shoulder. 'Oh, Jane, dear,' said Mary, 'there, dear. I'm sure we never meant to hurt your feelings.'

In the lounge, they watched television together, and laughter cackled behind the glass. 'You know what I'm saying?' a slim dark girl exclaimed. 'It's just *unreal*,' and the laughter cackled again. 'Well, look how late it's getting,' said Mary, checking her watch. 'I think it's time we all turned in for the night.'

Jane said goodnight to her grandparents, went upstairs and closed her bedroom door. She got the paraphernalia out from under the mattress, unwrapped it and looked inside. An absolute despair that felt almost like apathy overcame her. Suddenly she'd never had a desire in the world, and even the compass point held no temptation, and there was nothing else to do but go to bed. Between the sheets, she lay awake for a long time. She didn't want the music to wake her in the middle of the night, but it did. It always did.

17

The following days passed slowly without school to go to. She went on long, solitary walks to the beach road and back, and looked out across the shifting water, and tried to remember what it felt like to believe. The hatred had faded into something like a dull ache. For days on end, she was conscious of nothing but exhaustion.

A towering sense of purpose followed her everywhere she went. She couldn't make out its name or nature, but it was always there – in the corner of her eye when she least expected it but nothing there when she turned. It felt like being watched. One time, she found herself standing outside Maxine's nightclub on a Wednesday afternoon, staring at the glossy poster in the window. 'XMAS EVE FANCY DRESS BALL,' it screamed at her. 'TICKETS ONLY – 7 TIL 3!' She looked around, and saw that the club was on the furthest outskirts of town, and a narrow alleyway faced its entrance directly across the road. She didn't understand why she'd come here, and couldn't remember the walk that had brought her. For maybe ten minutes her mind had simply shorted out.

It was the exhaustion. It haunted her, and made everything look like a dream. When she got out of bed, the colours were all wrong. These days she hardly slept at all, and when she did she had such dreams. Such terrible dreams. One time she dreamed that she'd been buried alive and she was trapped screaming under the earth while people strolled and chattered above her. On the beach road, gulls shrieked, as if they were trying to tell her something.

Back home, the decorations were all up. There were Christmas cards on the sideboard. Frost settled on the flowers in the garden overnight, and Alf complained over dinner about the weather. The world played on like a song in the wrong key. She couldn't hide the deep shadows under her eyes with concealer. Mary asked her if she was feeling all right, and Jane said she thought she might be coming down with something, and suds glittered in the sink. How empty the world seemed now. How terrible to know there was nothing else left.

She stood outside Maxine's nightclub and felt something watching her. One evening, she was sitting up in her room after dinner, and it showed her what it was.

18

She sat at the dressing-table–desk. Outside the window it was pitch dark, and she could hear the static of the rain. She hadn't drawn the curtain. She could see angular black rooftops silhouetted on a sky as black and empty as outer space, and something in the sight pierced through her drugged listlessness with entirely unexpected clarity. How cold and majestic it all looked, out there in the darkness. How heartless.

She sat alone in her room. From downstairs, she could hear the cackle of the television. It combined with the almost unaudible sound of the rain, and hatred kicked deep in her guts – the aching loneliness in that sound enraged her. She thought of the golden advert girl, laughing far away. On Christmas Eve, Beverley Green would be going to Maxine's, Jane thought, and she felt the hatred seize her like a cramp.

She was turning her head and eyes away from the panorama through the window, when her gaze was caught by the teddy-bear she hadn't quite been able to throw away. It sat on her pillow, round and smug. Something in the lamplight caught its button eyes and gave it an arrogant, sneering look, made its vacant smile hateful. For the first time, Jane saw its ugliness. How cheap it was, this prized memento from the golden advert world, how thin and tacky its bright blue fur. It was no better than the golden advert girl, she thought, and she went over to her bed, and reached under the mattress, and unwrapped the little package, and her hand clenched round the compass till her knuckles whitened.

In the grip of a savage fury beyond anything she'd felt in her life, Jane grabbed the teddy-bear off the bed. The compass point winked in the lamplight. Slowly, almost methodically, she hacked and slashed at the blue fur, the small complacent smirk that dared her to do her worst. Hacked and slashed till her fury was joined by a swirling euphoria and blood sang in her ears and white fibres dribbled and leaked. The compass point twisted. The compass point tore.

When she'd finished, she let the teddy-bear fall to the ground. It landed as lightly as a pillow, its belly a white, shredded ruin, its button eyes staring into space. Jane's breath came slow and deep as she looked at it. Her own eyes were both vacant and terribly alive. At last, she had been summoned, and she knew exactly why. On Christmas Eve, the golden advert girl would be going to the party at Maxine's.

19

The following day dawned fresh and cold and sunny. When she came downstairs, Mary was cleaning the cooker. Through the window, she could see her grandfather busy in the garden. 'Morning, Jane, dear,' said Mary, looking round. 'You know, you still don't look very well.'

'I know, but I'm feeling better. A bit better than yesterday.' In the bathroom mirror, Jane had seen the hectic flush on her cheeks and her overbright eyes. She spoke quickly, with an urgency she hoped would sound like excitement. 'Listen, Nan, I don't want to scrounge, but can I borrow ten pounds?'

'What for, dear? Are you going into town?'

'Yeah,' said Jane. 'I'm meeting Beverley and Anita. We're going Christmas shopping.' There was a brief silence. Alf's electric shears whined on outside. 'I sort of wanted to get you and Grandad something for Christmas. Something nice, you see. But I haven't got any money.'

'Well, of course, Jane, dear. To think we never thought. Hold your horses. I'll just go and get my purse.'

Mary walked out to the neat little lounge, and came back with her battered leather purse. She fished out a crumpled tenner. 'You don't have to spend it all on us, dear,' she said, handing it to Jane. 'Keep a fiver or so for yourself. Buy yourself something nice.'

'Oh, no. Really. I couldn't.' Jane stuffed the note into her anorak pocket, then stood around awkwardly, not quite knowing how to say what she wanted to.

'Nan,' she said eventually, 'you don't mind if I go out on Christmas Eve, do you?'

'Well, so long as you're back early. Nine thirty at the *latest* now, Jane. It's not safe for a young girl, out there at night.' Curiosity followed hot on the heels of warning. 'What have you got planned?'

'There's a party in town,' said Jane. 'I'm going with Beverley.'

'Oh, that's nice, dear. She seemed like such a lovely girl. I half thought you two had fallen out again. She hasn't rung for you in such a long time.'

'We meet up and arrange stuff,' said Jane. 'Anyway, I'd better go now, Nan. I don't want to be late meeting the others.'

Jane left by the back door. A picturesque frost had settled on shed roofs and bushes, and the chill stung her fingers raw and numb. Alf bent busily over his roses, and she saw him with indifference. He didn't look up or speak as she passed him. He didn't seem to notice her.

Out of the gate and down the road she walked, hugging invisibility round herself like a mink coat. It warmed her, protected her. A group of small heavy-coated children shrieked and squabbled on the pavement, and didn't acknowledge her movement. She walked past them quickly. Raw urgency tugged a magnet in her head as the road widened ahead of her, and she recognised the busier road that led on to the town centre.

She walked. It was such a lovely day, clear and fresh and bright, and the jollity of the Christmas season ho-ho-hoed from strangers' windows. She saw the little newsagent with a couple of chattering housewives outside it, the second-hand-clothes shop and the furniture shop with a letter missing from the sign. The furtive rapture of something she shouldn't be doing over-whelmed her, and she was pleased that nobody seemed able to see her. It was good to feel this kind of urgency when you'd been betrayed and abandoned. It gave you a purpose in the world.

She passed the little church that looked as perfect as a pastoral painting, and the water of the little harbour glinted in the light. She saw the distant official buildings towering against a clear blue horizon, and something lifted in her heart. Then she was entering the town centre, and approaching the pretty little kitchen shop she'd noticed on her very first day here, and seeing the bright jumble of aprons and rag-dolls in the window. They weren't important to her. They weren't why she'd come.

She had another purpose here today.

20

'They don't sell fishnets,' said Bev irritably, as she came back from the counter. 'How hard can it be to find a pair of fishnets?'

It was a Saturday and they'd broken up over a week ago. Right now, the five of them were milling around in Top Shop. 'They'll have some in the fancy-dress shop,' said Adele. 'I've got to get my top hat from there, too.'

'Well, let's get going, then,' said Louise, then stopped, pointing. '*Shit*, that dress is repulsive.' Past the endless racks of sequined partywear, they walked out of Top Shop and into the cold. 'You got your snowman costume yet?' Louise asked Charlie.

'Of course I've got it,' said Charlie, with some irritation. 'I ordered it last *week*.'

Bev clung to familiarity and friendship like a lifebelt. Life was good with your hands stuffed in gloves in your pockets, seeing glossy special-offer signs in shop windows, and crowds of people, and the gradual approach of something good. There was no place for thoughts of Jane Sullivan here.

'I hope they have got fishnets,' she said. 'I can't be a proper St Trinian's girl without fishnets.'

The little fancy-dress shop on the outskirts of town was crowded and noisy. They recognised a couple of girls from their year, and said hi.

'Thank God,' said Bev, 'they've got them,' and she went to the till to pay. When she got back, Louise and Charlie were gathered round Adele, discussing the top hat squashed down on Adele's head.

'It's too small,' Adele was saying. 'I know I won't find anything better, but it's still too *small*.'

Emma was browsing through a shelf nearby, and Bev went up to her. 'You getting anything here?' she asked.

'Don't think so. I've pretty much got my costume sorted,' said Emma. 'Only four days left, now.'

'Tell me about it,' said Bev. 'I can't *wait*.'

'It's going to be great,' said Emma. 'Hey, I meant to ask. You seen that girl around lately?'

Something cold crawled up the back of Bev's neck. 'What girl?' she asked, but she knew.

'You know. The one who waited for you by the gates, week before last.'

'Christ, no,' said Bev, and fought for indifference. 'If you want to know, I've told her to stop following me around. She gets on my nerves.'

'I feel a bit sorry for her,' said Emma. 'Waiting all that time for you. She was being bullied, you know. I heard some people talking about it.'

Emma was kind, sympathetic, knew nothing. Thinking back to that bared and terrible arm, Bev spoke callously. 'That's *her* problem,' she said. 'Anyway, I think she got the message. I haven't seen her since then.'

'It's a shame,' said Emma vaguely, and the world turned up around them like music – the plastic colours and the ice-cold sunlight, the inconsequential festive bonhomie.

'Of course I'll get it,' Adele was saying crossly. 'It's just too *small.*' Then she went to pay at the till, and they all waited by the racks for her to come back.

21

Jane stood in front of the racks of kitchen knives. The variety bewildered her. For endless seconds, she stood indecisively, her eyes panning slowly from side to side.

She supposed she could always have snuck a knife from the kitchen drawer at home. But somehow, the idea of doing that hadn't felt quite right. Her grandparents might notice its absence too soon – but there was something else there too. She wanted something clean and new, devoid of resonance. A knife that felt like her own.

She stood there, hearing her breath slow and hard in her ears.

Dry, beguiling smells of pot-pourri and scented candles filled the narrow aisle, and people came and went around her, talking loudly. Jane barely heard them. Finally, she decided her choice didn't matter. She picked one out that looked about right, and took it over to the queue at the counter.

The elderly lady behind the till wore a Santa hat and an air of ardent sociability. She spoke chummily. 'Present for your mum, love?'

Jane nodded and smiled, and the elderly lady smiled back. She wrapped the knife in a carrier-bag, and Jane paid with Mary's tenner. She put the carrier-bag into her rucksack, and walked out of the shop into the raw December sunlight.

At the bus-stop, she waited for some time. She stood with a knife in her mind, and saw people coming and going around her like ghosts – the colourless fair-haired girl she vaguely remembered from another life, Anita's sisters, Michelle and Chandra and Stephanie. It seemed everyone was out Christmas shopping today. She stood and looked and felt her motives blur around her. It wasn't just about a pair of indifferent blue eyes any more, but a sunny little bedroom and a third-floor flat, a bathtub streaked red and pastel-striped wallpaper. It was about all of it and none of it, adoration and loneliness and maybe even envy. She couldn't separate the precise emotion that drove her on to the unthinkable. Just something that found its reflection in her inability to kill the golden advert girl outside that house in the suburbs, her need for impersonal surroundings that stirred no memories. Above all, Jane was driven by a need to destroy the specific and the past, like and yet far beyond the escape of the compass point, the chaos in her head flying in the wind for one last time. And maybe her motivation went beyond even that. Perhaps, after all, it was just about two girls.

When the bus came, Jane paid her fare and went to sit down. She looked out of the window at the dry frozen chill. Garish Christmas lights looked back.

22

When she let herself in through the back door, she could hear voices from the lounge. She tried to sneak up the stairs without anyone noticing, but Mary called to her when she was on the second step. 'Jane, dear? Come on in. We've got guests for tea.'

Jane pushed open the lounge door and entered unwillingly. The little room glittered like a magpie's nest, and tinsel sparkled from every corner. Her grandparents sat with Bob and Joyce Andrews.

'Hello, dear,' said Joyce. 'Bob and I were ever so sorry to hear about your trouble at school.'

'I was saying to Bob and Joyce what a disgrace it was,' said Mary. Suspending you for standing up for yourself.'

'It's a disgrace,' said Bob. 'I don't know what these teachers are thinking of.'

'But it's a very good school,' said Mary. 'I think Jane's been missing it. She's been like a dog without a tail lately. Haven't you, dear?'

'I suppose,' said Jane. 'Listen, I'm just going upstairs for a bit. I've got some stuff to do.'

'Well, come down when you've finished, love,' Alf said jovially. 'You're not in prison, you know.' He laughed, as Bob and Mary and Joyce did. Jane dredged up a thin smile and turned away. As she walked up the stairs, she could hear them talking in the lounge. 'She spends too much time up there on her own,' Alf was saying. 'Still, I suppose they're all like that at her age.'

Up in her room, Jane closed the door behind her and got the carrier-bag out of her rucksack. She unwrapped the knife from its plastic packaging. She held it in her hands and turned it over. She looked at it for a long time.

From handle to blade, the kitchen knife was just shy of eight inches long. Its handle was matt-black plastic, and when she unsheathed its blade, it glittered like silver and diamonds in the fading evening light. Its most lethal feature wasn't its point, but its edge: it was thin and keen as a razor-blade.

Jane stood in the bedroom that had never really felt like her own. In front of the mirror, she raised the knife and stood as if hypnotised. She was still frozen in the same position when Mary called up the stairs, and told her to come and say goodbye to Bob and Joyce before they left.

23

It was the Greens' first Christmas Eve without Jack. Putting the final touches to the dinner in the kitchen, Melissa realised it with a poignancy that mingled uneasily with her new contentment – a feeling that life had been safer once, the future less uncertain, the imminent New Year full of guarantees. A part of her wanted to turn back to the way things had used to be, but she couldn't do that and knew it. She was different now. Stronger.

The phone rang in the hallway. She turned down the gas under the saucepans, and went to answer it.

'Hello?'

'Hi, Mel,' said the voice down the line. 'It's me.'

'*Jack.*' She thought he sounded unhappy, subdued. 'How are you?'

'All right, I suppose. How are you?'

'I'm all right.' She felt shocked and slightly guilty to realise that it wasn't the conventional lie it should have been, that her words were true after all. 'I'm fine.'

'And the kids?'

'They're okay. Toby's got Tiffany round. Bev just got in,' she said. 'Do you want to speak to them?'

'*No.*' At first he spoke tightly, then continued in his normal voice. 'Not like this. Not now.'

'You *can*,' she said.

'No.' There was a long uncomfortable silence down the line. 'I was thinking,' he said at last. 'Do you mind if I come over for lunch tomorrow?'

'Of course not,' she said, startled. 'If you want to.'

'I want to. It gets lonely. I'm no good at being on my own.'

She'd never known him admit weakness before. It should have pleased her, but instead she felt upset and sorry. 'Well, of course. You're more than welcome.'

'What time'll you be starting?'

'About two o'clock,' she said. 'Come whenever. It'll be nice for the kids to see you.'

'Okay. I'll see you then.'

'Okay. 'Bye, Jack.'

Melissa replaced the receiver and went back into the kitchen. When the dinner was ready and the table was laid, she called the kids in from the living room. 'Your father rang,' she said, as they came in with Tiffany. 'He's coming to lunch tomorrow.'

'Whatever,' said Toby. 'I suppose it doesn't matter.'

'But it should be nice,' said Bev. 'I suppose.'

Melissa watched them eat and talk and laugh among themselves, and was touched by an infinite contentment. A festive, mellow mood seemed to have settled throughout the house, and the kids seemed happier than she'd ever known them. Through the french windows, fairy lights glittered round the patio.

'What time are you going to your party?' Tiffany asked Bev, as they finished eating.

'Oh, God, yeah,' said Bev, checking her watch. 'I'd better start getting ready. I'm meeting Emma and the others outside the club at seven.' She rose from the table and hurried from the kitchen.

When Toby and Tiffany had gone back into the living room, Melissa cleared the table, scraped the dishes and stacked them in the dishwasher. Smells of gravy and roast meat lingered pleasantly, and the small sounds of the approaching morning filled the world: the gentle rumble as the dishwasher started, the guffawing TV from the living room, the vague overhead murmur of Bev's stereo. It sounded good. On impulse, she went upstairs and knocked on Bev's door.

24

'Who is it?' called Bev.

'It's just me,' said Melissa. 'Can I come in?'

'Sure,' said Bev. 'Door's open.'

Melissa walked in. The room was in a state of extrovert disarray, and bits and pieces littered every possible surface – torn-off wrapping-paper, red and green envelopes with Bev's name on the front, the packaging from the toiletries and novelties and chocolates Emma and the others had given her for Christmas, and that she'd opened early.

'Look at this mess,' said Melissa. 'God, Bev.'

'Don't worry. I'll tidy up later.' Bev sat in front of the dressing-table mirror wearing her white school shirt and tie, a blue mini-skirt and fishnet tights. She was drawing large brown freckles on her cheeks with an eye-pencil. 'Could you drive me down there, Mum?' she asked.

'Of course.' Melissa sat on the window-seat, and met Bev's eyes in the mirror. 'I'll come and pick you up. I don't like to think of you getting a cab back that late on your own.'

'No, Mum, it's okay. I told you last week. Emma's mum's driving us back.'

'Beverley, *please*. I wasn't born yesterday,' said Melissa. 'Just you be careful, all right?'

'Of course I'll be careful. You know I'll be careful.'

'And stick with your friends. Don't go wandering around on your own.'

'Mum. Like I'm going to.' In the mirror, Bev's eyes were distracted, and she started arranging her hair in two thick plaits – her fingers moved quickly, with a hairdresser's ease. 'Don't worry,' she said. 'I'll be all right.'

'Well, I hope so,' said Melissa. 'I hope so.'

For a few minutes, Melissa sat and watched her daughter getting ready in silence. Bev applied an exaggerated Cupid's bow of red lipstick, and tied red ribbons round the bottoms of her plaits. 'I don't know about this tie,' she said eventually, adjusting it round her starched white collar. 'It doesn't look real enough.'

'But it's your school tie,' said Melissa.

'Maybe that's what's wrong. I should have got one from the fancy-dress shop. I just never thought.' Bev was about to say something else when the phone rang by her bed. 'Hello?' she said. 'Oh, hi, Adele, you getting ready?' and she settled down on the bed, obviously preparing to talk for some time. Melissa rose from the window-seat. 'Give me a shout when you're ready, and I'll run you into town,' she stage-whispered, and Bev nodded and smiled, before returning her attention to Adele. 'Well, of course that hat's too small. You said it was too small in the *shop*.'

Melissa went back downstairs. Through the half-open living-room doorway, a slice of Christmas twinkled like Aladdin's cave, and Toby and Tiffany's voices were almost drowned in the television noise. Melissa walked past, into the quiet of the kitchen. She sat down at the table and waited for Bev to come down.

25

'You off, then, dear?'

Jane had just opened the back door when Mary came into the kitchen. She stood, framed in the shadows, feeling defensive. 'Yeah,' she said. ''Bye, Nan.'

'You're very pale, Jane, dear,' said Mary. 'Sure you're all right?'

'I'm fine, Nan.'

'Well, have a nice time with Beverley, dear. And be sure you don't stay out too late. I mean it, now, Jane. Nine thirty at the *latest*.'

'I know. I won't be any later.'

'Good girl,' said Mary. 'Well, bye-bye, dear.'

When the back door creaked shut behind her, Jane heard the bolt being drawn. They'd start talking about her soon, she knew, and experienced a mixture of revulsion and longing for their world – Mary's curiosity as to why she hadn't been wearing her pretty new dress and Alf's gruff reassurance, a glass of Irish Mist in front of the telly as the cosy little over-decorated lounge glittered and rustled in the gathering night, and china dogs smiled out from the sideboard with empty eyes. It wasn't her world any more, and she suddenly realised it more deeply than ever. She'd chosen something else. What she was about to do would lock her out for life.

Doesn't matter, she thought, *not now,* and as she walked she felt both cold and feverish, and blood beat in her ears like jungle drums.

In the long streets that extended between the housing estate and the town centre, the world was dark and silent. Earlier that day it had rained, and the lights from passing cars caught red and white in puddles. A misty glow shone from the ever-open newsagent's, and fairy lights sparkled round a thousand curtained windows. Otherwise the darkness was unrelieved. It suited her. Soon, she'd be there.

She walked. It felt as if the volume was being slowly turned up around her – the steady escalation of noise and life as she approached the heart of light. A group of shrieking women passed her by the harbour, none less than thirty, dressed up for a big night out. 'And Delia's shagged him!' one of them cried, and the others exploded with laughter. 'And Karen said –' and then they were gone. Beyond them, a couple somewhere in their teens walked hand in hand, their smooth young faces cruel and beautiful under the festive lights, neither speaking. Brief gusts of noise and laughter emanated from pub doors as people came and went. It was a cold night. Jane's breath plumed white on the air.

When she reached the alleyway that faced Maxine's nightclub, she walked approximately half-way down, then stopped. From where she stood, she could see both ends clearly, narrow rectangles of bright light. People would pass her and see her, but she wouldn't be remarked on – perhaps she was lost, or hiding, or preparing for a crafty smoke and waiting for a friend.

Nothing sinister in a lone teenage girl. An image of the suburbs flashed for a second in Jane's mind. She leaned back against the dank brick wall and touched the silhouette of the knife beneath her anorak. It was almost half past six.

26

At twenty to seven, Bev came hurrying down the stairs, buttoning a coat over her fancy-dress. 'You ready to go, Mum?'

'For the last half-hour,' said Melissa, rising from the table. They walked through the hall, towards the front door. Outside the living room, they stopped. ''Bye, Toby,' said Melissa. ''Bye, Tiffany. I won't be long.'

'I'm going home in a minute,' said Tiffany. 'Have a good Christmas, Mrs Green. Thanks for the dinner.'

'And me?' said Bev, poking her head round the door. 'What about me?'

'Oh, you look wicked, Bev,' said Tiffany. 'Have a good Christmas and all, yeah? Hope you have a good evening.'

'I expect I will,' said Bev. 'Have a great Christmas, Tiff. See you later, Toby.'

'Yeah,' said Toby, ''bye.'

In the Shogun, Melissa put the heater on, and the frozen chill melted away quickly. Outside it had started to rain. 'Where do you want me to drop you off?' she asked, as she started the car.

'Outside Charlie Brownsish. Just sort of down from McDonald's.' Bev fastened her seat-belt and sat back. She looked out of the window and saw the suburbs racing away. She was surprised by how little traffic there was on the road. 'It's quiet tonight,' she said. 'I'd have thought it'd be busier.'

'Well, it's early, yet,' said Melissa. 'It's not seven o'clock.'

Towards the town centre, the Christmas season began in earnest, and the first of the evening's partygoers paraded between pubs with arms linked. Bev sat and watched the night through the window, feeling the first fizzing bubbles of excitement as the car slowed across the road from Charlie Brown's. 'You want me to drop you off here?' Melissa asked.

'Sure,' said Bev. 'Here's great.'

Melissa pulled up and parked. A mist of rain flickered in the headlights, and the windscreen wipers stirred and rested. Across the road, the queue for the under-sixteens' party was already growing. 'Where are you meeting your friends?' asked Melissa.

'Right outside the club. At seven.'

Melissa glanced at her watch. 'It's almost seven now.'

'Oh, God, yeah,' said Bev, checking her own. 'Listen, Mum, I've got to run.'

'So what time do you think you'll be home tonight? Shall we say one a.m. at the latest?'

'Oh, Mum, I don't know,' said Bev, wishing her mother wouldn't make such a fuss. 'Before two a.m. some time, all right?'

'I know, I know, you'll be sixteen next year,' said Melissa wearily. 'Still, it wouldn't be natural if I didn't worry about my own daughter now and again. You'll see, when you're older and have children of your own.'

'Mum, I'm going to be late to meet the others.'

'You'll see them from here, surely?'

'I don't know. I might not. It's getting too dark.' Bev kissed her mother's cheek and opened the passenger door. Wind howled and spat rain into the Shogun's interior. 'See you later, anyway,' she said. 'Happy Christmas Eve.'

'You too, darling,' said Melissa. 'Have a lovely evening.'

Bev closed the door and stood in the deepening rain watching her mother drive off. When the powerful headlights had vanished into the distance, she crossed the road. She bypassed the growing teenage queue outside Charlie Brown's. Then she turned down the alleyway that led straight to Maxine's, to the laughter and the lights and the others who'd be waiting for her.

The dank narrow passage was deserted. Her footsteps echoed hollowly. She told herself she was just hurrying so she wouldn't be late to meet her friends. Then there was a movement in the corner of her eye, and she turned.

27

Jane stepped forward. Bev stepped back. Bev felt horror and hatred and exasperation, but no genuine fear or urge to run. She didn't know there was anything to run from, until the knife flashed in the yellow light, and by then it was too late for that.

At first, the gathering inhalation on the near-silence.

Then the screaming.

Epilogue

When you're driving out of Underlyme, past the beach road, on the road into the next town, you'll pass a pair of open metal gates, which lead into a mismatched collection of buildings of which you only get a brief glimpse. Peeling paint and red brick, new concrete and glass. If you didn't know it was the local A-level college, you'd realise it from the people milling around the gates. Rucksack-carrying sixteen- and seventeen-year-olds wear jeans and Doc Martens, and chatter in groups that aren't quite as ostentatiously cliquish as the ones they formed at school. They hold thick ring-binders adorned with pictures of Gomez and Shirley Manson, and talk of essays and UCAS forms and imminent nights out at Charlie Brown's as they spill out of the gates, their bright voices and clothes catching the light in the somnolent, melting summer.

Perhaps you don't recognise the dark-haired girl who's coming out of the gates now, approaching two others who are sitting on a low wall and talking. There's no reason why you should. She wears a red-checked shirt and dark-blue jeans, and looks much like anyone else. She never appeared in the papers two years ago, after all, and you never read her name.

So you pay her no more attention than any of the other milling small-town students, and she's just a tiny part of this pleasant, somehow nostalgic afternoon as the college gates fade in the rear-view mirror, and you put your foot down as the open road extends in front of you, and you continue on your way.

Louise and Charlie are waiting for Emma by the gates. Adele

isn't. She married her boyfriend earlier that year, and is now expecting their first baby.

'Took your time,' Louise says waspishly, as they start walking together. The sunlight is glorious. 'What kept you?'

'Mr Park was going on about university applications,' says Emma. 'I'll have to fill in my UCAS form this evening.'

'What's your first choice?' asks Charlie.

'King's College,' says Emma. 'In London.'

'They sent that girl to London,' says Louise abruptly. 'I read about it in the paper this morning.'

'Who didn't?' Emma takes a long deep breath. 'I thought we'd never hear of her again. I can't believe she killed herself.'

'Didn't have much to live for,' Louise says callously. 'Not in a mental home or whatever it was.'

'A psychiatric unit,' Emma corrects her, but the look in her eyes is faraway and absent. 'Did you read about the note she left?'

'Yeah,' says Charlie. 'It just said Beverley.'

'That's scary,' says Louise. 'I always thought there was something wrong with her.'

'No, you didn't,' says Emma. 'Nobody did. Not even Bev,' and a long silence falls between them as they get the bus into town.

In town, they go into a florist's and pay a fiver each towards a spray of lilies – it is a transaction they have completed often, over the last two years, and has now become a monthly ritual. 'Poor Bev,' says Charlie quietly, as they leave the shop. 'I think about her sometimes, you know.'

'We all do,' says Emma, and she holds the flowers on the bus out of town. They get off at a little unsheltered stop, and walk to the cemetery in companionable silence.

Underlyme Cemetery is a neat well-tended place, all bright flowers and shiny headstones and weedless gravel path. For all its landscaped peace, it touches Emma with a profound sense of tragedy. Death doesn't belong here, she thinks, in the warmth of a summer afternoon. 'I saw her mum in town, the other day,' she says, as they approach Bev's grave. 'She's getting married again.'

'Who to?' asks Charlie.

'I don't know. We didn't talk long,' says Emma. 'She looked well, though. Younger.'

'That's good,' Louise says uncertainly, and then they are there. The headstone is black marble, with greyish-silver specks like shiny granite. Its top describes two sloping arches, the crux of a heart shape. The writing on it seems to have been carved out in gold. 'BEVERLEY GREEN 1983–1998', it says, 'IN LOVING MEMORY'. As always, the sight of it moves Emma with a sense of tragedy beyond tears – a hundred giggling afternoons in a pink-and-white bedroom stir in her mind as she registers the carnations that have already been laid there. 'Hey,' she says. 'Someone's been here. These flowers look fresh.'

'Who are they from?' asks Louise.

'I don't know. I'll read the card.' Emma sets the lilies down, and stoops to make out the writing. ' "From Mary and Alf Sullivan," ' she reads aloud. ' "Rest in Peace." '

'You know who they are?' asks Louise. 'Jane Sullivan's grandparents.'

'They've got a cheek,' says Charlie hotly. 'To leave flowers here.'

'I don't know,' says Emma. 'I think it's nice. It wasn't their fault.'

'Then whose was it?' demands Charlie.

'I don't know. Maybe nobody's.' Emma steps back from the grave, and looks at the lilies and carnations lying side by side. 'Well,' she says, 'that's that, then.'

'Yeah,' says Louise, and they stand and gaze for some time, then turn away.

As they walk back along the gravel path Emma's thoughts are distracted. The pupils of nearby St Andrew's often use the cemetery as a short-cut on their way home, and she can't help but notice them as they chatter past. Faces jump out at her from the uniformed, rucksack-swinging crowds. An impossibly pretty blonde in the centre of a laughing trio reminds her of far too much – the resemblance to Bev isn't quite uncanny, Emma tells herself, she has a black streak through her hair, is wearing too much makeup. Further back, a small bespectacled girl scuttles spiderlike and keeps sneaking glances behind her, as if expecting to see someone or something she dreads. Something in the eyes and the movement make Emma think of a girl she'd seen and barely noticed long ago, waiting for Bev in half-forgotten hallways, walking beside Bev through a playground she hasn't seen in almost two years. A clammy apprehension touches her deep inside at the sight, because it feels for a second as if time has rewound, and the Christmas term of 1998 has never gone away.

Then the chattering teenagers are vanishing into the distance, and the three students are waiting at the bus-stop. They while away the time by talking about college.

And you're going home.